From the Chicken House

I've never lost my head, or any other part of me for that matter, to a girl. Honest.

C.J. Skuse shows us how finding the best bits of a boy is surprisingly difficult – especially when it's a heart of gold that you truly, deeply want. This is a hilarious, moving, tiny bit sad, gloriously redemptive (yes!), unique mix from a totally brilliant new talent.

You'll never ask for a . . . hand . . . with anything again!

Barry Cunningham
Publisher

DEAD ROMANTIC

CJ SKUSE

Chicken House

2 Palmer Street, Frome, Somerset BA11 1DS
www.doublecluck.com

Text © C.J. Skuse 2013
First published in Great Britain in 2013
The Chicken House
2 Palmer Street
Frome, Somerset BA11 1DS
United Kingdom
www.doublecluck.com

C.J. Skuse has asserted her right under the Copyright, Designs and Patents
Act 1988, to be identified as the author of this work.

Cover design and interior design by Helen Crawford-White
Typeset by Dorchester Typesetting Group Ltd
Printed and bound in Great Britain by CPI Group (UK) Ltd, Croydon, CR0 4YY

The paper used in this Chicken House book is made from wood
grown in sustainable forests.

1 3 5 7 9 10 8 6 4 2

British Library Cataloguing in Publication data available.

ISBN 978-1-908435-41-5

No human being could have passed a happier childhood than myself. My parents were possessed by the very spirit of kindness and indulgence . . . the agents and creators of all the many delights which we enjoyed. When I mingled with other families I distinctly discerned how peculiarly fortunate my lot was.

VICTOR FRANKENSTEIN

For my mum, Jen Skuse

'Alone, bad. Friend, good.'

The Bride of Frankenstein, 1935

The Girl in the Graveyard

It had been the worst night in the history of the world ever ever ever. A giant mistake, a BFG meets Hagrid kind of big mistake. I shouldn't have even gone to the freshers' party, full stop, let alone done what I did there. Ugh. The smell was making me feel sick. Every now and again as I walked along the dark streets from college it would hit me and for a split second I'd wonder where it was coming from. And then I'd remember. It was coming from me.

I wanted to be by myself, so I took a short cut through the graveyard, still sobbing my heart out. My sobbing had been the only sound in the world until I rounded the corner of the church and heard a different one. A scraping sound.

Scrape. Scrape. Huff. Scrape. Huff. Scrape. Huff. Scrape, scrape, scrape.

I tried to ignore it at first, what with it being ten o'clock at night – prime time for old men dragging chains and floating women in wedding dresses. But it kept on.

Scrape. Scrape. Huff. Scrape. Scrape. Huff. Huff. Scrape. Scrape.

'Who *is* that?' I shouted. It wasn't like me to be so stroppy but on this occasion, I did have the right. After all, I was dripping with the poo of a thousand cows. I went to investigate, picking my way through the grass. And then, I saw a figure. There, by the wall. A figure digging.

I went a bit further along the path where it was shaded from the moonlight, desperately trying to turn on some carrot-fuelled ability to see in the dark. I saw a girl digging.

A girl my age, digging.

She was wearing a hooded jacket and was partly hidden by the overhanging willow tree, but it was definitely a girl and that was definitely what she was doing. Digging.

I thought I ought to tell her I was there, so I didn't scare her.

'Hiya.'

She snapped her head around. 'What?'

I gulped. 'Hi?'

A headlight, like the kind miners wear, was strapped to her forehead and when she looked at me it shone into my eyes.

'What are you doing here?' she barked.

'I . . . what? Nothing,' I said, shielding myself from the glare. I said it like *I* was the one who should feel guilty. 'I'm walking home. What are you doing?'

She didn't answer, just lowered her headlight and kept on digging. I noticed a Marks & Spencer's cool bag beside her on the grass.

Scrape. Huff. Scrape. Huff.

'Why are you doing that?' I asked her. 'Do you work here or something?'

'Too many questions and I don't want to answer any of them,' the girl huffed. She sounded posh. And intelligent. Intelliposh, I guessed.

Scrape. Huff. Scrape.

'I'll tell,' I threatened, not very threateningly though. I actually just wanted to watch what she was doing, thinking maybe at some point I'd see a body, but I folded my arms to look like I meant business, because that's what you should do when you find someone doing something they're not supposed to. Though it was pretty difficult to look like you meant business when you literally looked and smelled like crap. 'You're breaking a law. Probably.'

The girl stuck her shovel into the dirt so it stood up straight. She shone her headlight at me again. 'And who are you, the church warden?'

'No.'

'You have a vested interest in this particular plot?'

'No, I . . .'

'You're the town sheriff? This town ain't big enough for the both of us?'

'No!'

She turned down her headlight so I could actually open my eyes. 'Then what does it matter what I'm doing?'

I stepped closer. 'I don't know. Because it does. It's weird.'

She stood with a foot perched on her shovel, her gloved hands neatly folded on top. 'And walking through a grave-yard at night dressed as excrement *isn't?*'

Oh, she had noticed. Of course she had noticed. '*I* have an excuse,' I said. 'I've been to the freshers' party at college.'

'Figures,' she said. 'Some halfwit tried to hand me a flyer for that in the cafeteria on Wednesday lunchtime.' She went back to digging.

'You've started Hoydon College too?' I said.

'Yes,' she puffed. 'I'm assuming you were forced to engage in one of the many . . . hilarious initiation ceremonies they like to put on for new students, just to see who's the most . . . desperate to win friends.' *Scrape. Huff.*

'They made me do it,' I said, slapping my soaking wet dress at the sides. My eyes stung and there was a pain in my throat as I remembered what I had just done. 'They were all cheering and chanting and I felt so alive.'

'I heard of one initiation rite called the Eat, Drink and Be Merry,' the girl interrupted. 'I believe it involves eating something disgusting, drinking something disgusting and jumping in something disgusting, usually a paddling pool full of —'

'Poo,' I finished.

'Hmm. Apparently only the most desperate of "losers" will actually do it.' The pain in my throat gave way to floods of so many tears. I never knew I had so much water in me. 'I take it you were crowned this year's Queen Loser.'

Their words kept circling inside my brain like a whirlpool of diarrhoea.

Camille will do it. You'll do it, won't you? Go on, eat it!
Come on, Camille, eat it. Go on, drink it down, drink it all!
Down it, down it, down it, down it! Wahey, she downed it all!
Shove her in. Go on, Camille. Look at the state of her!

Stupid dares. Stupid A levels. Stupid friends. I actually big fat hated them all, and I didn't big fat hate anything usually. Except hard-boiled eggs. And people who were mean to animals. And velvet.

'I thought they'd think I was cool.'

'I presume you were trying to impress some boy.' *Scrape. Huff.*

I nodded. 'Damian. He's in our Sociology class. He's awesome. It was him doing the handbrake turns on the hockey pitch on the first day of term. And he can jump the train tracks in a Tesco trolley. He's just the best.'

'The best at what precisely?' said the girl. 'I think you should wake up and smell what you're covered in.'

I wiped my nose on the back of my pooey hand. 'I saw him, Damian, when I was in the paddling pool. Stupid arm around Tamsin Double-Barrelled. Someone else was filming it for YouTube. Even Damian had his phone out. And I lost my cherry scrunchie. I loved that cherry scrunchie. It matched my new dress.'

'I wouldn't expect anything less from that halfwit,' I

heard her mumble.

'No, Damian's different. He's not a halfwit.'

'Hmm, because only brain surgeons try to jump train tracks in a shopping trolley. This would be Damian de Jagger, I'm surmising?'

'It's pronounced Dee Yay Grrr actually,' I said, pleased that she had got it wrong. 'Do you know him?'

She stared at me again. 'Yes, I know him. The boy is bacteria.'

The moonlight bounced off the gravestones, shimmering on the marble. I was cold. My poo coat was no longer keeping me warm. 'How much longer will you be?'

She sighed. 'And you need to know that because?'

'Because . . . I . . . one of my best friends lives at the vicarage and I won't be able to sleep thinking about someone digging up the graves here.'

'Where was your best friend tonight?' said the girl.

'What?'

'Where was your best friend while you were at the party?'

I glared at her. 'She was . . . there. Somewhere.' I couldn't remember seeing Poppy at the pool for the Be Merry. But she was definitely there for the Eat and Drink. She hadn't been chanting or anything. She'd just been watching with everyone.

'Seems to me that a best friend would have stepped in at some point and stopped you.' *Scrape, huff, scrape . . .*

'Look, can you stop doing that, please?' I said louder, not quite shouting but still cross all the same. That's what drink did to me. I became someone I didn't like. Someone shouty. Someone who had realised they didn't have a friend in the world.

'If you're so concerned about time, you could offer to help.' The girl stopped and threw something over to me and it clattered on the footpath. A small spade.

I stared at it. I stared back at her. 'You want me to dig with you?'

She sighed again, like I was really getting on her nerves. 'I'm not digging. I'm filling in. Many hands make light work, don't you know.'

So I picked up the spade. And I walked over to where she was under the willow tree and I helped her shift the dirt into the hole. The hole was big and long. I still didn't know exactly what she'd done there. I mean, people only carry shovels in graveyards for two reasons: to bury something or dig something up. Or someone.

So there we both were. *Scrape, scrape, huff, huff, scrape, scrape, huff, huff.*

'Have you been having a picnic?' I asked, nodding towards the cool bag.

'No,' she said. I was waiting for her to say something else, but she just carried on digging. Well, filling in.

'So what's in the picnic bag then?'

'I think I said I was finished with questions.' She began kicking the earth to get more of it in the hole.

'So you *are* doing something wrong,' I said, copying the kicking thing.

'Wrong in *your* book, maybe,' she said.

'What does that mean?' No answer. I brandished the spade. 'If you've robbed a grave, it's wrong in anyone's book.'

Scrape. Kick. Scrape. 'Not in mine it's not.'

'So you *have* robbed it?'

She looked at me. 'I like to think of it as reclaimed.'

'Ugh!' I cried, and my cry echoed around the graveyard. 'You can't!'

'You can,' she said. 'I can. Needs must.'

'Needs must?' I cried. 'I know there's been that crunchy thing where everyone's lost their money but you can't go around prising wedding rings off dead bodies, that's just horrible! Ugh!'

Before I could say another word, she took the spade from me, slung her shovel on top of the cool bag and left me, alone, standing there, stinking of poo and staring into the coal-black air. Well, the air wasn't black, the sky was. Air is just air. Come to think of it, *what* is dark? The air's not dark, cos if you trapped night air in a jar you wouldn't have a dark jar. And the sky's technically not dark either. But it felt dark.

Everything felt very dark indeed that night. But in a really weird way, I kinda liked it.

So this is me, Camille

There were lots of things I was afraid of – one-man bands, balloons, hammocks, sharks, velvet – but death wasn't one of them.

At primary school, everyone had thought I was a freak because I kept dead insects in my locker. And because I was chubby. And because my parents were old. But mostly because of the dead insect thing. I used to bring roadkill inside when I was little too. I'd kept them as pets. Mum and Dad had bought me this kitten once but it got run over in the road. They'd been horrified when they found me in my Wendy house playing tea parties and wearing the flattened cat like a scarf.

Mum said I was into dead stuff because of my name.

When she was fifty, she and Dad had gone on this old folks' Mediterranean cruise and they'd been at this art gallery when I'd started kicking the hell out of her. She hadn't even known she was up the duff, so I guess it was a bit of a shock when she suddenly found herself in some foreign chemist working out the Italian for 'pregnancy test'. Anyway, at the time of my kick-fest Mum had been looking at this painting of all these dead mermaids on a beach by this Italian painter called Camille Posticcio. She'd thought Camille was a woman so that's why she'd called me Camille. Posticcio was actually some crusty bloke with a white beard who was famous for painting dead things and being mad. He used to run naked through Florence feeling up nuns. But Mum hadn't known that.

So that was me, Camille. Named after a freaky bloke obsessed with dead things, and a little obsessed with dead things myself.

Anyway, one morning a few months back, I'd met Death up close and personal for the first time ever.

We lived in Hoydon's Bracht (apparently, Bracht is an old English name for beach) and the town was famous for three things: its pier, a cafe called 'Wonkies' that leaned twenty degrees to the left, and an incident when a mad cow had run up the high street and killed three people. There was a sign on the road that said '*Welcome to Hoydon's Bracht – the Town Where a Smile's Never a Frown.*' Last time I saw it, someone had crossed out the last bit and put '*the Town They Forgot to Close Down*'. It was twinned with a place in Belgium I couldn't pronounce, and most of the stores were pound shops or sold those chairs that tipped old people up.

My mum, Francine, used to be a nail artist and my grey-haired dad, Stephen, liked recycling. He was the only person I knew who at parties preferred the bit when you recycled the wrapping paper to opening the actual presents. They had run Sea View Guest House since the eighties, way before I was born. It was a four-storey town house, just off the seafront – handy for the beach and crazy golf, but annoying if you hated sand and seagulls. It was also a pain in the arse if you hated child labour, as I was called on at any moment to change beds or wait tables. Still, I had the whole third floor to myself, and my own shower, so that was nice.

Anyway, one day, Mum had asked me if I would take breakfast up to Mrs Cleak in room six: scrambled eggs, a pot of tea and the paper. I'd knocked three times on the door before I tried the handle. I'd gone inside, calling her name in case I caught her doing something old and saggy-butt naked that would scar me for life.

'Mrs Cleak?'

I'd known she was dead as soon as I saw her. She'd been completely still. Whenever she'd fallen asleep downstairs in the guests' lounge, she'd been all twitchy and farty. But this had been something completely else. I'd put the tray down and gone and sat beside her chair and I'd watched her be dead. I'd touched her cheek. It had been hard. I'd touched her hand. It had been cold. It had been so peaceful, sitting there with her. But after a bit I'd realised that I wasn't really sitting with Mrs Cleak, I was just sitting with her body, which she'd left behind like an old suitcase. Then Mum had come in and screamed the pictures off the walls.

Ever since then, my fascination with death had got worse. I just thought it was awesome. Not awesome like roller coasters, but awesome like it filled me with awe. I wondered what it felt like, to breathe a last breath. I wondered if it hurt in that second when your heart stopped beating. I wondered what my final thought would be when I croaked. My thoughts just before going to sleep were usually about food or boys, so maybe it would be the ultimate thought – a boy made of chocolate or something.

I wasn't into ghosts, even though I thought Mrs Cleak was now haunting our airing cupboard. Every time I opened the door it squeaked, and it sounded like Mrs Cleak saying, 'Oh hello, dear!' No, I was more into real death. Actual bodies. It boggled my mind. Lots of things boggled my mind, but death did more than anything.

I knew it was weird for a girl like me to be interested in that stuff. I was a big softie who got all squiggly over Christmas and liked cuddles and romance novels. I even had a dolls' house that I still liked to poke my head inside and pretend I was small. Someone like me shouldn't gawp at car accidents or peek through funeral parlour windows. She shouldn't feel happy in graveyards or tape programmes on the world's worst serial killers. But that's just me, Camille Mabb. I was a freak.

And now I'd met another freak. In a graveyard, digging. And she was all I could think about.

Monday Mourning

My phone had been off all weekend. I didn't want to speak to Lynsey or Poppy, my two best friends. I didn't know what I would say to them after freshers' night, when they'd left me to stew in the poo with everyone laughing at me. The three of us had been so close all through school, and last summer had been the best. We'd met at the pool a few times a week to get fit and ogle the lifeguards, gone down to the Bracht to get tans and ogle the coastguards, and hung around the Asda cafe drinking iced teas and ogling the security guards. There was definitely something about men who guarded things.

Now, only two weeks into A levels, I could feel us growing apart. My mum said it was natural for friendships to 'come unstitched at the seams as you get older'. But she also said Johnny Depp had a house on the hill by our dentist's, so I wasn't sure what to believe. The fact was that we were all into pretty different things these days. Lynx, that's what Lynsey liked to be called these days, had her sights set on the Olympics. Poppy wanted to be a violinist. We were all taking Sociology together, but that was the last stitch really. We didn't have to be friends any more. We could branch out, be who we were supposed to be in life. I didn't know what I wanted to be yet. When I'd had my careers interview, I'd been told I came across as a 'quite like'. I quite liked throwing the discus. I quite liked romance novels. I quite liked death. I'd asked if there was a job where I could throw the discus, read romance novels and study dead people, but they'd said there wasn't.

But that morning as I walked to college, I couldn't think about anything else but Digging Girl. The hems of my jeans were soaked and my bridesmaid's dress and pink coat were spattered with pretty, clear jewels of rain. Yeah, I still wore my first bridesmaid's dress. I'd had it since my mum's best friend's wedding when I was seven and it still fitted so now I wore it as a top. Poppy said it was a fashion statement. Lynx said it was a death wish. I didn't know what that meant.

That day I didn't care. I was all on fire looking for signs of Digging Girl. In every bus that passed me on the road, every girl I saw with her hood up. I even walked through the churchyard, just in case she was there. But she wasn't there.

The awful thought arrived that maybe she had been a ghost. Maybe it had been a dream? Maybe I was like that bloke in that film who meets this mega-cool bloke who you think is just some mega-cool bloke who he gets to be best friends with but it turns out to be just a pigment of his imagination all along. An imaginary friend. I'd been quite drunk that night, thanks to Damian de Jager, who'd kept pouring this green stuff down my throat. I'd only let him to feel his fingers on the back of my neck as he was doing it. I'd liked that. But perhaps Digging Girl had been right. Perhaps Damian de Jager wasn't the one for me.

The rain was hammering down when I reached college. Lynx and Poppy were huddled under a red umbrella outside. I could see Poppy's neat centre parting a mile away. I went over. They both looked at me, coloured red with umbrella glow.

'Hi,' I said, scuffing towards them.

'Hi,' they said. Lynx looked at Poppy, who was munching her way through a giant chocolate muffin with the most massive chocolate chunkies I'd ever seen.

'I'm soaked through,' I said.

'Me too,' said Lynx. 'My hems are soaking.'

'Mine too,' laughed Poppy, flicking her spare-rib-coloured hair away from her mouth as she galloped another acre of muffin.

We all watched the rain as it bulleted the concrete.

'Have you done the Sociology homework?' I asked.

'Yeah,' said Poppy. 'Have you?'

I nodded. 'You?'

Lynx shook her head. 'You still thinking of quitting and doing Media Studies?'

'Yeah, maybe,' I said. 'Or something else. I haven't decided yet.'

There was only so long we could talk about subject choices and how wet our hems were. One of us had to say something about Friday. It turned out to be Lynx.

'I texted you loads on Saturday,' she said, zipping her jacket to her chin.

'Yeah, me too,' said Poppy.

'Are you mad at us for freshers' night? You were so determined, Mills . . .'

'We'd all drunk too much,' I said. 'That snakebite thing Damian was passing around went straight to my head.'

Why was I making excuses for them? It *was* their fault. They *should* have stopped me eating that sandwich, drinking that … Ugh, my stomach lurched just thinking about it. They *should* have stopped me getting in the poo pool. They hadn't even been drunk, so it wasn't as though they could use that as an excuse. Lynx never drank because of her training and Poppy's parents forbad/bedded/bidded it, them being all churchy and stuff. But for some infuriating reason, I gave them both another chance. 'It's fine, really. I'm my own worst enemy. Don't worry.'

A group of boys in football kit breezed past us, and one of them called out, 'How was your sandwich, Camille? Make a nice *meal*, *Camille*, did it?' The other boys laughed. *Hur hur hur.*

'Ignore them,' said Poppy. 'None of them had the courage to eat it.'

'Or the stupidity,' giggled Lynx.

I fiddled with my coat zip. We stood in silence. Me and

my best friends, without a clue what to say to one another.

Tamsin Double-Barrelled and her clicky-clacky brunette Daddy-pays-for-everything crew breezed past with mumblings about Friday night, giggles galore. I knew they were laughing about me. I heard the word 'pube'. But I didn't have time to dwell. Lynx dropped a bomb on me.

'Damian's asked me to the Halloween party,' she blurted.

Poppy gulped down a mouthful of muffin.

'Oh right,' I said, my guts coming to the boil. 'Wow.' My mouth was saying wow; my brain was saying *You utter backstabber.* The Halloween party was the next big event on the college social calendar. It was bigger than freshers'. I had hoped Damian would ask me and we'd arrive in his dad's orange Ferrari and totes blow everyone out of the water. Or at least, blow the memory of freshers' out of everyone's minds. But it was not to be. And I felt sick.

'No hard feelings, Mills,' said Lynx. 'I know you liked him and everything.'

I screwed up my face to look not bothered. 'Nah, he's not really my type.'

I'd just said that so Lynx didn't know how much it hurt me. In truth, Damian de Jager was anyone's type, and he knew it too. I was deeply in something with him, that I knew. Whether or not it was love, I knew not. But I'd Googled my symptoms when I was watching him play football a few weeks before – my heart rate sped up when I looked at him, my knees went to jelly and when I looked in my little compact mirror after he'd winked at me when

I'd thrown the ball back to him, my pupils were massive – I had all the signs of being in love. So it was a pretty safe bet that I was.

I remembered how Digging Girl had wrongly called him de Jagger. Where *was* she today? I peered through the rain at the students stepping out of buses and parked cars. I wanted to see her more than anyone else in the world.

'And guess what,' said Lynx. 'Splodge Hawkins has asked out Pops!'

My guts boiled over. They *both* had boyfriends now? I couldn't believe it. They started OMGing over a text Poppy had got from Splodge, one of Damian's mates.

'I just can't believe he actually asked,' Poppy chuckled, over and over – phone in one hand, muffin in the other. At one point she went to take a bite out of the phone. I didn't know what Poppy saw in Andrew Hawkins. He and Poppy didn't really fit together. She was all neat and prim and never swore, and he swore a lot and looked like a grubby blonde baby who'd fallen face first into a pizza. But they were both churchy and did orchestra, and lately they'd been Tweeting quite a bit about some band they both liked called Little Maniacs, so I guessed it worked for them.

'Read it again. Tell me exactly what it says,' said Lynx, all squealy-voiced.

Poppy squinted her enormous eyes behind her glasses as she read the text again. '*Do u want 2 go 2 Halloween prty wiv me? Luv Splodge* and there's a kiss.'

'One kiss?' said Lynx.

'Yeah, but capital X. And a full stop.'

'Oh my God, that's so definitive!'

My attention wandered the third time Poppy read out the text. I saw this figure, striding across the concrete where the buses pull in – long black coat, hood down, hair covering its forehead. As the figure got closer, I could see it was her. It was Digging Girl! In the daylight, I could see she had the most intense blue eyes, bluer than swimming pool water, and they fixed on mine as I stared. If she had been in one of my romance novels, she'd have been the princess, no question. She was Cheddar Gorgeous. Maybe not with that hair though. It was black and matted and looked like every so often she just grabbed a handful and hacked at it with a knife. She strode straight past us, soaking wet and stinking violently of bleach. I could barely breathe.

'Camille? Camille? Mills!'

I don't know how long Lynx had been saying my name but when I looked, she and Poppy had started walking towards the Humanities block where our Sociology classroom was.

'Sorry,' I said, scurrying over.

'Where did you go?' she laughed. 'Death Watch sucking you in, was she?'

'Who?' I said, catching up with them.

'I don't know her name,' said Lynx, 'but she glared at me in the hall on Friday and I full on checked my pulse. I thought she'd struck me down dead. Weirdo.'

'Isn't her dad that mad bloke?' said Poppy.

'What mad bloke?' Lynx and I said in synchro, smiling when we'd said it.

Poppy's voice dropped to a whisper. 'That mad

professor who lived up on the hill. Went on a mmmm and mmmmd all those students.'

'Mmmmd?' I said. Poppy did this whenever there was a word she couldn't say. She didn't like swearing or saying any word which had a harsh meaning. I think it was because her dad was a vicar. They had to say grace before meals and everything. So she mmmmd instead.

'Yeah, he was a professor at that university in London. He went on a killing spree,' she whispered. 'Killed his students.'

'Oh I know,' I said.

'No!' Lynx gasped.

'They found . . . things,' Poppy continued. 'At his house. The police came out with boxes. Boxes and boxes of bits. Bits of people. Heads and arms and mmmms.'

I knew all about it. I'd been all over that story when it had first broke on our local news. His name was Thomas Lutwyche. He'd been a professor at this big university and he'd gone totally bonkers and started living in the trees. I went up to his spooky-looking big house on Clairmont Hill the day they started bringing out the boxes of things the police had found after they'd taken him to a psychiatric hospital. I couldn't get closer than the police tape, no one could. But we all saw the boxes being brought out. Digging Girl was *his* daughter? Wow. Just, wow.

'It's absolutely true,' said Poppy as we rounded the main building and came to the square next to the Humanities block. It was raining a lot harder now.

'So what was he doing with the body parts?' asked Lynx.

'Nobody knows,' said Poppy, in the spooky way she

always used to tell us ghost stories when we slept over at the vicarage. 'They couldn't identify the bodies. He went to a loony bin though. The day the police broke the door down, I swear, you could smell that house from here. I heard they'd been eating bits too.'

'Ugh!' said Lynx. 'Freaks!'

'So what happened to the professor?' I said, folding my arms.

'That's the most frightening part of the whole story,' said Poppy. 'Nobody really knows.' Her grey eyes were double-wide behind her rain-spotted glasses. 'Some say he escaped from the asylum and went on the run and mmmd people and allsorts. I heard one rumour he cut off his own head to see how long his body would live without it . . .'

'Gross!' shrieked Lynx, as she checked the flatness of her stomach in a passing window, then checked her ponytail in the next one along.

'. . . and another rumour that he's actually living back in the woods on Clairmont Hill, like Tarzan. And that *she,* the daughter, is looking after him. Feeding him human flesh and stuff.'

I laughed. 'A professor who eats people and lives in the woods? That's mad.'

'Yeah, so is he,' said Poppy. 'And so is she.' We all watched Digging Girl as she disappeared into the Science block. 'I'd keep your distance from her if you want to keep your organs where God intended. Who knows what goes on up at that house.' Poppy took out some mini Jaffa Cakes from her blazer pocket as we followed Lynx into the Humanities block and along the chattery, locker-slammy corridor towards Sociology.

'Do you know her name, Pops, the professor's daughter?' I asked, like I really didn't care.

'No,' said Poppy, as two Jaffa Cakes committed double suicide in her mouth.

'Bet it's something like Elvira or Morticia,' Lynx chuckled, stopping to remove a stone from her trainer.

'It's Zoe,' said a deep voice behind us.

Damian de Jager, sexy-faced footballer extraordinaire, was behind us, flanked on both sides by his usual bookends, Splodge Hawkins and Louis Burnett. We stopped walking as Damian grabbed Lynx by the waist and gave her a kiss so tonguey and wet I almost felt a bit of sick come up. He had on a tight white t-shirt that showed off the hard shape of his chest beneath it, all toned and perfect. My heart went predictably *bang-bang-bangy* in my chest, which was annoying cos I didn't want it to. I couldn't help it though – he was still sexy with sprinkles on and I wasn't in the least bit ready for his jelly.

'Yeah, she lives up at Spook Central on Clairmont Hill,' he said in his Cockney twang. 'Second most expensive house in the town, my dad reckons. After ours. D'you have a good time Friday night, Camille?'

'Yeah, it was good,' I laughed. 'Made a bit of a fool of myself I suppose though.' I was going a shade redder with every word I said.

'Nah, nah, it was good. Well funny,' he said. 'You're funny when you're pissed.'

I felt my pulse – it was going banana cakes. I bet my pupils were dilated too. I wanted to get my pocket mirror out of my bag to check my eyes but Louis Burnett was looking at me like I was on the blink.

Damian and Lynx were talking and I caught the tail end of their convo.

' . . . totally, yeah, they're in the back of my car. It's half what you'd pay in the canteen here. Twice what I paid for them though.'

He grinned the sexiest grin in the world. I could just look at him all the livelong day. The way his brown hair stuck up at the back. His eyes like the bluest marbles. His diamond ear-stud. His jaw-line so sharp you could cut your birthday cake with it. I couldn't help feeling the same sicky pang in my stomach I always felt at the sight of him. *Damn you, sicky pang!*

I watched his lips as he spoke. I always watched boys' lips when they spoke. I imagined what they would feel like on mine. Damian was talking about how last night he'd broken into a sweet shop in town and stolen all this stuff. He had his own business, selling sweets, drinks, stationery, sim cards, whatever students wanted – for half the price they would pay for them at the college. He was making a fortune, even though his family already had one. His dad, Jeff de Jager had come down to the Bracht from London a few years ago and gone around buying up most of the town like he was in a game of Monopoly. My dad said it was because of Jeff and his 'friends on the council' that we couldn't have planning permission for a porch on the front of our guest house. The de Jagers were 'power-crazy greedy bastards', according to my dad.

Louis Burnett was still staring at me, so I totally gave

up on getting my mirror out and zipped up my bag. Louis was in my History class but he never spoke. He always sat on his own at the back, trying to look like he wasn't there. I knew of him from primary school but we'd never hung out then either. He was a bit weird. Cute in a brown-eyed puppy-left-out-in-the-cold kind of way but his dress sense was wacko. Today he was wearing a faded green Bride of Frankenstein T-shirt, a hat like my grandad wears, chimney-sweep boots and a kilt. Even Splodge dressed better in his jeans and grubby rugby shirt, despite all the fat rolls and stains. He and Poppy were doing some weird flirting thing with their Jaffa Cakes.

'So yeah, Splodger spent all of yesterday eatin' my bullets on Call of Duty. Cig?' said Damian, and offered me his packet of Marlboros. I shook my head. I didn't smoke. Not since I'd taken a sneaky drag of my auntie's cigarette at a party when I was ten and had such a tickly cough for a week afterwards, I convinced myself I had lung cancer.

'You can't smoke indoors, baby,' Lynx reminded him.

'You can't,' said Damian, lighting up regardless. 'What they gonna do to me?'

I still had one of Damian's old Marlboro dog-ends at home in a matchbox. I'd seen him chuck it down on the second day of term. I thought maybe one day I'd be able to clone a boy just like him, from the spit. I just had to learn to clone first.

'You hooked up for the Halloween party yet, Camille?' he said, biting his inner lip. I really didn't know why he kept singling me out when I was saying nothing at all. It seemed like the more I was trying to be invisible, the more noticeable I was.

'Uh, no, not yet,' I smiled, once again Miss Cherry Tomato Features.

'Loser needs a date, don't you, Lou?' said Splodge, wiping his mouth with his hand and draping his arm around Louis the way people do when they're acting like you're friends but really they just get a kick out of watching you go red. Lynx did this all the time and I hated it.

Louis swept his emo fringe aside and shrugged, shoving his hands in his cardigan pockets. He had loads of friendship bracelets on his wrists, which I thought was weird seeing as he only had two friends and never actually spoke.

Poppy wiped her glasses and giggled. Splodge went red in both cheeks and scratched his nose with his thumb. Louis Burnett looked at me and I looked away. It was a carousel of awkwardness for what felt like forever but was only about five seconds.

'How about you two hookin' up then?' Damian went on, as though trying to bulldoze through the unease.

I shrugged. Louis did a kind of half-nod.

'Sweet. You and Loser can come together then, can't you? Everybody's happy,' said Damian, looking at both of us in turn and striding off, his arm slung around Lynx's shoulders and his magnificent arse framed beautifully by the tightness of his jeans. Suddenly he looked back at me. 'And you know where I am if you need help with that thing, Camille, yeah?' He winked at me as he walked away.

'What's the "thing" Camille?' said Poppy, sucking the flimsy orange disc of her last Jaffa Cake.

'Nothing, he's just being stupid,' I said, scratching the back of my head to hide my blushing cheeks with my arm. 'Come on. Let's go and learn how to sociologise.'

So this is the thing . . .

O kay, so 'the thing' I needed help with was my virginity, which the life-ruiner Damian de Jager had found out I still had through sheer cheek on my third day of college. I'd been in the library trying to find this stupid book we had to read for English and he'd just appeared, cornering me at the dark end of the short-story section, his shirt collar all up like Dracula.

'All right? I'm Damian. Your name's Camille, right? Lynsey's mate?' he'd said.

I'd nodded, blushing fiercely of course, clutching my books to my chest.

'I'll come straight to the point. I'm in the virginity business. You got it; I want it. You need hookin' up, I'm your boy. You still got your V-plates, I'll take you out on the roads, show you what's what. Here's my number.' He'd handed me his card. 'You'll meet a lot of scrotes in this place. A lot of knuckle-draggers who don't know how to treat their women. Half of 'em couldn't find their way to a girl's G-spot with a sat nav.'

'Uh . . .'

'So what I'm saying is, don't worry about any of them. I got the sat nav. And I got the goods.' He'd looked down at his crotch, then back up at me.

'Wha . . .'

'I can deal with it so you ain't gotta worry about it, then you can just enjoy the rest of your A levels without it hanging over you. Do ya know what I mean?'

I'd nodded, my mouth doing a guppy impression. He'd had a green t-shirt on under his shirt that said MAN WHORE in really big white letters and he had been staring at me so hard I couldn't catch my breath. If stares could make babies, I'd have been having his triplets.

'No pressure, no refusal, guaranteed good times. You keep that card safe and text me when you need me.'

'Uh . . .'

'Don't worry. It's a free service. And I'll always answer.' And he'd walked away, one hand in his pocket.

I hadn't said one word for another six hours.

I'd thought about calling him, I really had. But it wasn't right. Although I had all the feelings of love – my pupils dilated, my cheeks blushed, plus I fancied his face off – something felt wrong. I was scared. I was properly scared. What if I called him, we did it and I was completely rubbish at it? What then? Would it be all round college that I was rubbish at it? And how did you *know* if you were rubbish at it? Maybe I wasn't ready. But I was sick of just thinking about it or reading about it in one of my romance novels. It wasn't enough anymore. I wanted it to happen to me. I didn't want to keep gazing at people in the street holding hands or snogging on coffee shop doorsteps, wondering, always wondering. How they did it. *Where* they did it. How many times they'd done it. Everyone I knew must have done it. The woman on the till in Sainsbury's. My dentist. Johnny Depp. My parents – ugh! But *I* hadn't. And now the perfect, sexy-faced opportunity was there for me to grab and I wasn't at all sure that I wanted to.

That was me, Camille Mabb. A sixteen-year-old girl who didn't want to do sex stuff with Damian de Jager. Freak. The weirdest kind of sixteen-year-old. I let my race down. And this was when I realised there was something really quite seriously wrong with me.

However much I fancied him, he actually quite scared me. He was so easy about s.e.x. and I really wasn't. Lynx was pretty whatever about s.e.x. too. She was always talk-ing about things she'd done, things she'd touched, things she'd tried. I didn't know what half of it meant but I always nodded along, and afterwards I'd have to look it all up on the Internet.

The last Sociology lesson, I was so *grrrrr* about both my best friends dumping me for boyfriends that I decided to unpick the last stitch. The Sociology classroom and the Chemistry lab were opposite one another but in different blocks, and from my seat I could look across the way and see Zoe through the window. I barely heard a thing our teacher, Mr Atwill, who looked a bit like a nerdy Jesus, was saying about crime and deviancy. I was too busy gazing at Zoe pouring liquids and examining jars of blue stuff. I wanted to be where she was. I wanted to be near her. Everyone gave her a wide berth in the corridors. She didn't seem to be bullied or ignored; people just stayed away, like they'd stay away from someone with a disease. But I was desperate to be in her orbit in some small way. And to find out exactly what she had been digging up in the churchyard on freshers' night.

So after a lesson where the only things I'd really learned were that Splodge now puts five kisses on every love text to Poppy and that Damian's texts to Lynx were, well, let's just say 'photos', I told Mr Atwill I was quitting and taking up Human Biology instead. He laughed. Poppy laughed. Lynx laughed.

But I wasn't actually joking.

And it was all because of Zoe Lutwyche.

By Wednesday lunchtime, having done my own head in with my confusing fears about sexy times with Damian and my sudden lusting over Digging Girl, I'd fully convinced myself I must have become a lesbian overnight. There was no other explanation for it.

I wondered if that was a recognised thing – if it *did* come over you all of a sudden or whether it had to be something you always knew, like when you were a baby or something. Did babies know they were lesbians? All I knew for sure was that I couldn't stop thinking about her, couldn't stop looking for her in the corridors. I also really liked the way she did her eye make up and I wondered if I could borrow her eyeliner when we became friends.

I did the tests to see if I was actually in love with Zoe. Did my heart rate speed up when I saw her? Yes it did. Did my knees go to jelly? A bit, yeah. Did my pupils get bigger? I didn't know – I was too busy staring at her to check. So I had all the signs of being in love even though I'd never fancied either Lynx or Poppy or any other girl for that matter. I was in a 'tumult'. I'd remembered that word from English.

A highly distressing agitation of mind or feeling; a turbulent mental or emotional disturbance.

That was me, Camille. In a tumult.

I couldn't concentrate on anything, couldn't focus. At lunch, I left half my ham salad with no dressing which was really odd for me because normally I'm so starving I start chewing on a napkin once my food's gone. I knew I needed help. I decided to go to the counsellor's office at the end of the day, see if he had any advice or leaflets about rapid-onset lesbianism.

But I forgot to go to the counsellor. My first Human Biology lesson saw to that.

When Zoe walked into that Biology lab, it was like I could breathe again. And she went from my fastest ever girl crush to a code-red all-out bleach-stinking obsession.

What she did in that lesson was, in a word, electrifying. *She* was electrifying.

Weird Science

Two girls ran out of the lab crying. Others pressed their hands over their mouths like they were going to puke. Most just went all squinchy-faced and jumpy on their stools. I thought one girl with glasses was going to pee herself. Mr Chaney, the Human Biology teacher, was striding between our desks with a jar of dead hamsters, leaving one on every workstation. He came to me and plonked one down.

'Thanks,' I said.

The door at the back of the room burst open and everyone, including me, turned around to see Zoe walk in. I actually smiled. I didn't know anyone else's name in the class and suddenly I felt like I had a friend there. Dressed all in black and keeping her head down, she made her way to the only free seat in the room: the seat next to mine. Something in my chest swallowed something else.

'See me after, Zoe Lutwyche,' Chaney boomed, as he took up position behind his desk, scrunching up his crotchety face to read his notes. Zoe scrabbled in her bag for a tatty black book and pen. She didn't seem to notice me at all.

'You have before you *Phodopus sungorus*, the Russian winter white dwarf hamster. We will examine the digestive and respiratory systems, skeleton and muscle groups. On your worksheet, note down the organs you can identify and their primary functions . . .'

I caught my breath as I leaned over to say something to her. I couldn't believe how nervous I was. 'It's me. From the graveyard,' I whispered. She was rubbing her hands with an antiseptic wipe. She looked at me and then back at the teacher.

'Take your dissection pins . . .' said Chaney, and he went on to describe what we had to do. 'Lie your specimen ventral side up on your dissection pan and pin the four paws to the baize . . .'

Zoe Lutwyche had already taken out some squiggly organ stuff before I'd even worked out what a dissection 'pin'? was. I just wanted her to speak back to me. Say anything, just so I could hear her voice. I leaned in to her again. 'Wow. You're really good at this, aren't you? You've done this before.'

Chaney tapped the board diagram. 'Pinch a skin fold in the mid-ventral line as seen here and take your scalpel to make your incision down through the centre . . .'

I had a little go at snipping open my hamster's stomach but I made a bit of a mess of it. I couldn't get a nice clean cut like Zoe. I looked at her. She was full to the brim with concentration. I so wanted to talk to her about the other night, maybe ask if she wanted an assistant with whatever she was doing.

I leaned in yet again. 'I haven't told anyone, you know. About . . . that night at the graveyard. About what you were doing.'

'What was I doing?' she murmured, still focussed on her hamster surgery.

'I don't know,' I said. 'But I won't tell. I won't tell anyone.'

She didn't say anything.

'If you tell me what you were doing . . .'

She stopped briefly, threw me a blue-eyed glare and went back to her work. She was so cool and intelligent. And not to mention pretty. And it amazed me how . . .

'Miss Mabb, pay attention to your own specimen, please,' came Mr Chaney's crackly old voice suddenly.

'Sorry, sir,' I said, almost falling off my stool. A smile split Zoe's mouth.

'I mean, I won't tell anyone what you were doing. Not that I know anyway. Can I . . . come with you, next time? I want to see.'

'See what?' she said. By this time, her hamster had been skinned so perfectly he looked like a sausage lying on a tiny fur rug.

I whispered, checking to see if Chaney had turned back to the board. 'Bodies and stuff. I don't want to rob anything though . . .'

'You'd better make a start,' she said, looking across at my hamster. 'He tours the workstations.'

I frowned, looking at my hamster every which way. 'I don't know how to do it without slicing into anything. You don't fancy doing mine as well, do you?'

Chaney's crackly old notes rose again into the lab's pet-shoppy air. 'Now the inner organs are exposed. Can you identify the liver? Yes. Good, very good.'

Zoe had already identified the squiggly organ stuff and started stitching her hamster back up the middle. When she was done and when Chaney's back was turned again, Zoe switched her dissection pan with mine and started on my hamster, all without saying a word.

'Thanks a really lot,' I said.

She sliced down my hamster like she was cutting into a tiny pie and picked up her magnifying glass to get a closer look. Chaney started doing his rounds, so I picked up my scalpel and poked at Zoe's hamster sausage like I was interested. He stopped at our table. For a split second I thought he was going to make some comment about us switching hamsters, but amazingly he didn't.

'Excellent, Camille. You're a natural, it would seem!'

'Thanks,' I said, my voice breaking in shock. He moved on to the next desk and I twirled my scalpel around in my fingers like a baton, rather pleased with my first ever praise from Chaney. I looked at Zoe. 'Thanks, Zoe.'

She turned her head, stared at me, and went back to her surgery.

I continued to twirl my scalpel until the knife nicked my thumb.

'Ah!' I unzipped my pencil case and reached in to grab a happy flower dressing. 'Are you going to the Halloween party?' I said when Chaney had clacked back towards his desk.

'Pardon?' she asked.

'The Halloween party. It's at the end of the month.'

'So why are you asking me at the beginning of the month?' she muttered.

'Well, it's quite a big event,' I explained, 'and I heard people usually start asking people out now and hiring their fancy dresses and limos and everything. It's like a second prom. We have to have special outfits and masks and stuff, which the Art Department are making, and the boys have to ask us to dance, it's like the law of the party. And we have, like, a buffet and one of those horse things you hit with a stick. I've got an orange dress and I'm going as a pumpkin.'

She looked up. 'And you have to go, to dispel the memories of the Eat, Drink and Be Merry, I take it?'

'Pretty much,' I nodded.

'Is that all people care about here, parties?' she said. 'Is that all they like to do, stumble from one party to the next? Freshers'. Halloween. Christmas, Valentine's?'

'Pretty much,' I said again.

'What types of human waste will they persuade you to ingest for that one?' she muttered.

'Halloween will be different,' I said, trying not to let her comment sting me.

'I'll have to make sure I'm either dead or in jail by then,' said Zoe.

The strip light was flashing above Mr Chaney's chair.

He set down his papers and stood on top of his desk to wiggle about with the little thing at the end of it.

'I suppose he's the preferred dancing partner,' said Zoe, tapping the spine of my ring binder where ages ago I'd written 'Mrs de Jager' in bubble writing.

'Yeah, totes,' I said, going violently hot in the cheeks yet again as I tried scratching over the bubble-writing with my Biro. (One day, I'm going to have surgery on my cheeks to take the blush out of them, it's so annoying.) 'Except Damian's asked Lynx to go with him. Lynx is – was – one of my best friends . . .'

'De Jager,' Zoe interrupted. 'Yes, he's in my Chemistry class,' she murmured. 'I caught him in the teachers' store cupboard last week, stealing chemicals.'

'Did you report him?'

'No,' she scowled at me.

'Why were you in the teachers' store cupboard?' I asked her.

'I hope you've been listening, Camille. You won't know what to do next.' Chaney stepped down from his chair but the strip light was still flashing.

'Yes, sir.' I really wasn't listening any more though, it had to be said.

'And here we have it,' he announced, pointing to the whiteboard diagram of a squiggly brain thing. 'When you have cut through the abdominal wall you will have exposed the large intestine . . . What's so amusing, Tamsin?'

Mr Chaney was telling off Tamsin Double-Barrelled for laughing at her hamster's bottom, while Harvey With A Squint and Kayden No Neck were in hysterics, having stitched both their hamsters together. I watched Zoe working on her hamster and within seconds, she had stitched it totally back up again, her fingers so furious they could have been playing a really fast tune on a piano. Chaney went back to fussing about the strip light and announced he was going to have to get a new bulb from the store cupboard.

'Damian's cute though, isn't he?' I grinned. 'I mean, he's a bit of a head case but he is lush. I thought I might be in love with him but . . .'

'I'm not really interested in boys,' said Zoe.

'What?' I said, trying not to let my face in on the fact my brain was shocked. 'Well, that's great. That's really cool. But I wouldn't tell anyone that you're . . . like that if I were you. Not yet anyway. Your old school was probably really relaxed about it but girls here might get funny. You know. It might stop you fitting in.'

'Funny about what?'

'Well, girls worry when they know a new girl might . . . fancy them.'

'Why would I *fancy* them?'

'You said you weren't interested in boys.'

'I'm not interested in boys. And before you ask, I don't *fancy* girls either.'

I chuckled. 'Well, what else is there?'

'Science,' she said. She removed a black zip-up case from her bag and opened it. Inside were lots of syringes filled with a blue liquid, as blue as her eyes.

I frowned. She, in her starey way, stared back at me. How weird. I'd never met anyone who fancied science before. I'd watched this documentary once about a woman who was in love with the Berlin Wall but cheated on it with the fence post in her garden. Sometimes I wished I could be happy with a fence post. But I wasn't. I wanted a boyfriend. A sweet, sexy, funny, warm boyfriend who'd treat me well and hug me all the time. Was it too much to ask? I'd love to hug a boy. Or just have my hand held for a bit. I dreamed about it. I ached for it. Hang on, I'd thought boy. Not girl. Maybe I wasn't a lesbian after all?

Clink clink.

When I looked up, Zoe was standing before the store cupboard. She had slid the top bolt across. Chaney's muffled shouts were coming from inside.

'Gather around, everyone. I want to show you something,' she announced.

'Zoe, you open this door right now!' Chaney's cries from the cupboard again.

'Mr Chaney!' Tamsin Double-Barrelled screamed, lunging for the door.

Zoe stood in her way. 'I think we'll leave things as they are, for now,' she said, slowly producing from nowhere one of the syringes, three-quarters full of blue liquid. Tamsin Double-Barrelled backed away, before darting towards the main door and out of the room. Two other girls followed and all three of them ran crying past outside the window. Everyone else from the Three Joshes to Oliver Big Hair stayed put.

Duff duff duff. 'Help! Someone get help!'

'Now, as I said, gather round,' said Zoe again, smiling.

'And bring your hamsters, whatever stage of dissection they are at.'

We all did as she said, like she had cast some spell on us. My hamster looked pretty gunky but I scraped it off my dissection pan and brought it to her.

On the desk, Zoe had placed two leads with crocodile clips at the ends, a small black bag and a block of wood with knobs on. She took her hamster and laid it in front of her. She circled over its heart with her fingertip.

Duff duff duff duff duff.

'He wouldn't appreciate this. But I know you will.' She smiled, and for a second I thought I saw a glint on one of her teeth. She took a pair of thin rubber gloves from a box on the desk. 'Now, this hamster is dead, do you all agree?'

Silence.

'Your hamster is dead.' She pointed to Laura Yellow Boots. 'And *your* hamster is dead.' She pointed to William Pratt. 'And *your* hamster is dead.' She pointed to me. 'You all saw me open this hamster up and put it back together, yes?'

I nodded again. My hamster was probably deader than anybody's. Chaney was still going ballistic in the cupboard. *Duff duff duff bang!*

Zoe looked at all of us in turn. 'You will all look back on this day and say, "I was there." You won't believe you are seeing this. But you will see it.' She was laughing. I thought someone had told a joke I'd missed.

I started laughing too, because mad laughter is kind of infectious. No one else did though. Another girl stepped quietly out of the room.

Holding up the syringe, she announced, 'I have injected this hamster with some of what is in this syringe. I administered it to its lower extremities and directly to the heart, which I checked was healthy when I opened it up.'

'What's the blue stuff?' I asked, then put my hand over my mouth, thinking maybe it wasn't the time to ask questions.

I could have sworn she smiled at me before saying, 'Good question. Inside the syringe is Ambystoma zoexanthe serum 651. This serum has the power to not only regenerate damaged tissue, but also repair wounds, fissures and abrasions. It is also a magnificent electrical conductor and it is the glue that is starting to put this little hamster together again.'

'Woah, sweet,' Hindu Josh With The Headphones muttered.

'And now . . .' Zoe announced, brandishing the two leads. She clipped one end of each lead on to the hamster's front paws, attaching the other ends to the battery in the middle of the wooden block. 'We apply electrical pulses to prompt muscle contraction. This is galvanism. Electricity, you see, holds the very key to life.'

'But that hamster's dead,' said Skinny Josh On Crutches. 'It's so dead.'

Watching the wall clock, Zoe flicked the battery switch up to five.

'Oh. My. God,' breathed William Pratt.

We watched the hamster's body. It was still as a stone. After a second, it twitched. Sparks crackled from the metal clips on its paws. The paws fluttered, then flopped. Zoe took the clips off. The paws fluttered again. The eyes opened.

'Oh my God!' It was the most amazing thing I'd ever seen in my entire life. I know judges on talent shows said this kind of thing every time someone sang in tune, but this actually especially was amazing. The amazingest.

The long cut on the hamster's stomach had disappeared. I hadn't noticed when, it had just gone. The hamster moved. Stretched out. There were gasps. Within seconds, its body was squirming to right itself. Scratchy Max ran out. Josie With The Humungous Handbag started crying and Emma With The Nose Ring slapped both her hands over her mouth. Within a minute, the hamster was sniffing around the desk, finding a peanut Zoe had put there for it.

'You see what has happened?' said Zoe, switching off the battery. 'The serum, or Ambystoma zoexanthe serum 651 as it is properly known, has worked its way through this creature's body and repaired the dead tissue. The electric impulses have reanimated its musculature and restarted its heart.'

'That's . . . incredible!' I said.

'That's science,' she said.

'But, it was definitely dead, wasn't it?' said Blonde Josh In The Liverpool Shirt.

'Yes, it was,' said Zoe, her face alive with excitement.

Duff duff duff duff. '*ZOE LUTWYCHE, OPEN THIS DOOR IMMEDIATELY!*'

'As you can see, this hamster is alive when moments ago we had all taken it to be deceased. With the help of this,' she said, picking up the empty syringe, 'we have achieved the unthinkable. Stroke it. Feel its *warmth*!'

It was the most amazing thing I had ever seen since I'd been alive. It beat all the magic tricks I'd ever seen and all the cartwheels I'd ever done and finding a dead woman. Anyway, it was truly awesies.

'Aaaaaarrrrgggghhhhh!' William Pratt's delayed scream set several girls off screaming and this set off Chaney's banging again. *Duff duff duff duff duff.*

In his haste to get out, Oliver Big Hair fell backwards over a stool. Josie With The Humungous Handbag crashed straight into Laura Yellow Boots, who'd already pushed over Hindu Josh With The Headphones in her hurry to get out of the room. Hindu Josh now looked like he was going to throw up in the fish tank. All the commotion must have frightened the poor hamster because he scuttled to the edge of the desk and took a running jump.

Everyone not puking or fainting hurtled around the classroom, searching for the tiny fur-ball as it darted along the skirting boards. Stools clattered to the floor, tables scraped back, brooms brushed, glass smashed, feet stamped, arms flapped.

'It's there, quick, get it!'

'Stamp on it!'

'There it is, there, there, there!'

'Aaaaarrrrgggghhhhh!'

'Kill it!'

'Get it!'

I stayed beside the teacher's table with Zoe, watching the madness unfold. She looked at me. 'You must really think I'm crazy now, don't you?'

'Huh?' I said. 'I think it's amazing. I think . . . you're amazing.'

A shadow of a smile appeared on Zoe's face. She held out her hand.

'Camille Mabb,' I smiled back and shook it.

'No,' she said, frowning. 'I want your hamster. I'm going to do all of them.'

Pier Pressure

So Zoe was put on 'indefinite suspension' for the hamster shenanigans, and for locking a teacher in the store cupboard *and* because the hamsters she had brought back to life turned out to be mad. Like, proper mad. Chewing through concrete kind of mad.

Holes were appearing in pillars around college two days later and there was talk of college closing so they could get pest control in. Unfortunately, talk was all it was. I still had to go in for classes, which all sucked when there was no promise of seeing Zoe before, during or after them. I missed her a lot. It's not very cool to admit you're lonely, but I'm not very cool, I know that, and I was very lonely. Like that man in that film who's stranded on a desert island and his only friend is this ball he's drawn a face on. And all the way through the film you're thinking, *That's just a ball he's drawn a face on*, but it's all he's got to talk to and then he goes and shouts at it and the ball floats off on the sea and he's so upset. I tried drawing a face on the dry chewing gum ball I'd parked on the edge of my desk during History but it wasn't the same. It was just a lump of chewing gum; it wasn't my friend.

Anyway, Poppy did eventually send me a pity text asking me to meet them all at the pier that Friday night and because I didn't want to stay at home watching *Gardener's World* with Mum and Dad, I decided to go. I showered, Impulsed my knickers and put on my lemon bridesmaid dress, yellow leggings, black Mary Janes and second-best lemon Alice band. It was my *I'm On My Own But I'm So Confident I Don't Care* outfit. It made me feel good, like I'd made a real effort.

When I got to the pier entrance, I wished I *hadn't* made so much effort. It was cold and everyone was in jeans and hoodies so I immediately looked weird. All except Louis Burnett, I noticed, who was still wearing his Scottish-chimney-sweep-with-cardigan combo, with a scruffy black leather jacket on top. Splodge and Poppy were holding hands and feeding each other green candy-floss, and Lynx was batting her eyelashes at Damian and touching his chest.

'All right?' said Damian, looking me up and down again. 'You scrub up well.'

'All right?' said Louis Burnett and Splodge together.

'Hi, Mills,' said Lynx, laughing at something Damian had said before I arrived.

'All right?' I said, fidgeting and generally being seven sorts of awks.

My blushing cheeks and lemon dress turned me into rhubarb and custard.

Lynx and Damian started strolling up the boardwalk with their shared box of chips. My heart pulsed. They were kissing, barely watching where they were walking. Oh to be that happy and in love, I thought. To be so hung up about someone all you want to do all day is hold hands and kiss.

'Look what Splodge got me, Mills,' squealed Poppy, running over with a brand-new touch screen phone. 'Well, I bought it but his dad runs Fone Frenzy in the High Street and he got me a really good deal. Isn't it awesome? We can Skype on it.'

'I don't have Skype,' I told her.

'No, me and Splodge, I meant,' she giggled. She'd always been happy with her old phone with the crappy Snake game on it until now.

'Wow,' I said, about as un-wow as I could get away with.

The little land train that took tourists along the board-walk pulled in, and Splodge took Poppy by the hand to run for it.

'See you up there, Mills!' she called, and ran with him. A fist clenched in my chest. Everyone had someone except me. I was as spiky as a hedgehog.

Louis Burnett was ordering a Hoydon's Hug from The Bracht Shack. A Hug was made up of two blobs of vanilla ice cream, drenched in melted caramel then wrapped up in a thick buttermilk pancake. They were truly scrumble-shanks but I didn't have them often cos of the fat, especially with all the free toppings you could get. Louis was adding all of them – cream, chocolate sauce, sprinkles and hot jam.

He turned to me, a long dribble of ice cream down the centre of his Dracula T-shirt. 'Guess you must be the spare girl,' he said, spooning up the ice cream dribble with a fish fork. 'Nice to meet you. I'm the spare boy.'

This was the most words I'd ever heard Louis utter. I didn't even think he could speak. Damian usually did all the talking for him and Splodge. We started walking towards the end of the pier, which was all lit up red and blue for the night and looked so beautiful. I wanted to cry. I wished I hadn't come.

'History this morning was boring, wasn't it?' he said.

'Yeah,' I said. 'Always is. I don't know why I chose it really.'

'Me either,' he said, as his boots went *clomp clomp* on the boardwalk. Then he talked about the weather for a bit and I talked about how I wished I'd brought a coat but pretty soon our conversation ground to a halt.

'Do you like fish?' he said suddenly.

'Um. They're all right in batter. Not keen on tinned.'

Louis held up his phone and showed me his screen saver. It was a picture of a large fish tank. I recognised it as the big one from inside the Chinese fish restaurant in town. 'That's the main tank at Fat Pang's,' he told me. 'I'm trying to convince my dad to get a bigger one for the reception area of our place.'

'Yeah, I've seen it in there before. It's got sharks in, hasn't it?'

'Yeah, tinker sharks,' he said as his boots clonked in time with my Mary Jane heels along the boardwalk. 'They're vegetarian ones.'

'Oh right,' I nodded, trying so hard to be interested my brain was hurting.

'They've just got in the most amazing shoal of samurai carp in it too.' He held out the phone to show me another picture. 'Damian thinks I'm sad. I love it. I'd love to, like, live underwater or something. I'd love it if humans could do that.'

'Yeah,' I said, looking at a picture of some little blue and yellow fish nosing about in a clump of rocks. 'It's really . . . full of fish, isn't it?'

There was nowhere to go with the conversation. I wasn't interested in fish. I'd had a couple of guppies once upon a time. We used to keep them in a tank in our kitchen. They weren't very friendly and the tank was such a pain to clean out. One of them flung itself into our waste disposal unit and got mangled to death.

'Do you want some?' he said, nodding towards his plate. 'I got another fork.'

'No thanks,' I said. 'I'm watching my weight.'

'I'll never understand girls and weight,' he laughed. 'In the water, we're all the same weight anyway. Whales can eat up to a tonne of fish every single day. They don't care how much they weigh.'

'Are you saying I'm a whale?' I asked flatly.

'No, no,' he said and our conversation came to another halt.

I sighed. 'I was a chubby little girl and I don't want to

go back there. I have to be strong about what I eat.'

'Why?' said Louis. 'You were quite happy as a kid. I remember.'

'How do you remember?' I snipped.

'Cos I was at the same primary school as you, wasn't I? For a bit.'

I couldn't remember much about him from school. Quiet. Scruffy shoes. Peed his pants at Harvest Festival. They were the only memories I had. 'Didn't you leave?'

'Yeah. I had to in the end,' he said, but he didn't say why.

'And we didn't hang out, did we? So you can't remember me that well.'

He scooped up a forkful of pancake and ice cream and golloped it. 'You always used to hang out by yourself, eating sweets and collecting insects and stuff.'

'Yeah,' I said, slightly cringing at the memory of my evil school enemy Jessica Runnybum throwing my favourite snail shell over the garden wall. And her friend Lucy Eggybreath crushing my ladybird under her stupid flat foot.

'I remember that day you found me in the boys' toilets,' said Louis.

I stopped walking. 'I've never been in a boys' toilets in my life.'

'You did,' he said, chewing. 'I was in the toilet, hiding . . .'

'Why?'

'Just playing hide-and-seek,' he said. 'And I was sitting up on a toilet seat and all of a sudden this thing came whizzing under the cubicle door. Do you remember what it was?' I shook my head. 'It was a sweet. A peppermint. You came racing in, looking for it. And that's when you found me.'

The penny dropped. I did have another memory of him. It burst into my mind like a firework. 'Oh I remember now!' I said. 'I used to love those peppermints. Pee Wee's they were called. They were really hot and then all chewy.' Then I remembered something else about that particular peppermint. 'You were crying.'

He snorted. 'Yeah, I thought you'd remember that. These boys were picking on me. One of them's at our college now – Will Pratt, do you know him?'

'Yeah. He's in my Human Biology.'

'Anyway, I ran in there to hide and then you broke the door down to find your peppermint and when you saw I'd been crying, you gave it to me to cheer me up. I think. Either that or you decided you didn't want it cos it had been on the floor.'

'This girl called Lucy had kicked it into the boys' toilets,' I told him. 'She and her friends used to bully me. What happened after? Did we play together?'

'No. You went and got a teacher, then you left.'

'If only I'd known you were being bullied. We could have been friends.'

'Yeah,' he said, with a laugh.

Lynx's shrill laughter interrupted us and my eyes fixed on her and Damian again. He had his hand on her bottom, and then he moved it up to her waist and kept it there, and she didn't mind. She wasn't worried he'd grab a handful of fat or twang her knicker elastic or anything, not that Lynx had any fat to grab and was probably not wearing any knickers. The land train *beep beeped* behind us and we moved out of its way so it could rumble past. Splodge and Poppy were sitting at the back, chewing each other's lips off.

I caught Louis looking at my dress. 'What?' I snapped.

'Nothing, sorry. Just . . . your dress. It's nice.'

'Thanks,' I said, as he tripped over his trailing bootlace. I realised then that he had been drinking and I could smell it on his breath.

'I'm freezing,' I said. I thought he might offer me his coat or at least drape his manky cardigan around my shoulders in a gesture of gentlemanliness. But he didn't.

We caught up with Lynx and Damian and I could hear what they were saying.

'. . . I could take you to Fat Pang's. They do an All You Can Eat Bottom Dwellers Buffet on Saturdays. It's so they can clean the crap out of the tank.'

'Yeah, that would be lovely,' said Lynx, not even trying a hard-to-get act.

Damian draped an arm around her shoulders like a rope. 'I can see we're going to have fun together, my little morsel.' Lynx giggled.

We passed an old couple, holding hands. Two dogs sniffing each other's bottoms. Love was all around me and it blowed. There was no one holding *my* hand. No one sniffing *my* butt. It made me cross, the unfairness of it all. I noticed some graffiti on a bench. It said 'I Love Minge.' I wished I was Minge. I wished someone loved me enough to scrawl on a bench for me. I wanted that squizzy feeling people talked about. I wanted to walk around a garden centre at Christmas, holding hands with a boyfriend and listening to carols. I wanted to watch DVDs and eat ice cream and have marathon cuddle sessions in our matching onesies. I wanted what Jack and Rose found on that boat – pure, wonderful, romantic, I-would-die-for-you kind of love. Even though Rose didn't die for Jack – actually she let him freeze to death cos there wasn't room for him on her raft thing, but before that they were totes in love.

Louis coughed, interrupting my thoughts. 'Did you have a good time at freshers' the other night?'

I threw him a look, waiting for the cocky comments. 'Yes, I'm so glad I went and made a complete fool of myself. I wouldn't have missed it for the world.'

He sidestepped a squashed potato wedge. 'Yeah, I had a crap time too. Damian brought his snakebite. I was puking in the hedge all night long. It was nasty.'

'Yeah, I know. I had some too,' I said, looking out across the beach. It was a dead romantic beach, if you could see past the dog turds and rubbish. Someday I wanted to go down there with a boy. Gallop along together on a strong white steed, the wind in my crinkly hair. His strong hands on the reins. Him shouting, 'Hya!' That would be so romantic. But tonight was not romantic. It was blustery and cold and I got a mouthful of sand and sweet wrappers when I breathed in.

'Damian's not really worth the fuss, you know,' came Louis' voice as I scanned the beach. There was a single figure down on the sand. A figure with a dog. I shivered. 'He's a bit of a slut and I can't see that changing really.'

'That's your best friend,' I said, and then sighed. 'But you are right.'

'He's never been faithful to a girl,' he said. 'Never known him any other way. Did you know he's on a mission to "do" every girl in college.'

'Yeah,' I said, feeling a little sick and regretting how I felt about him a little more every second that ticked by. 'How long have you been friends with him?'

'Since secondary school. I had no friends at all until him. He was the only one who was curious about what my parents did for a living.' He hesitated. 'Well, at first, anyway . . .'

'Oh really?' I said, barely listening. I looked back out to sea, trying to find the dark figure again on the sand. It had gone. 'What do your parents do?'

'You remember, don't you?' he said. 'We own Burnett & Sons, next door to Lugosi's Pizzeria. Just opposite Fat Pang's?'

He worked in a funeral parlour? Suddenly I found Louis terribly interesting. 'Oh Burnett, yeah, of course. Should have known. Wow. That's really interesting . . .'

'Yeah, yeah . . .'

'No, honestly, I'm genuinely interested in dead things.' He looked at me. 'I mean, I don't mind them, like, at all. They're necessary, aren't they? I'm quite fascinated by death. Someone died at our guest house a few months ago. You probably did her funeral, Mrs Cleak?'

He frowned and shrugged at the same time. Frugged, I guess. 'We do a lot.'

'Sure, sure. That's so cool that your parents own one. So how's business?'

He nodded. 'Good, yeah. Thanks to the care homes and the cokeheads around here, it's never been better. Don't tell Damian you're into dead stuff though. He had a bad experience at my twelfth birthday party and now he won't go in there. Splodge locked him in our embalming room to teach him a lesson for looking up my cousin's skirt. He's had a total phobia about the place ever since.'

I laughed. It was funny hearing someone talk about Damian as a human being with fears. It was nice. Refreshing. 'Fancy being afraid of dead bodies,' I said.

'It's not that unusual,' said Louis. 'Most people are. But Dame is petrified.'

'I'm not scared of them.'

'Neither am I.'

We smiled. I even started to get the feeling I was enjoying myself.

'Let's go in the pavilion and warm up,' said Louis as he ran on ahead to get the door.

'Thanks,' I said, going in, and as I looked back at him, he smiled, and snapped his hand away from the door and it swung back into my face.

Schbaaaang!

The pain was immediate and thick and spread from my nose outwards to the rest of my face. It felt like my whole head was on fire.

'Ahhhhhhhhhhhh!' I gasped, holding my nose. 'Oh! Oh God! My nose!'

'I'm sorry!' cried Louis. He had folded his arms across his chest, his wrists in his armpits, like he was stopping his sides from splitting.

'You idiot! That's not funny, you complete idiot!' I cried.

His forehead creased up. 'My hand slipped, I'm so sorry. Camille, my hand totally just slipped and the door's on a sprung hinge . . .'

Blood poured from my nose. I could hear Damian and Lynx laughing somewhere inside the pavilion as Louis ushered me inside to sit at one of the two-player racing games, Zombie Road Rage 3: Kill or Be Killed.

'Wait here. I'll get an ice pack.'

I didn't care where he was going. I sat in agony and cried. The pavilion was loud and stank of burnt sugar and fried onions. Every sound made my brain bang about inside my head. The clinky penny pushers. The clicky neon air hockey tables. The laughing fortune teller. The Whack-A-Mole where a girl was merrily *bang-bang-bang* bashing a plastic brown thing on the head every time it popped through a hole.

Tucked into a corner was a new game I hadn't seen there before called 'Electrocutie'. In the glass case sat a grinning life-sized dummy in a boiler suit. Strapped to its head was a tin hat with wires coming out of it. Two boys were putting coins in the slot and flicking the lever over and over to watch the dummy scream and fizz and shake, all tongue hangy-out and horrible.

Damian and Lynx appeared. He slipped down into the seat beside me, and started racing and killing zombies. Lynx frowned at my face.

'What the hell have you done to yourself, Mills?'

'Door. Banged on my face. Louis did it,' I sniffed, and winced at the same time. Sninced, I guess.

Splodge and Poppy turned up and stood behind Damian's seat to watch him. They started warning him of zombies and blood slicks. Poppy looked at me and at the blood running through my fingers as I tried to shield my face from them all.

'Are you okay, Camille?' she said, but she didn't come over to me or try to help. Nothing was going to un-glue her from Splodge.

'Yeah, I just had an accident. Louis has gone to get an ice pack.'

SPLAT. VROOM. SCREEEECH. UGH!

'Yeah, eat that you mother . . . smash his brain in you stupid . . .'

UGH UGH UGH.

'Damie baby, I'm gonna go and get a Slushie, you want?' said Lynx, resting her cheek on Damian's.

'Yeah, go on then,' he said, not looking up from his game.

When she had gone, he started on me. 'How's your conk, Mills?'

I tilted up my bleeding face to look down at him. 'What?'

'Loser gets like this when he fancies a bird. Clumsy tosser. Don't tell him I told you, he'll go well mad.' He cackled as he drove into a zombie, crushing him against a wall until he exploded. 'You thought about my offer?' *UGH UGH.* 'I haven't had any little emergency phone calls. Thought you'd be hurtin' for a squirtin' by now.'

'Leave me alone,' I sniffed, tasting blood in the back of my throat.

Louis came back with a bored-looking boy in a red Hoydon's Pier uniform and a blue squidgy cold thing, which he tried to put on my face. I snatched it away from him and gently held it over my nose. The pain in my face clawed me like a bear.

'Well, you'd better hurry up, I don't hang around forever,' Damian carried on. *THUNK.* 'Go on, it'll make your fortnight, a shag with me. I'd go easy on ya.'

'Dame,' said Louis, quietly.

My brain throbbed in my ears. All down my chest were bloody red drips. I got up from my seat. 'I wouldn't go out with you if you were . . . dipped in chocolate.'

'That can be arranged,' he said. *UGH UGH. Two hundred points. UGH UGH.* 'And I'm only talking about a shag. I don't wanna go out or nothing.'

I threw the squidgy thing down and stormed out, snorting blood as I went.

Louis came outside after me. 'Camille, please come back, I'm so sorry . . .'

I turned to him, my nose dripping freely. 'I'm always the joke, aren't I? The laughing stock.' *Sniff.* 'The girl whose face you smashed with a door. Big fat hilarious that is. Ow.'

'No, please. Come back.' He was shivering. Typical

stupid boy to come out on a freezing night wearing a kilt. 'We can hang out without that lot. Like friends.'

I stopped. 'You're NOT my friend,' I told him, pushing his offered hand away and wiping my tender nose with my arm. 'Ow. I've only got one friend. And monsters like you and Damian de Jager can jump off the end of this pier. GoodBYE.'

As I stomped off down the boardwalk, the heel of my Mary Jane caught in one of the wooden slats and broke. I ripped both off and threw them over the side into the raging sea. I started to run. *Bam bam bam* went my bare feet on the slats.

'Camille!' I heard again behind me on the wind, but I was running like the pier was crumbling under my feet. I ran to the seafront, my face throbbing. That was it. That was absolutely IT. I was NOT putting myself through this embarrassment any more. I was going to be like that nun in that film who's just happy serving God and dancing in the hills. Boys were a big fat NOTHING to me now. End of.

I sprinted towards the bandstand and collapsed on one of the benches. My sobs echoed around the walls.

Before long, I felt a presence. I looked up to see a dark figure and through my tears I saw it was someone in a hood. A girl in a hood. *My* girl in a hood!

'So how was *your* night?' said Zoe, looking at my face and bloodied lemon dress and bare feet. 'I think we can rule out "a success".'

'Oh Zoe!' I said, jumping to my filthy feet and flinging my arms around her. She didn't hug me back though.

In fact, she was frowning as we pulled apart. 'It was horrible. Louis Burnett opened a door on my face and I think he broke my nose . . .'

'It's not broken,' said Zoe, looking at it.

'Yeah, and then Damian and the others didn't even care what had happened, they just carried on playing in the arcades and Damian kept on about when we're going to have sex and . . .'

'Why do you associate with them?' she said. 'Have you no self-esteem?'

I couldn't stop crying, but now it was with relief. The relief of seeing Zoe. 'Oh God it's so nice to see you, where have you been?'

She looked at me, wide-eyed. 'I'm not sure that is any of your business but I will say that there's more to life than A levels.'

I looked down. She was holding something by her side. 'What's that?'

'Are you the hysterical type?' she asked.

'No. I don't think so anyway,' I replied, wiping my nose.

Zoe held up her right hand. She was holding a puppy's head.

My hand immediately sprang to my mouth. 'Oh my . . .'

She held up her left hand. Dangling by its tail was the rest of the puppy.

'. . . God.'

Spook Central

I knew where Clairmont House was. It was on the same road as my dentist, high up on the hill above the town. It looked like the haunted house on the cover of one of my romance novels, *Romancing the Bones,* or a stately home that my parents might visit, except it had a 'Keep Out' sign on the gates and no gift shop. After what Poppy had said about Zoe's dad, Professor Lutwyche, about the body parts they'd found at the house, about the people he'd killed and how he lived in the trees like Tarzan, I was a bit nervous about meeting him. I tried not to show it though.

'Thanks for inviting me back, Zoe,' I said, sniffing up a fresh trail of snotty blood as I puffed my way barefoot up the steep streets of Clairmont Hill. 'I'm really excited about meeting your . . . family.'

'I didn't invite you. You invited yourself,' said Zoe, not even out of breath and still clutching both parts of the Jack Russell puppy. She'd told me she found him in the woods, lying in an animal snare, and that he had probably run off from a local farm where they train them as ratters. I believed her.

'Will anyone be home?' I said.

Puppy Part Two dripped on the pavement. What with my nose and the headless dog, the night had been a blood-bath.

'Just my Aunt Gwen,' said Zoe. 'She will be asleep.'

'No one else?'

'No.'

'Oh. We've made a lot of mess,' I said, looking behind me at the pavement.

'It will rain soon,' said Zoe.

'Will it?' I said, trying not to worry. 'Mum says Johnny Depp lives up here.'

'Who?' said Zoe.

'Johnny Depp.'

'I've never heard of him.'

Was I having an out-of-body experience? 'You've *never heard* of Johnny Depp? *Pirates of the Caribbean* and . . . that one about the pies.'

'We don't have a television set.'

My mind went into meltdown. Never heard of Johnny Depp and didn't own a television. Blimey. Just, blimey.

Before I knew it, out of breath and spattered with new raindrops, we had arrived before two tall black gates. The driveway beyond was lit up by a super-huge full moon lying low in the sky. I thought the grounds looked quite pretty at first, until I started noticing all the weird stuff going on. There was an odd sort of whooping coming from the trees. Not quite birdy sounds, but not human either. And there was a piano rotting away in a clump of ivy. Cracked mirrors nailed to tree trunks. A naked woman, peering out from behind a bush. I looked again before I realised it was a clothes mannequin. No signs of Mad Dad though. I expected him at any moment to leap down from a tree, beating his chest. Luckily, he didn't. It was just me and Zoe.

'Wow, this is nice,' I said, beginning the painful walk across the gravel.

Zoe didn't even blink. 'No, it's not. We inherited this place from my grandfather. He was into antiques. We're not.'

Everything went silent except for the distant whooping. There was a river flowing alongside the driveway, and by the light of the moon I could see its shimmering path through the garden. She handed me the dog's head and unlocked the front door. 'Mind the step.'

'Why? What's it going to do?' I jumped, grimacing as I looked at my hand, which was now thickly covered with blood.

The hallway was dark and smelled like my dad's old war books. Zoe lit a big candlestick thing on a small marble table next to a big pile of unopened letters with red writing all over them. When my eyes got used to the light the first thing I saw was this massive stuffed bluey-greeny lizard in a glass case on the shelf. The walls were high and red and the carpet was mossy green. All around were stuffed animals in glass cases. And when I looked again, I saw some of them weren't any old stuffed animals. A goat had huge white swan wings coming out of its back. There was a cat with duck feet. A crab-like creature with a mouse's head. A two-headed piglet with a tortoise's shell.

'Blimey O'Riley,' I said, as under-my-breath as I could. 'What kinds of animals are these?'

Zoe looked at me as though she couldn't fathom what I was so shocked about. 'My mother was a taxidermist. She used to experiment with some of the specimens my father . . . didn't get quite right.'

'She used to?' I asked. 'What does she do now?' But Zoe didn't answer and I was too unnerved by the goat, which I was sure had just winked at me, to press her on it.

All the cases were numbered. In a corner of the hall stood a large stuffed polar bear with deer-like legs, its front paws holding out a dusty tray of drinks. He had a number seven pinned to his ear.

'Wow,' I said, whispering like I do in museums. 'Your parents must have been really clever. My mum can't even sew up a turkey's arse to keep the stuffing in at Christmas.'

Zoe led me up an endless Hogwartsy staircase by the light of her many-candled candlestick, passing glass cases full of china dolls with scratchy faces and toys from the olden days and butterflies pinned to boards, all covered in cobwebs. There were horrible faded green velvet curtains at the windows and every single stair was piled up at one end with a stack of paperback books.

'So you live with your Aunt Gwen?' I whispered,

shrinking away so the velvet curtains didn't infect me with their velvetiness.

'Yes,' said Zoe. 'She moved in just after my father . . .' She stopped talking.

'Went away?' I said, thinking maybe it was hard for her to talk about him going into an asylum – if that's where he was.

'Yes,' she said. 'I can't bear the woman but she keeps the under-age squad at Social Services happy.'

I was more than a bit relieved to hear about the lack of dad. I never liked meeting people's dads anyway, cos they're always a bit weird, but mad dads who stored people's body parts and lived in trees I especially didn't want to meet tonight.

Zoe went and knocked lightly on the door of one of the bedrooms. She poked her head around it. A grandfather clock chimed midnight on the landing. Zoe closed the door. 'She's asleep. Good. That'll keep her out of our hair for the night.'

'What are we going to do?' I asked. She held up the puppy's headless body. 'Oh right, yeah,' I laughed, looking at the head. 'Pin the head on the doggy.'

It was so dark in Zoe's room my eyes again had to strain to see. She lit some more candles and slowly it all started to come to life. It looked like a museum. There was a bookshelf covering a whole wall, and more shelves with cases of smaller stuffed animals on it. Dotted here and there were glass bottles with labels with long science words I couldn't pronounce on them, and what looked like pickled-onion jars, except they had little skulls in them not onions. A sign on the back of her door read '*The only thing that interferes with my learning is my education –* Albert Einstein.'

'I like your room,' I told her.

She laid the two-part puppy carefully on her desk next to all kinds of instruments and knives and stuff I'd only ever seen at the dentist's. She lit lots more candles and set them down beside her patient.

'Don't you have electricity?' I said.

'We're trying to keep costs down,' she said, washing her hands in a little basin in the corner and snapping on a pair of disposable gloves from a small cardboard box. 'Aunt Gwen only has her pension. Times are hard and it's an expensive place to run.' She sat down at the desk and reached for the headlight she'd been wearing the night in the graveyard and put it on her head, then took the end of a little tube dangling from a hanging packet of blood and inserted a needle into the end of it.

'The credit crunchy thing.' I nodded. 'Yeah, my dad's all, "If it's brown, flush it down; if it's yellow, let it mellow."' And my mum's started buying value washing-up liquid. It's well depressing.' I picked up the anatomy model from the end of a bookshelf and tried to prise out the heart. 'She used to do mobile nail art but she had to give it up. She had to do like a thousand nails a week just to pay for the petrol for the van so it wasn't worth it in the end. We've still got the van though.'

The beam from Zoe's headlight flickered as her hand moved back and forth with a needle and thread. Slowly but surely, the puppy's head began to join its body.

'Are you on Facebook?' I asked her.

'No.'

'Oh. You should join, then we could chat. Look for me. I'm Camille Omnomnom Mabb at the moment. That's not my real name though. Last week I was Camille Hufflepuff Mabb and the week before that I was Camille EverybodyLovesaParty Mabb. It's just something me, Lynx and Poppy are trying out.'

'But not any more,' said Zoe.

'No,' I said. 'Guess I'll always be Omnomnom now. Damian's on Facebook too. He's got all these pictures of himself in front of mirrors. One of his photo albums is just of his six-pack. I can't help fancyng him though, even though I know it's wrong. Why am I still in love with someone who's such a . . . ?'

'Runt?'

'No. Someone who treats me so badly?'

Zoe stopped sewing and turned to me. 'People in love, or in your case lust, go slightly insane for a time. It's scientific fact.'

'Are you saying I'm mad?' I asked, fumbling with the model and organ bits.

'Yes, in a manner of speaking. Love or lust makes one so. I don't have any truck with it. Can't take the risk of suffering such intellectual impairment. My father always kept me away from boys when I was home-schooled.'

'Wow, I've never met anyone who was home-schooled,' I said, still fumbling with the model's plastic heart, until my hand slipped and the organs burst out over the floor. Zoe didn't stop working. I scrabbled round the carpet, collecting them up. 'I bet you know the names of all these organs, don't you?'

'Yes,' she said.

I stood up and replaced the model on the bookshelf, not really sure if I had everything back in correctly. I was pretty sure nothing was supposed to stick out. 'Is that easy to do?' I asked her, leaning over the desk.

'Fairly easy,' she said, repositioning the dog. 'In the grand scheme of things, the head's the most straightforward part to attach.'

'And then you inject the blue stuff and it sticks everything together, right? Like you did with the hamsters?'

'Yes,' she said. 'Glad you were paying attention.' She tapped the hanging blood packet. 'I'm giving him a transfusion as he's lost some blood in transit.'

'Where did you get the blood from?' I asked, but she didn't answer.

I was looking around her room, and on the shelves above her desk, in amidst all the science books and jars of pickled bones, there was a photograph in a wooden frame of a man with a baby. The baby looked like Zoe. And the man had Zoe's eyes. Not in a jar or anything, just his eyes looked like hers.

'Is that your dad?' I asked, picking up the frame.

Zoe looked up. 'Yes.'

'He looks like you.'

She stopped working. It was then I realised just how silent it was at the house. There were no cars going past, no seagulls squawking like they do at all hours at our place. Only the distant grandfather clock *clonked* on the landing.

Outside in the trees, a little bird twittered for all he was worth. What was a bird doing twittering at night? Birds didn't twitter at night. It sounded like he was going for a world record. I wondered if Mad Dad was up there too, squeezing the tweets out of him.

'Black pouch. There,' said Zoe, pointing at a small black zip-up bag on the end of her bed. The same small black bag she'd had with her in Biology. I handed it to her. Inside were seven syringes bundled up with an elastic band. They were all filled with the blue liquid Zoe had called 'the serum'. She took one of them out and aimed it over the puppy's heart.

'So you're going to inject him with that one now, yeah?' I checked.

Zoe rolled her eyes and plunged down five millilitres into the little dog.

We waited. Nothing happened.

'Nothing's happening,' I said.

She looked at me. 'You don't say. What was the next thing I did with the hamsters, do you remember?'

'You put clips on their paws. And you electrified them!' I cried, remembering.

'Electrocuted them, yes. Pass me the clips,' she said, pointing at four black leads, also laid out on the end of her bed.

Zoe attached two clips to the puppy's front paws and two to the flesh on his back legs. She then clipped the other ends to a battery block at the back of the desk. She flicked a switch and the puppy's feet jumped. His whole body juddered and his tail shook and went all pointy like a ballerina's leg, and then loose and wavy like a skipping rope. A nose twitch. A whisker flutter . . . An eye opened.

'Oh my God, you did it! He's alive!' I cried, hugging her. 'He's alive!'

The puppy looked up. Zoe pulled out the blood tube and put a little plaster over the hole. 'Welcome back, little one,' she said, tickling his chin. His eyes narrowed with glee. She picked him up off the desk and handed him to me.

He immediately licked my face. 'Ha ha, silly boy, silly boy.' I felt all around his neck. Smooth. Bloody, but smooth. 'There's no join,' I said. 'There's actually no join where it was cut! You'd never know! How did you . . . ?'

'The serum,' she said, scribbling down some notes on her notepad. 'It's the world's best-kept secret. They thought my father was a deranged madman. And who listens to the mutterings of the deranged? Only the deranged.'

'Shall I give him a bath?' I said, seeing as the puppy was at that moment a brown and red Jack Russell, rather than a brown and white one.

'Yes, could do,' she said, tapping her pen. 'You can keep him if you want.'

'REALLY?' I cried. I cuddled him close and he licked my neck, which was weird but sort of enjoyable. 'Wow, oh thanks, Zoe! What shall we call you?' He licked my neck again like he was so relieved to see me and I wanted to cry. I already knew I loved him more than anything. 'I'm going to call him Pee Wee, because he's so small. And because of Pee Wee Peppermints.'

'Fine,' said Zoe. 'He'll need looking after. He might be

out of sorts for a while.'

'Oh yes, yes, I'll look after him and train him and every-thing!' I said, squeezing him tightly, but not too tightly in case his head came off again. 'I can teach him some tricks and give him lots of cuddles.'

'Yes, that kind of thing,' said Zoe, slowly starting to collect up her instruments from the bloody desk. That wasn't swearing. I mean, the desk had blood all over it.

'You don't seem very excited,' I said, putting Pee Wee down on the floor. He immediately darted under the bed. 'You've just brought a puppy back to life. A headless puppy! That's incredible. Aren't you happy?'

'It's not the first time I've done this, Camille,' she said, removing a tiny bone-shaped biscuit from a drawer and putting it on the floor. Pee Wee ran out, scoffed it and darted back under the bed. 'I watched my father many times. I learned from him. I owe everything to him. You saw the animals in the hallway. Some of his prototypes. Failures and false starts. Now it's my turn. I've perfected the serum now, so no more zombie mice, or squirrels that climb trees backwards, or cannibalistic cats. I'm going to find a way to really prove to them just how important my father's work is.'

'Who's them?'

'The authorities who . . . took him away.'

'I'm sure it was a misunderstanding. Your dad is a bril-liant scientist.' Pee Wee trotted out again with a tartan slipper in his mouth and swiftly began tearing it to pieces. 'He must be.'

'Yes,' she replied, more calmly. 'And once I prove that

the serum works on more substantial creatures, they'll *have* to acknowledge that. He'll be vindicated a thousand times over.'

'What do you mean? You want to try it on a bigger dog or something?' I said.

'Hmm, maybe,' she pondered. 'Maybe bigger.'

'A cow?'

'Maybe not. We've always found that the serum works better on male specimens for some reason.'

'A man cow then?'

'A bull.'

'Yeah.'

'Not substantial enough.'

'A rhino?'

'Where would I get a rhino from?'

I shrugged. 'The zoo?'

'Don't be ridiculous.' Zoe walked over to the window and I joined her and we looked down at the town. It was raining. The town was still all lit up. The pier was still open and little ant-sized people were still walking along the seafront towards it. It all looked so pretty from a distance, even though it had been the scene of such hideousness earlier that night. 'No, I need to go one step further. Do something no one's ever tried before.'

'Like a fish finger or something?' I said. 'Like, if you gave a fish finger the brain of a mouse, maybe?'

Zoe looked at me. 'No. You can't reanimate something that was never animated in the first place.'

'Oh right. Why not? A fish finger used to be a fish.'

'A subject has to have a circulatory system, a brain,

musculoskeletal and nervous systems. And preferably no breadcrumbs.'

'Just a suggestion,' I said. 'Can I help you do it? Would you let me be involved?'

She looked at me. 'Yes. You can. You said you trusted me?'

'I do, Zoe, I do. For deffs.'

'Then you can't disapprove if I decide to do something a little . . . off the wall?'

'No, of course not. I promise.'

Suddenly her face was a concrete building with a flaming blue fire flickering in the upstairs windows. And then she just said it.

'I want to try it on a human.'

'A what?'

'A human.'

'A human what?'

'A human being,' she said. 'I've been considering it for a while. Imagine if I applied these methods to a human and it worked. I wouldn't just break down the boundaries of science, I'd obliterate them!'

'But, how?' I said. 'Do you mean digging someone up?'

'No, I need to push the science as far as it will go. Really put my father's methods into action. How about we create a human as near perfect as we can imagine? Perfect face. Perfect body. Perfect brain. How about I create *you* the perfect boyfriend?'

'What?'

'For your Halloween party. We could assemble from all the best parts of different boys – a strong body, healthy lungs, good legs, a superlative brain – and electrocute him back to life as a complete human being. And of course I will be able to present him to the British Medical Association and restore my father's reputation. And you, well, you could finally have your perfect boyfriend.'

'Really?'

'Yes, really.'

My very own Electrocutie. Bliss, I thought. 'But hang on a minute, isn't this all a bit . . . impossible?'

'You'd have thought bringing those hamsters back to life was impossible not so long ago,' she said.

'Yeah, but . . .'

'You'd have thought reattaching a dog's head and having him run around and chew slippers again was impossible an hour ago.'

'Yeah, I guess.'

'Imagine all those faces at the Halloween party when you walk in with the most desirable boy any of them has ever clapped eyes on. Think how jealous all the other girls at college will be. Think how jealous *Damian* will be.'

I looked down at Pee Wee who sat beside my feet, chewing happily on Zoe's slipper. Maybe it was because I'd had a door slammed into my face or maybe it was my loneliness, but it was all actually making sense to me. A whole new boy, just for me. A beautiful boy who would make everyone totally jelly pants, and completely wipe away the hideous memory of tonight and freshers' night and every other hideous night forever. 'You really think it could work?'

'You doubt me?' she said.

'No way. I just . . . can't imagine someone as perfect as the boy you're talking about. And even if I could, I can't imagine him falling in love with me.'

'Well, start imagining,' said Zoe.

I felt a bubbliness in my stomach. Suddenly, I was dead excited. 'Oh my God, yes please, let's do it!' I said, launching myself at her for a hug. 'I'm no good at science though, stitching and chemicals and all that. You'll have to teach me.'

Zoe looked at me. 'Your role as my assistant will be to aid me in obtaining my components, hand me my instruments, clear away detritus, etcetera. And of course, keep our secret. I can't present this to our A level group like the hamsters.'

'Why?' I said. 'It would make a great joint coursework project.'

'Well, there's the tiny problem that we will be breaking the law. We won't have the consent of the previous owners to make you a boyfriend from their limbs or organs, so it will require some degree of stealth.'

'Okay,' I said. Love against all the odds it would have to be. Criminal, forbidden love. Love at a high price, but totes worth it.

'But once I've proved it works, it won't matter one jot. Nobody will care because what we will have done will be so awe-inspiring, so unbelievable that the law will be irrelevant. So this must remain between us for now, until I'm sure it works.'

I nodded. 'But where will we get all the different boy parts from?'

We stood at the window as lightning flashed in the sky outside. I followed Zoe's stare back down towards the town lights.

'They're all down there, somewhere,' she said, grinning, 'like the pieces of a jigsaw, just waiting to be put together.'

The Plan

Even though the parentals were pretty worried about my purple nose when they saw it the next morning and did the whole 'Maybe we should take you down the A&E' bit, I somehow managed to keep Pee Wee away from them. I fed him the cereal meant for room three when Mum was out of the kitchen and then we headed to Wonkies, the seafront cafe overlooking the Bracht, where Zoe had asked to meet up for a planning session. On the way there, Pee Wee attacked a Pomeranian and I had to tell him off. But I gave him a treat for letting go of the Pomeranian's leg eventually, and because I felt really bad about telling him off.

Zoe had got to the cafe before me. We settled ourselves at a four-seater table by a window overlooking the beach.

They'd just switched the fryers on, and rather than going for the usual doughnuts or bacon and eggs you were expected to eat at this time on a Wednesday morning, I asked for cod and chips and a hot chocolate. I was celebrating the end of dieting forever. Zoe asked for a glass of water.

'Why did you want to meet so early?' I said, taking off my arm warmers and tucking them inside my bag beside Pee Wee's sleeping body.

'Because there's much to do,' said Zoe, as I lined up my condiments in front of me. I was going to have ketchup, brown sauce, tartare sauce, curry sauce and mayo. I'd always wanted to try full fat mayo on chips and now I had my chance.

The waitress came over with our order. I'd forgotten I'd asked for buttered bread with my fish as well and my heart did a little leap when I saw it on the side plate. I gazed at the glorious squashy mess of crispy golden cod and the mountain of chips before me. Now that I didn't care about staying thin to find a boyfriend, it was faboosies to finally be able to eat as much as I liked. Our homemade boyfriend wouldn't mind if I was fat. He would think bigger girls who ate like pigs were actually the best and that's how every girl should be. I'd teach him that. Zoe said we could teach him anything if he had the right brain. Zoe was watching me.

'What?' I said.

'You're guzzling that like you haven't eaten in days,' she said.

'I love fish and chips,' I said, offering her my pot of

curry sauce. 'Dip a chip in there, it's awesies!' She shook her head. 'This is so good. I wish I'd got large now.'

'Camille, we have some serious matters to discuss now. Are you going to be able to leave your breakfast long enough to join me or am I doing this alone?'

'Yeah,' I said through my crammed mouth.

'Right, so, first things first. Here's what you need to know,' she said, taking a large lined notepad from her bag. The pages were filled with the messiest writing I'd ever seen. She thumbed through to a page where there was an inky drawing. She flipped the book round and showed it to me. It was of a blue lizard.

'Camille, say hello to Ambystoma zoexanthe. The blue-blooded salamander.'

'Hello . . . blue-blooded salamander,' I said. 'Hang on. There was one of those in a glass case in your hallway.'

'Well remembered,' she said. 'This is the main ingredient of the serum. My father went travelling early in his career and spent some time on an island called Tdk Benar in the Indian Ocean, where they are native. He was researching human stem cells in the brain and bone-marrow and methods of self-renewal in already existing organisms and he'd heard about this creature.'

'Coolio,' I said, still tucking in. She was talking about science; I was eating. We were both happy.

'He wanted to know if a restorative could be developed for a human being. He studied these creatures. Their habitat. Interactions. Reproductive habits. Gestational periods. And he learned something extraordinary about them.'

'Neat,' I said. There was a flood of spit in my mouth

and I just couldn't get the chips in quick enough to soak it up. I shook some more vinegar on.

'The blue-blooded salamander,' said Zoe, 'could replicate its limbs and repair its wounds in much the same way as an axolotl or a starfish or a flatworm can. If it loses a limb to a predator, it will re-grow that limb.'

'Wow, that's clever,' I said through my mouthful.

'Lumbriculus variegatus, a species of black worm, can regenerate an entirely new body. So if you cut it in half, each half will regrow. This salamander had a regenerative blood type, extremely rare in the natural world. My father harvested, tested and adapted it, and after six hundred and fifty attempts, he came up with serum 651. It's a combination of various coagulants, plus the blood and endocrine glands of this salamander, methadrelanol hydraglycerine, hydrocanthium, glycerol, distilled water, aloe vera, powdered metallinium and sulfa, which was a type of medicinal powder used to bind wounds on soldiers on the battlefield.'

'There were quite a lot of words there I didn't understand. Do I need to?'

'No,' she continued. 'You just need to understand the basics, that the serum can completely regenerate damaged tissue.'

'That's quite impressive, isn't it?' I licked salt off my lips and squinted at the sun pouring through our window.

'Quite impressive?' said Zoe, standing up the menu to shade our table from the sun's rays. 'My father discovered *the* key ingredient necessary for the regeneration of human tissue. And this is it.' She lightly tapped the drawing in her book. 'Ambystoma zoexanthe. I'm named after it.'

'Zoexanthe, that's your name? That's so cool.' I made a chip, curry sauce, mayo and batter sandwich. Utterly Yumsville.

Zoe nodded, brushing her black hair away from her face. 'So basically, this is the glue that will hold your perfect man together. Now I am no judge of male beauty, so that's where you come in. What are you looking for in a perfect partner?'

'Well, I want us to make an impression when we walk into the Halloween party together, like Cinderella does at the ball in the Disney film. He has to look like a man version of Cinderella, so he's got to have the face of, like, a model or something. A square jaw and all that.'

'Right,' said Zoe, making a note in her book.

'And a really fit body, like, super fit. Fitter than Damian de Jager. Fitter than *any* boy in college actually. A proper athlete's body. Like that lifeguard at the pool who's always doing one-handed press-ups. His body is UN-BE-lievable. He's got that lumpy stomach thing too. Dashboard.'

'Washboard,' Zoe corrected. 'Right, right.'

'And his hair has to be really soft and quite thick. And nice feet, no second-toe-longer-than-the-big-toe business going on. And above all else, he has to love me. Like, proper love me. Couldn't-live-without-me kind of love me. And a bit intelligent, I s'pose, but not more intelligent than me.'

'I pick the brain,' said Zoe. 'I just need you for the aesthetics.'

'I can't stand athletics,' I said, remembering my

disastrous 800 metres on sports day in the last year of school. 'I'm quite good at discus though.'

'Aesthetics,' said Zoe. 'What he looks like. The parts that really matter – the brain and the internal organs – I'll need to source myself. The fundamentals have to be correct before we go wrapping them in shiny paper.'

'But do you really think it'll work on humans, Zo?' I said. 'I mean, if surgeons could really stitch people's arms on or give dead people new heads and bring them back to life, well, wouldn't they have done it by now?'

'They *have* done it with limbs,' she replied, sketching some hair on the faceless boy she'd been drawing. 'They've done quadruple limb transplants, face transplants. Medicine is progressing so quickly in this area. We're just skipping over a couple of chapters.'

'I can't wait,' I squealed. 'I really can't wait.' I chewed my bottom lip. 'I'm going to buy him a suit too, to wear at the party. A really nice one and we'll get his hair done so it's all sweepy and sexy and bang on trend. But what about making him a good person and making him kind and, most important of all, making him love me? Could we really train him to be whatever I wanted him to be?'

Zoe sipped her water like the answer to this was at the bottom of her glass. 'Research has shown that monkeys and dogs that have undergone partial body transplants can be completely retrained. In essence, their memories have been wiped. Wild dogs became controllable. Good dogs became wild, etcetera.'

'So he might really love me?' I said.

'Anything is possible, Camille. My father was making

inroads in all of these areas and applying the electromagnetic principles when he was so cruelly snatched away from his research. So now it's up to me. With your help of course.'

'Cool beanies,' I said, 'my very own boyfriend. My sexy dead boyfriend.' I stuffed another chip into my already full mouth – a curry sauce-flavoured one – and it was heaven.

Some boys came in and sat at a table opposite, making such a noise I could barely hear what Zoe was saying. They ordered bacon sandwiches and Cokes. Two of the boys with spotty skin and greasy spiky hair were sitting with their legs wide open and their feet flat on the floor, leaning back in their seats and leering at us.

'But *how* are you going to do it?' I said, trying to ignore them. 'I just don't understand how it's poss—' I started to say, as Zoe swept aside my condiments and lay her notebook down before my plate.

'So, what do we have on our shopping list? A genius brain, a model face, a superlative body with organs in peak physical fitness,' she said, pointing to the little pictures on her boy diagram. 'We find the body, we find the head,' she said, circling the body and head sections, 'we stitch the head to the body. I source the brain,' she drew an arrow where the brain was going to go, inside the head, 'then we inject the serum here, here, here, here and here,' more arrows, 'into the peroneal, femoral, carotid, radial and vertebral arteries, which should regenerate the structural tissue and begin to repair blood vessels and musculature. Once the serum is injected, then we can think about galvanism.'

'Galvanism?' I said.

'Yes.' She turned the notebook back to face her. 'We will need to apply pulses of electrical current to his body in order to cause muscle contraction. Once we apply the charge and get the heart beating, it'll just be a matter of waiting for his eyes to open.' She stared at the boys at the opposite table who were sharing pictures of something on their phones and laughing. *Hur hur hur.* 'And you won't have to kiss any more frogs.'

'I *shall* go to the ball,' I said.

'Yes,' said Zoe, slamming her book shut, 'I'm certain you shall.'

We Want Your Body

I didn't hear anything from Zoe for days and college sucked without her. There were no body part news flashes, no *How about this for a square jaw?* updates, nothing. So I tried to keep myself busy in the meantime and not think about what was probably going to be the most wondrous thing ever: my brand-new sexy dead boyfriend.

Pee Wee was still Secret Pee Wee at home as I still hadn't worked out quite how to break the news to my mum and dad. Luckily, our house was three storeys and my bedroom was on the third floor, and Mum only ever went up there for washing and Dad only went up there if something needed mending, so it wasn't too difficult.

On Thursday I had to explain to my tutor, Jill Price,

why I had to bring Pee Wee into classes with me. I told her I was like the weird girl, Amanda Stones In Her Hair who'd been in my Sociology class. She was one of the 'special cases' who was allowed a canine companion to stop her having tantrums. I said Pee Wee had been given to me by a children's charity. Amazingly, she bought my lies, and even brought in a biscuit for Peeps next time I saw her.

But on Thursday night, there was a knock on our front door and it was Zoe. I was so excited to see her I wanted to hug her, but I stopped myself.

'Your mother used to do nail art,' were her first words to me.

'Uh, yeah,' I said, biting back my smile as best I could. 'Where have you been? You haven't phoned . . .'

'You said she had a van; a van for her nail art,' said Zoe. 'I presume to transport her table and assortment of polishes.'

'Yeah.' I couldn't remember telling Zoe about it but clearly I had and she'd remembered.

'Does she still have the van?'

'Yeah. It's in the garage.'

'We need to borrow it. Go and get the keys. I can drive.'

'But . . .'

'There are six garages around the corner. I'm surmising one of them belongs to your family?'

'Uh, yeah . . .'

'I'll meet you there in three minutes.'

'But . . . it won't have any petrol in it. And what about Pee Wee? I can't leave him here; if Mum finds him she'll chuck him out . . .'

'We can get petrol first and then we'll drop the dog off at my house on the way. Bring your purse. Come along,' she said and disappeared around the corner like a puff of smoke.

Zoe had found the perfect body, that's what all the mystery was about. So by half past nine that night, we were sitting in my mum's nail art van, in the archway opposite the funeral parlour, waiting for a good moment to break in. Our local paper, *The Herald*, lay on Zoe's lap, folded open at the obituaries page. In the middle, dead centre, there was an advert for *Burnett & Sons* and it showed four men – one old and fat, one black-haired and fat, one black-haired and moustached, and one young, shaggy-haired and square-jawed (Louis Burnett) – and they were standing in front of a black hearse, wearing black suits. The ad read: '*BURNETT & SONS: Hoydon's Bracht's most professional budget funeral service.*'

I switched on the overhead light so I could read it over her shoulder. She turned over the page to a news story with the heading '*LIFEGUARD KILLED IN FREAK POOL ACCIDENT*'. There was a large picture of a half-naked young man with floppy brown hair wearing dark glasses. He was smiling and flexing his bicep.

'That's our body,' she announced.

'*Well-respected Hoydon's Bracht lifeguard Luke Truss died last Saturday evening following a fall at the town pool,*' I read. 'Oh my God, I knew him!'

'You did?' said Zoe.

'Yeah! He was one of the lifeguards at the pool.'

'Evidently . . .'

'Me and Lynx and Poppy used to go down there during the summer and full-on flirt with him chronically.' I carried on reading. *The nineteen-year-old is thought to have slipped on a novelty Snot Monster called Big Greeny in the children's changing area at around 9.00 p.m. last Saturday night. It is thought he banged the back of his head on the floor. A cleaner discovered him later that evening and an ambulance was called. He was declared dead on arrival at Bracht General Hospital. There have been calls to ban the sale of Snot Monsters as well as all other slime-based toys. His funeral will be held on Friday 10 October.* 'That's tomorrow. He looks smarmy in that photo though, doesn't he? Bit like a paedo.'

'Hmm. A paedo in Speedos,' Zoe mumbled, setting the paper to one side.

'Do we really want a paedo's body for our project?' I asked, gently touching the end of my nose. It was still really painful to touch and a bit crunchy too but I kind of liked the sound.

'He's not really a paedophile, is he?' said Zoe. 'And anyway, his personality is immaterial. We just want his body. We won't be using his head or brain.'

'Why not?' I said. 'He was good-looking.'

'It's not that,' said Zoe. 'His brain isn't good enough. And his face is local. People know him around here. The head will have to come from much further afield. Like a wise man once said, the main function of the body is to carry around the brain. *That's* the most important part. And that's all we will need Luke Truss to be. The carrying tool. The body to carry around our perfect brain. Don't worry, I have everything in hand.'

'The body that I will walk into the Halloween party with, looking all gorge and making everyone hella jelly belly,' I said.

'Quite,' said Zoe, looking at me oddly. She rubbed a patch of steam on the windscreen and peered through.

'Do you think the coast is clear yet?' I said, wiping my side of the windscreen.

'There they go,' she said suddenly, pointing to some figures coming out of the side door of the funeral directors.

'That's Louis,' I said, wiping away the steam again. He was wearing a suit and tie. Another figure came out behind him: an older man with a black moustache. 'That must be his dad,' I said as the rain pitter-pattered on the van roof.

Zoe flicked on the air conditioning to clear our steam. Neither of us made a sound. After about twenty seconds I whispered, 'I think they've gone.'

'Right,' said Zoe, pocketing the van keys.

'Are we going in then?' I said.

'I'm going in first,' she said, pulling the door handle and stepping out. She reached across and held out her hand for one of the sacks of potatoes at my feet. She heaved it out and placed it on the ground. 'You count to a hundred, grab the other sack and follow me in. I've got the torch.'

'What? We're not going in together?'

Zoe shut the driver's door. I could feel my heart beating then, when it was just me alone in the van, and I could see Zoe walking across the road with the massive bag of potatoes weighing her down. I didn't even know why we'd had to bring two sacks of potatoes; she'd just said it was dead important that we did. The rain fell harder on the windscreen, and I couldn't see her any more.

'One, two, three, four, five . . .'

At one hundred, I clicked open the door and stepped out.

I could see Zoe's torchlight flickering inside as I approached the side door. My hand was on the handle. It wouldn't move. How on earth had Zoe got in, I wondered? A top-opening window was ajar. I set down the potatoes and tiptoed over to where the bins were, moving one underneath and climbing on top. I was just hooking my leg up over the top of the window when a voice stopped me in my tracks.

'OI! WHAT THE HELL ARE YOU DOING?'

'Aaaaarrrggghhh!' I cried, banging my head on the open window. I turned to the voice, one leg in and one leg out.

Louis Burnett was standing below me, his hair soaking in the rain.

'Camille?' he said and sort of laughed. 'I thought someone was breaking in.'

And out of nowhere, I started proper bawling. Like when I was little and Dad caught me in my Cook 'n' Learn Kitchen making soup with his seventy-year-old Scotch. It was a complete reflex, designed to stop Dad from going ballistic. And amazingly, it also worked on Louis.

'Aaaaargh haaaa haaa haaaaa,' I went, full on proper tears and everything.

Louis looked completely shocked. 'Oh God. Are you okay?'

I shook my head. 'Aaaaargh aaaargh!' I wailed, on and on.

'It's okay, I'm sorry. I'm so sorry.'

'I . . . I . . . I'm . . .' I said, between huffs. 'I just . . .' I didn't really know what to say. He'd caught me cocked-leg, trying to get into his family's funeral parlour and I had no excuse. Luckily, I didn't need one.

'The office is closed now. Did you want to view someone?'

I still didn't know what to say, so I nodded. Of course, yes, there was a dead person inside who I was upset about. That would do it.

'I just . . . came into town . . . to p-pick up some potatoes for . . . tea.' He took my hand as I stepped down off the bin and I showed him the massive bag of potatoes. He nodded. 'And I thought . . . I'd come and see . . . him.'

He smiled but looked totally what-the-hell at the same time. 'Oh. I'm sorry. Who was it you wanted to see?'

I sniffled a bit, and dabbed my eye at the corner, like my mascara was going to run. I wasn't even wearing mascara. 'L-L-L-Luke,' I stammered.

'Oh, Luke Truss, yeah? Was he your relative? Your boyfriend or . . . ?'

I nodded. 'Boyfriend.'

This was quick thinking. I could get away with saying he was my boyfriend, because there'd be no record of this anywhere, whereas if I'd said brother or cousin or something, this could be traced. Boyfriend definitely seemed the way to go.

'I loved him so mu-huh-huch!' I started crying again and going all shivery like in films when the woman's crying in the rain and the man wipes the hair from her face. I was quite a brilliant actress when I put my mind to it.

Louis didn't wipe the hair from my face. I'd hoped he might hug me, but he didn't do that either. He just stood there, fiddling with his friendship bracelets up his jacket sleeve. He didn't look right in a suit. A bit like a homeless person who'd won a night at the opera.

'God, I had no idea. I can't really let you in though,' he said. 'I've only come back to get my phone. I left it in the office. I'm supposed to be at Fat Pang's. He gestured towards the restaurant almost dead opposite and its smiling fat Chinese man welcome sign. 'It's my mum's birthday. I don't even eat fish but she really likes it there. Dame's there too. He fancies my cousin Madison . . .'

Louis didn't seem too thrilled at the prospect of going back to his family, but I nodded again, and tried to smile and look like it didn't matter. 'What are you going to eat if you don't eat fish?' I asked.

'Chips,' he shrugged. 'I guess five minutes would be okay, if you really wanted to see him.' I nodded again. 'Okay.' He took a bunch of keys out of his trouser pocket and found the one to unlock the door.

I'd never been in a funeral parlour before. I'd expected it to be all dark and cobwebby and for a big, meaty, dead-people stink to hit me. But the reception was warm and biscuit-coloured and smelled of tea and sweet flowers. There was a small tropical fish tank in the corner and a painting of a field full of lambs.

'How's your nose?' he asked, bringing the potatoes in for me and closing the door behind us.

I touched my face, then immediately wished I hadn't cos my nose started throbbing again. 'Hurts,' I said. He looked really guilty, and at that moment I would have said anything to make his face not go like that, even though he had caused both my nose to hurt *and* his face to go like that. 'Only when I touch it though. Otherwise, it's fine, really. So, what do you do here?' I asked him, looking around.

He looked at me. 'Well, we deal with dead people and stuff.'

'No,' I laughed, 'I mean you. What's your job?'

'Uh, a bit of everything really.' He tapped the side of the little fish tank in the wall. 'Preparing the coffins. Getting the suits ready. Dressing the clients. I'm allowed to drive the cars now sometimes but my dad still won't let me direct the funerals. He's kind of fussy about stuff and I'm not really. He doesn't quite trust me not to mess things up.'

'They're nice fish,' I said, nodding to the fish tank. I was just making conversation really.

'They're mine,' he said, wiping a sheen of rain from his forehead. 'I'm not allowed pets at home so Dad and Uncle Pete let me keep these instead. They're for the mourners really but I feed them and clean them out and stuff.'

'They're pretty,' I said. 'I'm not allowed pets either. But I . . . kind of found this Jack Russell puppy and he's mine now. My mum and dad don't know about him yet. I've been hiding him. It's hard though, running straight upstairs every time I come home. Running straight out first thing. I'm sure they're beginning to smell a rat. Or a dog.'

Louis laughed.

'I'm going to keep him though. They can't stop me.'

'Good for you,' he said. 'I wouldn't dare with my dad. Talking of which, we'd better . . . um, I'll just go and . . .' Louis chucked his keys down on the coffee table and disappeared into an office next door, mumbling about his phone.

Zoe popped up from behind a sofa. I clasped my hand over my mouth to stop from screaming.

'What are you doing?' she whispered. 'Why the hell's he here?'

'He came back for his phone. I didn't know what to do so I pretended I was all upset over Luke the Lifeguard. He's let me in so I can see the body. A last time before the funeral, kind of thing.'

Zoe sniffed. 'Well, boys'll do anything if you cry hard enough, I suppose.'

'Or maybe he's just being nice?' I snipped.

'Just hurry up and get rid of him,' she said, getting up. Behind her back, she was holding a large, scary-looking meat cleaver. She ducked down again.

Louis came back into the reception area, waving his phone to show he'd found it. 'We can go in,' he said. 'I've switched it all on. You can leave the potatoes here if you like.'

He led me along a small corridor to an unmarked door, opened it for me and I went in. The room was small and red and dimly lit by large candles. It smelled sweet, like summer pudding, and in the corner was a little CD player softly playing the theme tune to *Baywatch*. A large object painted orange and shaped to look like a dinghy stood on a stand right in the middle. I guessed it was a type of coffin. Inside it lay a man with his hands clasped over his chest. He was dressed in a wet suit and over his legs was draped a blue Chelsea flag.

'I'm going to back to the restaurant for a bit, okay? Otherwise Dad'll wonder where I've got to.' Louis whispered. I nodded. 'I reckon I could give you about ten minutes. Then I'll make some excuse and come back and let you out.' I thought he was going to clasp my shoulder in sympathy, but at the last minute he itched his nose instead.

'Thank you.'

He closed the door behind him. I heard his footsteps down the hallway and the front door closing. Then nothing.

Zoe appeared from behind a red curtain. 'About time.'

I stepped closer to the body in the coffin. It was weird how it still looked like Luke the Lifeguard, but not quite. Like Mrs Cleak had, except not old and wrinkly. His skin wasn't pink any more, it was sort of bleached. There was no expression on his face at all. Like a doll. Tucked into the sides of the dinghy coffin were some car magazines, a bottle of super-strength lager and a photograph of a group of sunburnt men with their tops off and pints in their hands.

'People always say they look peaceful, like they're asleep, but he doesn't look peaceful. He just looks dead.'

'Just as well,' said Zoe, pulling the meat cleaver from her waistband. 'He won't feel this then.'

And before I even had time to look away, she swung the cleaver high into the air and down again, hard onto his thick, pulse-less neck.

Kerrrrrrrr-chunnnnnnnk!

Rest in Pieces

A head on its own was pretty disgusting – so disgusting, it was almost funny. It was a bit like something you would see in the window of a butcher's shop, all bright red and cleanly cut and stinking of meat, until you remembered that it was not just some pig or some cow's head – it was a human head. A human head I'd been flirting with all last summer. A head that had laughed and cried and fallen in love and blown out candles on birthday cakes.

'I don't know how you can be so . . . fine about it, Zoe,' I told her. 'So cold. You've just cut a man's head off.'

'No, I've just cut a *corpse's* head off. It's dead meat, Camille. It has no nerve endings. No feelings anymore. Once you accept that, it's mind over matter. It's easy.'

I still couldn't quite accept that but, as it turned out, cutting Luke's head off *had* been the easy part of the process. Getting the body out of the coffin was major diffs, and getting it out quietly was even more diffs. Because the coffin was on a stand, we had to get it on the floor before we could lift him out of it. And I never realised just how heavy a coffin was.

'Come on, heave!' Zoe whispered. 'Bend your knees, one, two, three, LIFT!'

'I am. I'm trying as hard as I . . . can. It's not going to . . . budge!' We both let go and stood back. The dinghy coffin had shifted on the stand, but only slightly.

'Dead weight,' said Zoe. 'Blast.'

'Well, it moves *on* the stand, so it must be able to move *off* the stand as well,' I whispered. I rounded on it, standing at the head end, opposite where Zoe had spread a black curtain out on the floor.

'What are you doing?' said Zoe.

'Tipping him out. We're not going to get him out of it otherwise, are we? If we can't lift it, we'll have to tip it.'

'No! The force will bruise him!' she said. 'Help me slide it back.'

We both took the foot end of the coffin, pulled it backwards with all our might. With an almighty *THUD* the stand collapsed.

Kerrrrrrrrrrrrrrrrrrrrrumph!

We both stood absolutely still and silent, listening out for signs of Louis or a nosey neighbour or the police, but there came nothing. *Baywatch* still tinkled along on the speaker.

'Well, that's one way of doing it I suppose,' I said when the dust had settled.

'Okay, quickly, help me pull him upright,' said Zoe and we grabbed hold of the body by its arms and pulled it into a sitting position. As we did, the head rolled back off the shoulders and plonked into the coffin.

We dragged the body out and lay it on the curtain, where we wrapped it up and tied both ends with curtain cord. Then we put the coffin back on the stand and filled it with the two heavy potato sacks, plus a spare water-cooler bottle we found in the corridor to weigh it down more. Once we'd wrapped the potatoes and the bottle in the Chelsea flag, it kind of looked like it had been before, except a bit more lumpy, with just his head on show.

'There. That wasn't too taxing, was it?' she said, then stopped. She sighed and banged her eyes shut like she'd just remembered the answer to the million-dollar question when it was a second too late.

'What? Zoe, what is it?'

She turned to me, coming back to life and posting the cleaver back into her waistband. 'Right, when Louis comes back, I need you to get him to do something.'

'What?' I frowned, dreading what she was going to get me to do next.

'Nail the lid down.'

'What?'

'Louis must nail the coffin lid down, otherwise when they nail it down tomorrow morning for the funeral, they are going to know someone has tampered with the contents. It looks all right in this dimmed lighting, but in broad daylight it is not going to look like a body.'

'Well how am I going to get him to do that?' I cried. 'I'm only supposed to be saying goodbye.'

'Use your feminine charms on him. Cry again if you have to. You can do it.'

So I did it. When Louis came back, Zoe waited behind the altar with the headless body and I turned on the water-works. I got myself in a state, producing real tears, saying I was afraid Luke's ex was going to visit the funeral parlour the next day and put a lock of her hair in with Luke (I'd seen that on a film once) and that was why I needed him to nail the lid down tonight. And even though he knew he might get in trouble with his dad who didn't trust him with watering the flowers, let alone nailing down the lids, he did as I asked. I hugged him in relief. He hugged me back. And even though we weren't hugging for a real reason, it was the nicest thing that had happened all night long.

Louis walked me out of the funeral parlour and we said one of those awkward goodbyes where we didn't quite know whether to do a handshake or another hug.

'I can't thank you enough for, well, you know, letting me in and everything.'

He shrugged. 'It was no sweat, really.' He smiled and looked at his shoes.

'Will you get in trouble for nailing the lid down?'

'Probably. So, will you be okay now?'

I nodded, pretending to wipe my eyes with a tissue. 'I'll see you tomorrow.'

'Yeah. Triple History, isn't it?' I said, rolling my eyes like I really hated it, even though I didn't actually mind it too much.

He frowned. 'There's no point going in for it though. You won't be able to concentrate and you'd have to leave at ten anyway for the funeral.'

'Oh yeah, yeah of course, of course. No, I don't suppose I'll bother.' I mentally stapled it to my brain: *don't forget to show up at the funeral tomorrow morning*. Wherever it was. *Sniff*.

'Mr Atwill won't mind, under the circumstances,' he said.

'I guess not,' I said as he put his hand up to wave and then walked across the road and into Fat Pang's, which was buzzing with people and colour and light. On the doorstep, he turned to look at me and I made out I was starting to walk in the opposite direction. But once his back was turned, I stopped and watched him go inside. He walked over to a long table beside the wall with the huge fish tank in it. He sat down next to Damian, who looked especially Yumsville in his black suit with his shirt wide open. He was leaning back in his chair chatting to some blonde girl with black roots. Louis sipped his Coke and seemed more interested in the fish tank and I couldn't help myself smiling.

'So, that's Part One,' said Zoe, climbing into the driver's seat and carefully closing the door behind her.

'What's Part Two?' I said. 'The head?'

'Yes, but we should get some serum into him first to retard decomposition.'

'What's decomposition?'

'Rotting. He will have been taken out of the freezer at the funeral parlour around four for family viewing. That means he's been thawing ever since. If I get the serum into him tonight, that will give us at least a few more days' grace, provided he is kept at low temperature.' She started up the engine.

'I thought you only inserted the serum before you electrocuted?' I asked her as the van rolled out of the street and waited at the traffic lights to the seafront. 'We're not going to electrocute him without a head, are we?'

'No, of course not,' said Zoe. 'We need to do things a little differently with this one. The serum can be injected at any time before electrocution takes, but I want to give it longer to work in this specimen, so that it has less chance of going wrong. Like with the hamsters and your dog.'

'They didn't go wrong,' I said. 'The hamsters and Pee Wee are all alive and well thanks to you.'

'Yes, but they're flawed. They're not perfect versions of their former selves.'

The van turned onto the seafront. 'Pee Wee looks okay to me.'

'Have you seen what the hamsters have done to the college? A hamster should not be able to chew through concrete walls, Camille. And normal little dogs don't behave like Pee Wee.'

I looked behind me. The curtain-wrapped body was jumping off the floor as we scaled each speed bump on the road. 'Why, what's wrong with Pee Wee?'

'You'll see,' said Zoe. 'Maybe nothing's manifested itself

yet but it will. It always does. Did you ever hear about the cow that escaped up the High Street?'

And something did manifest when we got back to Zoe's house. Pee Wee was sitting on the doormat, like he was waiting for us, all sweet and smiley and panting.

And covered in blood. Again.

'Oh my god, what's happened! Oh Pee Wee, my baby!' I cried, clamoring to get out of the van and see if he was okay.

'*Raaaaarff raaaaahhf!*' he woofed at me as I lifted him up in my arms. I felt underneath him, all around his belly and his neck. Nothing. He hadn't been hurt, I thought, but it was so difficult to tell by moonlight. Zoe was standing on the grass when I looked back.

'Over here,' she called and I went to join her on the grass, cuddling my poor bloody baby in close to my cheek.

'*Raaaaarff.*'

'His woof sounds funny,' I said.

'It's not just his woof,' said Zoe. She pulled the torch from inside her coat pocket and shone it down on to the patch of grass in front of her. Black fur. And a collar. And mush. Red fleshy mush.

I could see what it was then. A dead dog!

'What on earth . . . ?' I cried.

'That's your poor bloody baby's dinner,' Zoe told me. 'Suki. The poodle from two doors down.'

'Ugh! That's disgusting!' I cried, putting Pee Wee down on the grass. 'Ugh! Ugh. UGH!' He sniffed around the poodle mess and started licking it.

'See what I mean now about electrocuting too quickly?

Come on; let's get this one in the chest freezer.'

Afterwards, Zoe dropped me and Pee Wee back at my house in the van and then drove on back up to her house. I wondered if we'd ever get the van back as I was pretty sure my mum was going to notice it was missing at some point. I didn't have time to worry about that too much at the time though, cos I had to get Pee Wee upstairs to my room before I ran into a parental.

I needn't have bothered. The next morning, I was just finishing up my shower in the en suite when I heard a scream. Pee Wee had escaped from my room, gone all the way downstairs, jumped out of the lounge window and mauled a passing sausage dog. I had a twenty-minute lecture from the parentals about how I was paying for therapy for the poor sausage dog's owner AND buying her a new sausage dog AND how selfish it was keeping a pet.

'He's mad,' said Mum.

'He's not staying here. And he'll poo everywhere and we've got to keep the place immaculate for the guests,' said Dad. 'You know they're the most important people in this place.'

'Yes, I know, but I'll look after him,' I said. 'I'll train him, properly. And he might be able to catch that mouse that lives in room three, Dad, you never know.'

'Bloody thing,' Dad muttered. At this point I think Dad was coming round to the idea. He'd been chasing that mouse with traps and cheese since we'd moved in.

Mum huffed. 'You know who'll be looking after it, don't

you? Muggins. Muggins here will be buying the pet food and the kennel and the . . .'

'He's not having a kennel and I'll buy all his food. I'll take him to the vet's and get him microchipped and everything.'

'Damn right you will.'

'And he can live in my room and sleep on my old baby blanket until I buy him a proper cosy bed.'

'No, you're not keeping him,' said Mum. 'We'll have to take him down the cop shop and see if anyone's reported him missing.'

'Remember how upset you were when the gerbils died?' said Dad.

'Only when I found them lying on top of the rubbish in the bin cos you couldn't be bothered to bury them,' I snipped, cuddling Pee Wee tighter.

'And when the kitten got run over?'

'I wasn't upset then.'

'And when Jasper had to be put down?' said Mum.

'So the only reason I'm not allowed a pet is cos they die? You're both going to die one day, why don't I kick *you* out as well just to save me the grief?'

Mum gasped. 'Camille!'

They both stared down at me. But I didn't care one jot. Well, maybe one jot, but I wasn't budging on the subject, no sir-ee. I decided to play the guilt card, which I only ever did when I absolutely positively had to.

'Mum. Dad. You never gave me any brothers and sisters, and while I respect you for that, I'm lonely living in a house full of old people. I love you both lots but Pee

Wee is mine and I'm keeping him. If you want to chuck him out, you'll have to chuck me out too. So that means you'll have to get someone in to do the breakfasts.'

I was just about to turn on the tears when they finally stopped arguing and let me have my way. I think they finally realised that, actually, having a dog wasn't too much to ask. As daughters go, I'd been a bit of a breeze. Compared to Lynx, for instance. She'd put her mum and dad through all sorts of dramas before they split up: drinking in the park, nicking earrings, all that business with our P.E. teacher at school. Reminding them of Lynx actually did help my cause. I kept quiet about the whole eating other dogs business though. They didn't need to know they were living with a cannonball.

I had triple History before I could go and see the body in daylight, so Pee Wee and I had to hop, skip and jump it to college. Louis wasn't in History and I was a little annoyed that I'd made the effort and he hadn't. Class was uneventful – I ran out of ink, got shouted at for forgetting who Goebbels was and tripped over a runaway hamster in the corridor. Pretty average day really.

On the way back into town, I stopped at the pet shop and spent the last of my chambermaid wages on a collar and lead for Pee Wee, some chew toys and a bag of food, and then decided to treat myself to some fudge at the Fudge Shack as I'd had my eye on some strawberry short-cake flavour fudge since my last diet.

When I got to Clairmont House, Zoe was in the freezing-cold kitchen, standing beside the kitchen table, upon which lay the naked, headless body of Luke the Lifeless Lifeguard. Only now he wasn't just headless. He was handless too. And footless. And organ-less: his torso was wide open and red and empty. He was a sorry sight really, like a car that'd had its engine stripped out and its wheels taken off.

'Yes, he's a bit of a work-in-progress, I'm afraid,' said Zoe, wiping her hands on a blue tea towel.

I picked up Pee Wee and moved closer to the table to get a better look. 'What . . . where are . . . why did you cut his hands off? And his feet?' Luke's wet suit was on the floor. Zoe had cut that off him as well.

'Well, we have a problem,' she said.

I had a mouthful of fudge. 'What problem?'

'These . . . '

She held up a carrier bag and opened the top so I could peek inside it. There was a pair of blacky bluey feet, cut off at the ankle, lying at the bottom, on top of a pair of bluey blacky hands.

'They rotted?' I said with a grimace I just couldn't control. The bag smell was utterly vile. If I'd had to describe it like my dad described wine, I'd have said there were notes of pork and blood and morning breath in it, and a rotting bin. I clamped my hand over my mouth.

''Fraid so,' said Zoe, putting the bag on the floor. 'I noticed last night as I was putting the serum in that they were slightly blue so I took them off straight away. No sense in delaying the inevitable. At least we know now he wasn't embalmed.'

'What's that?' I said, offering her my bag of fudge.

She shook her head. 'Sometimes funeral parlours embalm bodies to preserve them longer for family viewings. It delays decomposition and keeps the body looking like it did in life for as long as possible.'

'Grim.'

'Saves me an awful lot of work actually. Problem was, not only did I have to remove his hands and feet, he was also missing several key organs. Lungs, heart and kidneys have all been removed. Bloody organ donor. Luckily I had spares so I was just going to transplant some over now.'

'Spares?' I cried. 'Where did you get spares from?'

'You're in luck – they're all good specimens. Healthy.'

The Marks & Spencer's cool bag I'd seen her with that night in the graveyard was on the draining board and she went over to it and unzipped the top. I looked inside. Five plastic packages. Two kidneys in one. Lungs in another. All marinating in deep red blood. And two separate packages of hands. I put Pee Wee down on the kitchen floor, reached into the bag and picked out the top package.

'This is the heart, isn't it?' I said, squidging the parcel. 'The thing he's going to love me with. His actual heart. I've got his heart in my hands.'

'It's just a pump,' said Zoe, taking it from me and placing it carefully back in the cool bag. 'It's just a means of getting his blood from one part of his body to the other, that's all.' She went back to the table.

I poked around in the cool bag to see the hands more clearly. They were as bloody as the organs but they didn't look like they had just come out of a butcher's window –

they really did look like someone's hands. There was even what looked like a little mole on one of the fingers. I snapped my own hand away pretty quickly, suddenly not wanting it to be anywhere near the bag.

'The main problem is that his body is decaying much quicker than if he *had* been embalmed,' Zoe explained, going back to her syringe. 'In the freezer at the funeral parlour, he was probably kept at between two and four degrees. Decomposition will still have continued to occur, though at a slower rate. I've set the chest freezer temperature to minus twenty to reduce it further but without a cryogenic freezing chamber, we can't retard it for long. That's why I'm injecting him now. It should slow it down for a few days.'

I turned to her. 'I can't have a boyfriend with no feet, Zoe. I just can't!'

'Well, yes, I realise that,' said Zoe, moving around to the other side of the body with the saw and pinching at the skin on the body's legs. 'We will have to find some. I'll need some blood too. Where can we get eight pints of blood, Camille?'

'Um, um, um . . . Could you take some out of me?'

'I could only get one pint from you on a good day. Anyway you're A positive.'

'A positive what?' I said.

'No, your blood type is A positive. He's O negative. It's better to stick to the same blood type in any severed part to reduce the chance of rejection.'

'Oh right.' Pee Wee squirmed to be put down so I let him. He immediately went over to the wet suit Zoe had cut off Luke's body and started tearing it to pieces. 'How about the hospital for the blood?'

'Yes, good, now you're thinking like a scientist.'

I frowned. 'How do you know I'm A positive? I didn't even know that.'

'I tested it when you had your nosebleed. Just in case.'

'Oh right,' I said, rustling in my fudge bag for, disappointingly, the last chunk.

'You do still want this to go ahead, don't you?' asked Zoe. 'To hold one of these perfect piano-player hands when he leads you into the gym on the night of this Halloween party? The perfect feet to trip the light fantastic with?'

I nodded eagerly. My mouth was too full of fudge to actually say the word yes, so I just said, 'Yug.'

'Right, help me get the body back in the freezer and then we'll take you to the hospital. Grab his arms . . .'

'Me? I don't need to go to the hospital.'

'You do. You're going to have another nosebleed, I'm afraid.'

'I am?' Her medical genius never failed to amaze me. 'How do you know?'

She reached towards my face and gave my nose the quickest of tweaks. It crunched and the pain seared through my face like fire and the blood ran down my chin like rain.

Feet

So we left Pee Wee eating a Pot Noodle in the porch, locked in so he couldn't attack the stuffed animals like I knew he wanted to, and headed down to the hospital in the van.

It was very busy in A&E and my nose was still streaming. There were old people with broken arms, young people with broken collarbones, a couple of tombstoners who had fractured bones jumping into the sea off Madeira Cove, two pale-and-sweaties and a man with a beer gut who looked like he was fine, until he threw up black stuff all over the floor. Zoe knew what was wrong with all of them before they did. It was one of her talents, diagnosing any illness from a distance. She said it was why she never ate in public, even snacky foods.

'The smell of cancer and toasted teacakes don't really mix,' she said.

Three hours we were sitting in the dingy green waiting room, watching the doctors and nurses come and go, reading creased-up tea-stained magazines and ear wigging all the coffee-breathed conversations. I was holding a makeshift tea-towel-ice-bag combo over my non-stop nose. Zoe kept popping out. I thought she had bladder trouble she had excused herself so often.

'Are you all right?' I asked her, the fourth time she returned from 'popping out for a moment'. I noticed she was now wearing a white doctor's coat with one of those scopey things around her neck.

'What are you wear . . . ?'

'Miss Mabb. Come with me,' she said.

Zoe led me along the busy corridors until we got to a brightly lit area with lots of curtained cubicles and doctors rushing about. She took me right past them all, through a white door which led down another corridor. There were signs showing the way to pathology, oncology, radiology and maternity wards and, through another white door, a smaller sign read 'Mortuary' and an arrow pointed down a dim passageway.

'What's a mort-yoo-ary?'

'It's where they keep the supplies.'

'What supplies?'

'Bodies. It's where we can find some new feet.'

It had suddenly become the doorway into Wonderland. 'Wow. You mean there are real live dead people in there?'

'Of course,' she whispered nonchalantly, like we had

been shopping for cushions and now, logically, we needed the covers.

'Oh-kay,' I said. 'But won't it be a bit suspicious, just wandering into a mort-yoo-ary and lopping off someone's feet? And what if there aren't any feet worth taking?'

'I've looked already,' said Zoe, pushing through another white door. There was a concrete staircase leading down and at the bottom was a long, dimly lit corridor. The door to the mort-yoo-ary was at the end of it. My clacky shoes echoed loudly on the cold ground as I walked. Zoe peered in through the glass porthole and tried the handle. The door squeaked open.

Inside, the room was large and white and freezing cold and stinky with the bleachy Zoe-smell that always seemed to be in my nostrils these days. At the tops of all the walls were windows and the floor was wet. In the middle stood three really big steel tables, all with pipes attached and plugholes at the ends.

'Why are there plugholes in the tables?' I asked as Zoe made her way over to the other side of the room.

'Fluids,' she replied.

'Oh,' I said, not knowing what fluids she could have meant. 'Where are the bodies?'

'In there,' said Zoe, pointing towards a bank of eight large, heavy-looking white doors. 'There are supposed to be two technicians here at any one time. One is on a call; the other is at lunch. We have twenty minutes at best.'

'How do you know?'

'What do you think I've been doing for the past three hours? I've been surveying the hospital of course. Obtaining eight pints of O negative blood. Locating some more suture thread. Studying lunch rotas. Finding our feet.'

I got a little squiggle of excitement in my tummy. It must be all the death, I thought. And then I realised, it wasn't excitement, it was sick.

'Zoe, I think I'm going to throw up.'

'Why?' she said. 'I thought you said you weren't squeamish.'

'I'm not,' I said, rubbing my tummy. 'It must be the fudge.' I breathed in through my mouth, then out through my nose. And then the other way round cos that wasn't working. The bleachy smell was so strong I could taste it both ways.

'Okay, get some of those bags from down there,' she said, pointing to a box on the floor containing a ream of yellow plastic bags marked 'For Incineration'.

I grabbed a bunch and tore one off. She opened the clasp on the first door and pulled out a long metal bed, *clangy clink clank.* On the bed lay someone dead, under a green sheet. Their marble-white feet were sticking out the near end.

'How about those?' Zoe asked.

I read the toe tag. '*Peter Simpson, 32, renal failure.* No, he's got a verucca.' I pushed Peter back into the filing cabinet of death with a *clangy clink clank* and heaved out the drawer below. '*Michelle Victor, 27, female*, so no.' . . . *Clangy clink clank* . . . 'One leg.' . . . *Clangy clink clank* . . . '*Betty Brundle, 89, windsurfing accident* . . .' *Bang.*

I opened the next door and pulled out the first of the drawers in there. '*Martino Lugosi, 97* . . . aww, that's the old man from the pizza parlour!'

Martino's head twitched.

'AAAARRRRGGGHHH!' I shrieked, grabbing onto Zoe. 'Oh my God. He's alive! He's alive!'

Zoe shook her head. 'No, he's not. It was a muscle spasm. I should have warned you that kind of thing some-times happens with cadavers. It doesn't mean anything. I promise you, this man is very definitely deceased.'

I nearly was too. My heart was going so fast I didn't think the beats were ever going to catch up. I stood there and panted for a while before I could think about open-ing any of the other drawers.

Zoe was having none of it. 'Come on,' she said.

I swallowed down my fear and tried to concentrate on the job at hand: finding feet for my future husband. I pulled open another drawer, my hands shaking so much I couldn't see them properly. '*Frederick Benjamin, 74*. Ugh, yellow toenails.' . . . *Clangy clink clank* . . . '*Samuel Popplewell, 49, RTA*. Ooh, no legs or feet.' . . . *Clangy clink clank* . . . 'Oh, these ones are nice . . .'

'They're black,' said Zoe.

'Don't be so racist.'

'I'm just saying black feet on a white boy are not going to be the best look.'

'They're still nice. He's got a better body actually, too . . .'

'No,' Zoe sang-sighed, like my Mum did when I'd been keeping on for money.

I banged the drawer back in and pulled out the next one down. '*William Pratt, 17* . . . Ooh, Zoe, here we are. These are perfect.'

'Really? You sure you want those?' she said, looking at

the tag on his toe.

'Yeah,' I said, looking at the name on the toe tag again. 'I know that name. Why do I know that name? Of course! He's in our Biology class. Oh my . . . when did he die?'

'Must have been very recently,' she said, turning to a tray of sharp implements, and then to a table on which lay what looked like an electric carving knife, like the one my dad used to slice up the Sunday roast.

'That's so sad,' I said, again and again.

'Why?' said Zoe.

'Because I knew him . . .'

'Did you like him?'

I thought hard. 'Well, no, not really. He was a bit of a . . . he was one of the ones filming me in the poo pool on freshers' night. And he laughed. No, I didn't like him much at all actually.'

'Well then,' said Zoe, plugging the electric knife into a socket on the wall.

'I wonder how he died.'

'Tombstoning, I believe it's called,' said Zoe, starting up the buzzing meat slicer. 'I've seen them up there before at the top of the cove. Another world beater in the brains department.' She pointed to the toe tag. 'Rock fall. Now move out of the way, I've got fourteen minutes left to bag these.'

'But hang on, Zoe, we can't take these. We knew him. Don't we have to mourn and stuff first? It wouldn't be right.'

'You didn't mind us using the lifeguard's body and you knew him.'

'Yeah but he was older. William is, was, our age. He had so much more life left to live.'

She turned off the electric saw. 'Yes, well, his spirit can live on in his feet, can't it?'

She was so cool about it. So calm. So . . . doctor-like. She didn't care that she had probably walked past him at college or spoken to him or paired up with him for an experiment. She just didn't care. But I did. I really did, even though I knew nothing was going to stop her now.

She barged past me with the meat slicer and began sawing, just above the ankle to where you'd pull a sock.

Buzzzzzzzzzzzzzzzzzzzzzzzzzzzzzzzzzz zzzzzzzzzzzzzzzz nnnnnggggggggggggggggg.

'Wow, there's quite a lot of blood, isn't there?' I said. My mouth was so dry. Zoe said nothing. 'Not like chicken,' I said. 'It's really bloody, isn't it?'

I watched Zoe at work – in awe at her concentrating face, the buzzing, gnashing sound of steel sawing through cold bloody meat, through bone.

Nnnnnnnnnnnnzzzzzzzzzzzzzzzzzzzzzzzzzzzzzzzzzzzzzzzzz gnnnnnnnnnnnnnnnnnnnnn.

The sight of the frozen red flesh, the first foot as it came away . . .

Hospital car parks
can be so romantic

I woke up to whiteness and the sound of rattling. Wheels rattling. Tube lights flashing by on a long white runway. I was on a hospital trolley. Windows and walls were passing me at speed. I looked over to the side and saw Zoe was pushing me along.

'Zoe?' I croaked. I looked towards the end of trolley. My body was covered in a sheet. My feet were sticking out the end. They were big. And they were most definitely not mine.

'Zoe!' I cried.

'Shh! You're fine.'

'What's . . . did you saw me up? Please don't say you sawed me up!'

'Keep still. We'll be out in a minute.'

'Out where? Where are we? And what's wrong with my feet?'

Zoe leaned down to speak into my ear, pushing the trolley along all the while. 'We're still at the hospital. You fainted in the mortuary. Just as well you did, because one of the technicians came back and I had to pretend I was a junior doctor and you were a patient that had been brought down by mistake. I always find if you say something with enough conviction, people will believe it. And they're not your feet.'

'Where are my feet? What have you done with them?' I cried.

'SHH!' she said, all cross and speaking into my ear again. 'I haven't touched your feet; they're further up the trolley a bit. Just concentrate on being dead so I can get us out of here.'

It took me a minute before I realised the feet poking out of the sheet were the ones Zoe had just chopped off William Pratt. 'Oh my God. I think I'm going to be sick.'

Zoe flopped the end of the sheet over my face and wheeled me through the waiting room. I thought I heard someone call my name. I wondered if I really *was* dead and Zoe was just trying to be nice. I wondered if she was taking me to God. I did feel very cold all of a sudden. I could hear birdsong and the sound of my name on the wind. The trolley wheels on concrete, then softness – grass? – then concrete again. My name was called again.

'We've been seen,' said Zoe's voice. Then she yanked the sheet away and tipped me off the trolley. 'Right, help me with all of this. And hurry.'

We were at the back of the car park behind the bins, where we'd parked the van. Underneath the trolley, balancing on a tray, were some of the yellow incineration bags, a large picnic box marked 'Blood For Transfusion', some spools of transparent thread, a stethoscope and some bottles of clear liquid with labels with long words on them.

'You've been busy,' I said, scratching my head, and I started helping her load it all into the van. The fire was in her eyes again – the fire that showed she was happy, which made me happy. I did still feel a bit fuzzy-headed from the fainting, but I felt part of something again and that felt great. Mucho mucho great, in fact.

'Camille!' I heard my name again, this time clearer, and I could tell it was a boy's voice. I looked around to see Louis Burnett running across the car park towards us. He was still in his suit trousers and shirt from last night, except the top buttons of his shirt were undone and there were blood smears on it. 'Oh thank god, I thought something had happened to you. I saw you being wheeled along and then I saw Zoe and I thought . . . well, I didn't know what to think. I'm just . . . I dunno, glad you're okay.'

'Louis, what are you doing here?' I said, suddenly all flustered and not quite knowing what to say or do. Zoe was folding up the trolley into the back of the van.

'Damian had an accident last night,' he puffed. 'Someone tried to run him over as we were leaving my mum's party at the Chinese.'

I gasped. 'You're kidding! Is Damian okay?'

'Yeah, he's fine,' said Louis, rubbing his eye until it

looked red. 'His ego's a bit bruised but there's nothing broken. He rolled over the bonnet and everything. It looked quite cool.'

I saw the blood smears again on his shirt collar and I felt my chest clench. 'You were hurt too?' I said.

'No, I'm fine. This is Dame's blood. He's bruised and he's got a cut on his face, but he'll be all right. He's in there chatting up two of the nurses so I don't think he's been damaged beyond repair.'

I found myself breathing a sigh of relief, like I really cared. 'Did they get the driver?'

'Camille!' Zoe yelled, slamming the back doors of the van and marching round to the driver's door.

'No, it all happened so quickly. There were only us two there. I'm going to get so bollocked for missing History. Supposed to give my talk today on Hitler,' Louis rubbed his eye again. He looked tired. He'd obviously been at the hospital all night. 'So how did it go this morning?'

History? I thought. 'Oh, okay, you know. The usual. Boring. War, war and more war.'

He frowned. 'No, I meant the funeral,' he said.

'Oh,' I said and laughed, and then tried to make my face go as serious as possible. I'd forgotten about Luke Truss's funeral. 'I couldn't face it in the end. I think . . . I pretty much said my goodbyes last night anyway, so . . .'

He nodded, looking at me. 'So you're okay with it all now?'

I nodded. 'Yeah. Life has to go on, doesn't it?'

He smiled like he didn't really know what to say. 'I couldn't go cos I had to stay here with Dame but Dad rang me and said everything went well.'

'Good, good.'

'So what's going on with all that stuff?' he asked, gesturing towards the back of the van. 'Are you nicking it?'

'Uh, kind of, yeah. We need it for an experiment,' I said. 'Human Biology. We're just borrowing it really. For a bit. They said they don't mind.' Even *I* didn't believe that.

He laughed. 'Me, Dame and Splodge have nicked a hospital bed before, for a charity bed push. Dame kept all the money though. He wanted new golf clubs.'

'We haven't got time for this, Camille,' Zoe barked out of the window, starting the engine.

'I've got to go,' I said, making to leave.

'Wait . . . how's your nose?'

I touched it. It hurt. I thought it might bleed again but it didn't. 'Um, okay. Purple, as you can see. And a bit achey. Otherwise, fine.'

'Did you hear about Will Pratt from college? The whole place is in shock. It happened last night . . .'

'Uh, yeah, yeah I did. Really sad.' My eyes wandered towards the van where William Pratt's feet were. 'So sad.'

'I texted Splodge to see if he'd heard about it but he hasn't answered. He was good mates with him from rugby. Could you text Poppy and find out if she knows where he is?' he said.

'Uh, me and Poppy don't really hang out as much as we used to.'

'Camille!' Zoe called out again, revving the engine.

'Okay, I'm coming,' I yelled. I turned back to Louis. 'Maybe we should swap numbers?' In case either of us hears from them?'

'Yeah, that's a good idea,' he said, taking his mobile out of his pocket. I did the same and we swapped phones and put our numbers in each other's contacts. We swapped back. 'Okay, well, I'll see you later.'

'CAMILLE, WILL YOU HURRY UP AND GET IN THIS VAN, PLEASE!'

'Yeah, see you,' I said, suddenly feeling terribly sad.

'Bye,' he said, walking back towards the hospital, his hands in his pockets. He looked back at me and I thought he was going to smile, but he didn't. What was he thinking? I wondered. Was he thinking of telling on me and Zoe? Telling someone at the hospital about us stealing the trolley? No, it wasn't that. It wasn't a threatening look. It was a worried look. Like he was afraid of something. Of Zoe? Possibly.

As soon as my bottom was on the passenger seat, Zoe sped towards the hospital exit.

'About time,' she said.

I got my phone out and called Poppy's number. No answer. I texted: *Hi Pops. Hope u r OK. Hav u seen Splodge? Louis wants 2 talk 2 him. Bad things happened. DDJ bin in axident. Tlk soon. Cx*

A thought flashed into my mind. A mole. A small mole on a hand. Splodge had a mole on his hand. I'd seen it the last day we were all together at college, outside the Humanities block at college. He had been eating Jaffa Cakes though, so it could have been chocolate. I wasn't sure. The hand in the cool bag had had a mole on one of the fingers. Coincidence? Or something totally else?

'You're very quiet,' said Zoe. 'Aren't you excited? We have nearly all the pieces now to really get going. This time next week, you will have the perfect boyfriend.'

'Yeah,' I said. I stared at my phone. 'I can't wait.'

Zoe stared at me, hard. Did she know what I was thinking? What *was* I thinking? Poppy not answering her phone. William Pratt dying, Damian being run over. And now Splodge's mysterious non-answering-of-a-text. That's what I was thinking.

High Hopes and Nightmares

I had to leave Zoe at about four o'clock as Mum texted me to say Granny and Grandad Mabb were visiting and that I had to go home and see them. My heart sank. It was always the same whenever they turned up. My dad didn't even like them that much and they were his parents, but Mum said we had to be nice because they didn't have long left and she wanted their Royal Doulton crockery in the will.

They stayed for ages and I was forced to sit sandwiched right between them on the sofa, with him stinking of pee and talking about U-boats, and her stinking of attics and pinching my cheeks and asking me if I was courting. It was the boringest evening ever and it meant I didn't get to see Zoe and help with our project at all.

That night I had the most horrend dreams about Poppy and Splodge. In one dream, they were tied up in the boot of a car. In another, they were hanging upside down from the trees and being skinned like rabbits. Both times they were screaming out for help but no one could hear them except me and I was stuck in the mud, just watching. Helpless. I stopped trying to sleep at about four and played with Pee Wee.

After stealing some frying sausages out of the pan for breakfast, me and Pee Wee raced up to Zoe's house that Saturday morning to find Zoe just coming out and locking the front door behind her. She was carrying the cool bag.

'Sorry I couldn't come over last night; my grandparents came round and I couldn't get away . . . Where are you going?'

'Out,' she snapped. 'To get the next piece for the project.'

She was tetchy. I could tell she was tetchy cos no one says 'Out' before they say 'Hello'. So I knew I had to be careful. Normal Zoe was odd enough, Tetchy Zoe might be dangerous. 'Which piece are we going to get?' I asked her, following her up the drive.

'The head. And after that he will be ready for the most important piece: the brain. I have a train to catch.'

'Cool beanies,' I said. Pee Wee trotted beside us, looking adoringly up at me. I think he really loved me. Then I realised he could smell the sausages in my coat pocket. I let him have one.

We walked in step, all the way down the snaking bends of Clairmont Road, which overlooked Madeira Cove and the jetty, where we caught the electro bus. It was always driven by a crotchety old man called Alf. We had to stay on it all the way to its final stop, the train station. The name 'electro bus' made it sound quite exotic but it wasn't. It clattered, the seats were uncomfortable and its top speed was ten miles an hour. Zoe took the window seat. Pee Wee curled up in my lap.

'This is nice, isn't it?' I said.

'Yes, isn't it just,' Zoe sighed. 'There's nothing quite like a daytrip to London to steal a severed head. Shall we start singing?'

I giggled, more than a little unnerved. 'No, I don't think so. But at least it gets us out of Hoydon's Bracht for the day.'

'Thank Darwin,' she said.

We passed the Mercedes showroom and saw Damian and his dad standing next to a massive silver car, talking to some salesman.

'Oh look, there's Damian and his dad,' I said, not really thinking.

'Why would I be interested?' she sighed.

I shrugged. 'I don't know. I was just making conversation.'

'Can't see any conversation to be made there,' she said, staring ahead like a statue.

I couldn't say anything without her making some spiky comment, so I concentrated on chewing a piece of banana bubble gum and watching a chocolate football roll up and down the aisle of the bus, trying not to speak at all.

We went past Holy Trinity. The vicarage was behind it, where Poppy lived.

I didn't like silences and the longer ours went on, the more I thought I'd done something wrong. So I decided to speak just to test the water, see if I really had done something. 'I still haven't heard from Poppy,' I said. 'Louis hasn't heard from Splodge either. We're both quite worried about them.'

'And?' said Zoe, still staring straight ahead.

'She is still, sort of, my friend. I'm worried something has happened to her.'

'Why? She's evidently not in the least bit worried about you, or she wouldn't have dumped you, would she? Wouldn't have gone off with that Splat moron.'

I blew a yellow bubble and it popped, sending a light spray of banana rain over my face. 'Splodge,' I said. 'His name's Andrew, actually . . .'

She looked at me, her eyes as dead as coal. 'I. Don't. Care.'

'Sorry,' I said.

The cool bag she had brought along slid out from under our seat as the driver braked hard for some old people shuffling across the road. She tucked it back underneath. It amazed me how Zoe took up so little room. My stuff always seemed to be spread out all over the place. She was neat; I was messy. She wore black; I wore dresses and pink pumps. She liked reading surgery magazines or her weird dictionary of organs; I preferred my romance novels.

I thought about Poppy. She still hadn't texted me back. It wasn't like her at all. I kept my phone up the sleeve of my arm warmer, hoping at any moment I'd feel the little vibration and see the words on the screen: *Hi Babes, soz havnt called. Bin soooo bizi. Me n Splodge doin so much kissy stuff!!!* But it didn't come. Nothing came at all. Where was she? Where was Splodge? It was too much of a coincidence for them both to go missing. I was sure something had happened to them.

I scrabbled around in my rucksack for some more bubble gum. I managed to pull out everything in my bag I didn't need – my 3D glasses, lip gloss, a couple of romance novels, Pee Wee's tennis ball and poo bags – before I accidentally nudged Zoe's arm and she got all cross.

'For goodness' sake!'

'Sorry.' I found one Banana Bubba at the bottom and popped it in my mouth.

My phone buzzed in my hand. It said *Louis Burnett*.

'It's from Louis,' I told Zoe, cos I always think it's a bit rude if you're with someone and you answer a text from someone else and you don't at least say who it's from. Zoe stared out the window. The text said: *Hi Camille, hope u r OK. Still nothing from Splodge. Anything from P yet?*

I texted back: *Hi L. No not yet. I'll let u know don't worry. I'm sure they r fine.*

He texted back: *Thank u. C u soon.*

I wondered whether or not I should text back again and add a little smiley face, but then I thought perhaps not. We were both worried; it was no time for smileys. Then I thought I could do a worried smiley, to show him I felt like he did. So I texted back: *Yeah. Keep your chin up* ☺

And five seconds later another text came back: a worried smiley on its own.

I always had to wait ages for texts from Lynx or Poppy, but Louis was straight back every time. I liked that. I hated waiting for texts. I always thought in the meantime they'd found another friend and forgotten about me.

'Louis seems nice, doesn't he?' I said out loud. 'I don't think he'll tell on us for stealing the hospital trolley.'

Zoe said nothing and still stared out the window.

'Well, he's nicer than Damian, anyway.'

She looked round at me, slowly, like her head was going to twist all the way. 'Seems nice?' she said quietly.

I nodded. 'Yeah.' For some reason my heart started to pound and I felt the coldest, prickliest feeling all over my skin. I had said exactly the wrong thing.

'So this . . . Louis will do for you, will he?'

'Do what?' I said, swallowing.

'He will do as your "perfect" man, will he? I'm going to all this trouble – trying to collect a thousand different pieces, trying to put them all together in the exact right way – just so you have someone half decent to go to that stupid party with, and the boy in your History class will "do".'

Her words were like wasp stings. 'I never said that, Zoe. Why are you being like this . . . ?'

'Some scrawny know-nothing, one of the lads, one of those beer-swilling spotty-faced runts that you see on every street corner, every day of the week. One of them will do, will they?'

Her rant had winded me. 'Louis isn't like that,' I said. 'And he doesn't have spots. He's got quite good skin actually. And he's not scrawny. He actually has nice arms . . .'

'I'm generalising,' Zoe snapped. 'He may not dress like them but he colludes with them. That Damian de Jager amoeba. That Splodge Hawkins monstrosity. I've seen chemical spillages more appealing than those two. I heard Hawkins has got two younger brothers. What on earth made his parents think they needed to spawn two more when the first one looked like that?'

'How do you know Splodge has two brothers?' I said, though my voice was barely a whisper. The chocolate football had appeared again and Pee Wee leapt out of my lap and launched himself at it. He missed it and galloped down the aisle to get it, but it rolled back. Alf's driving got a lot more all-over-the-roady.

'I mean, Mozart composed his first symphony aged nine. Picasso painted *Portrait of Aunt Pepa* at fourteen. Blaise Pascal had written a theorem by the time he was sixteen. What has Damian de Jager ever achieved? Top scorer on Call of Duty and five wanks in one day?'

Weird. She had never heard of Johnny Depp but she'd heard of Call of Duty?

'I had to spend an entire half-hour listening as he regaled the Chemistry class with Tales in the Life of Damian last week.'

Ah, that explained it.

'The teacher did absolutely nothing to discipline him. But of course, we're encouraged to act like morons at our age, aren't we? God forbid we might actually read a book or achieve something every once in a while.'

'Zoe, calm down. Alf doesn't like a lot of noise.'

'And now you're in love with one of them, well how

convenient,' she growled at me. 'I should have guessed it that night on the pier. The stench of your pheromones made me quite nauseous.'

I hadn't understood much of what she'd just said, and I hadn't even tried to. I just got that she hated Splodge and Damian and for some reason she also hated Louis, even though he hadn't done anything at all. In fact, he'd been quite sweet to me, except smashing my face in.

I tried to change subject. 'Where will we get the head from?' I blew a bubble with my banana gum and it was so big that when I turned my head it touched Zoe's nose. I laughed.

She didn't. 'London. From a medical school,' she said. 'And *I* will get it. I don't think your heart is truly in this project anymore.'

'What? It is!' I cried. 'You said I could do the athletics. All the outward bits, face and hair and body and stuff.'

'Aesthetics,' Zoe spat. 'And I can do that alone. I don't need you. Not now.' Her words were like needles.

'What do you mean "not now"? What have I done? I want to be involved, Zoe. I'll try harder, I will.' I wished I knew how to break her anger mask. 'Maybe we can go somewhere and you can show me some heads and I can pick one out. I mean, you've done *everything* so far. You found Luke the Lifeguard, you sawed off William Pratt's feet, you got the blood and you even found new hands. I'll help you much more. You can rely on me, I promise.'

'Was your fontanel compromised at birth?' she said, lifting the cool bag from under the seat and standing up. The bus had arrived at the train station. 'I don't have access to an endless smorgasbord of boy-band body parts I'm afraid. My sources are limited. I take what I can get.'

I went to stand up but Zoe pushed me back down into my seat, so hard it hurt.

'Ow!' I said, even though it was only the shock of it that had hurt.

'You're not coming. Go home, Camille. Go back to your family and your Mr Adequate.'

And she left me there on the bench seat. I watched her march down the bus steps and through the train station doors, barging through people like they weren't even there. She didn't once look back.

I waited for tears to form in my eyes. Why was she so big fat horrible? Why had she brought my family into it, and Louis, my 'Mr Adequate'. What did *that* mean? What had I done to deserve her being so cross with me? I needed a hug. Poppy gave brilliant hugs. I missed hugs. I missed her. I picked up Pee Wee and gave him a cuddle instead.

'Ain't you gettin' off?' Alf the driver called back to me. 'I don't stop at Tanner's Knife or Pleinpalais on a Friday, you know.'

'No, I know,' I said, clearing my throat. 'I need to go to . . . Holy Trinity. The vicarage. I'll get off there.'

Cue the Tinkly
Suspensey Music

Mrs Lamp opened the door in her apron and lime-green Crocs. 'Hello, Camille love. Long time no see.' She zoned in on my conk. 'Ooh, you've had a nasty knock there.'

'Hi, Mrs Lamp. Yeah. A door. Is Poppy in?'

Pee Wee jumped up and started biting her tights. She frowned as she tried to push him away. She was normally quite glamorous and I'd never seen her without make-up on, but today her face looked like it had been wrung out like a soggy dishcloth and her eyes were puffy as though hadn't slept all night. 'No. Has she not phoned you?'

'No. I've texted her twice. She hasn't texted back. I was

worried. Has something happened?'

Mrs Lamp rubbed the silky bit on her apron. 'I was sure she would have told you at least.'

'Told me what?'

'Come in, love.'

It was weird how everything looked old in the house without Poppy there to young it up. Everything seemed so much more grey and vicaragey. The pictures all up the stairs were of her and her brothers as children. And of her friends: our day out at Splashy Manor four years ago – me, Poppy and Lynx on the rollercoaster, screaming; me, Poppy and Lynx at the aquarium aged about nine. I'd forgotten how fat Lynx had been as a little girl. I'd forgotten how freckly Poppy had been.

I followed Mrs Lamp through to the kitchen, where she let Pee Wee into the back garden and put the kettle on. She got down a cup and saucer for her and my usual mug, which she filled with three scoops of light hot chocolate powder without even checking I wanted it. She just knew. She placed it down on a doily coaster on the tabletop and took a piece of notepaper from the top of the fridge. 'This was on her bed yesterday morning.'

My worry was so big by this time that I physically couldn't read the note fast enough. I had to read it twice before I understood what it said.

Mum and Dad, I've gone to the West Fest with Splodge. I'm sorry, I just couldn't not go. Please forgive me. We're getting the bus to Abergavenny. I'll see you in a couple of days. Please don't worry. I love you, Poppy xxxxx

'Poppy wrote this?' I asked. Mrs Lamp nodded. 'I'd heard Poppy talk about West Fest back in the summer. Lynx couldn't bear the thought of not showering for three days and I didn't like any of the bands, but she had really wanted to go. Me and Lynx had doubted her parents would have let her anyway – they hadn't even let her have her ears pierced until she was sixteen.

'I can't believe she didn't tell you about it,' said Mrs Lamp, pinning her red hair back up into its clip as it was coming loose.

'No. Well, I haven't really seen her that much lately.'

She sniffed. 'Ever since this Splodge character came on the scene, neither have we. She even missed church last week, just so she could go and see him. It's just not like her, is it, Camille? She's never done anything like this before. We were always so sure with her. Her GCSE results were excellent . . .'

'I don't think this was planned, Mrs Lamp,' I said, touching her hand to comfort her. 'I just think . . . well, I think she's in love.'

'That's not an excuse, is it? Not when she's just started her A levels. There's no way she's going to that Halloween party with him, that's for sure. Oh no, not after this. What do you know about him, Camille?'

I shrugged. 'Not much, really. He's on the rugby team at college and in the orchestra with Poppy. He's quiet. Chubby. Bit of a lad . . .' I saw Mrs Lamp's face fall. 'But he's not a bad person. I think he really loves her too. And I'm sure he'll look after her.'

'I forbade her from going to that festival this early in a

new term. I looked it up on her computer, what goes on there. You can imagine. Drugs. Parties till all hours. Naked weddings . . .' Her voice dropped to a whisper and her cheeks flashed red. 'Not to mention the fact that they'll both be sharing a tent. They'll be having . . .'

'Sex?' I blurted out, before realising that Mrs Lamp really didn't need me telling her what they would be doing. I tried to make up for it. 'Poppy wouldn't do that, Mrs Lamp. She knows that you wouldn't approve. And I don't even think she approves of that before marriage anyway. I think she and Splodge just really like these DJs, Skitzy and Creampuff. And there's this band, Little Maniacs – I think they were going to be there too. They're like an electronic orchestra.'

Mrs Lamp shook her head. 'Just doesn't seem right to me.'

I bit my cheek. I had to say it. 'It is weird that she went when she knew you wouldn't let her, though. Poppy doesn't even swear because you don't like her to. It's very . . .'

'. . . out of character,' she finished.

I shrugged. 'Yeah. Totes.' I looked around at the blue and green kitchen tiles me and Poppy used to count when we were having tea in the kitchen, swinging our legs beneath the breakfast bar. 'But I really think they might, like, love each other, if that helps?'

Mrs Lamp's eyebrows rose up to her forehead and she sighed the longest sigh, like she was letting all the air out of her body. 'How would that make me feel better? I suppose being in love makes you do crazy things like ignore your parents' rules and take impromptu trips out of the country whenever one feels like it, does it?'

'Hmm,' I said. I turned the sentence over and over in my head as we sat there. *Being in love makes you do crazy things.* Like what me and Zoe were doing, building the body. It was all because of love.

'What is it, Camille?'

'Nothing,' I said. 'I was just wondering if she told Lynx or anyone else about the festival.'

'No, Lynsey was round here yesterday asking for her. Brought that rather forward young man with her. Jeff de What's-His-Name who owns the arcades and half the pier – his son. Dylan, is it?'

'Damian,' I said.

'Yes, Day-me-an,' she said slowly. 'Seemed rather . . .'

'Yeah,' I said, unable to think of an appropriate word to sum Damian up. 'I know Damian.'

I looked at the note again. I didn't want to worry Mrs Lamp until I was sure, but there were a few things I just didn't get. For a start, it was written on a tea-stained kitchen notepad with corners that had gone curly. The slightest crease on a page and Poppy had to use a whole new one. And it didn't really look like Poppy's handwriting either – it was scrawly and ink blotted. It could have been done in a rush, I guessed, but Poppy was always so neat. She was like one of those medieval monks about her hand-writing. It was her pride and joy. That scruffy scribbly note was not Poppy's style, of that I was the certaintest I had ever been about anything ever ever. A thought flashed into my mind – Zoe's notepad. Messy. Ink blotted. Like the note. Could it have been Zoe's handwriting? Could Zoe have written that note?

On the way back into town, the electro bus was packed so I had to stand up and hold one of the ceiling straps. Pee Wee sat between my feet. My phone buzzed in my pocket. I pulled it out and saw a text from Louis Burnett. My chest pulsed. Had he heard from Splodge?

But no. It just said: *R u OK?*

I texted back: *I'm fine. Went rnd 2 c P's mum. They went 2 a festivl in Wales. Her mum not happy. C.* And I put a happy smiley. Then I turned my phone off.

I didn't see the point in telling Louis my worries before I'd got everything sorted out in my head. It all just didn't add up, and I was no good at adding up anyway so I knew it was going to take me a while to work it out. Had Zoe written that note? And where had she got those hands for the project? Where had she got those organs from? You just don't have those kinds of things lying around, do you? Or maybe you do if you're someone like Zoe Lutwyche? Had she gone up to Madeira Cove and pushed William Pratt off the cliff just so she could steal his feet? Did I know who Zoe actually was? Was my best friend Zoe Lutwyche a murderer?

No, no, no, it was the terriblest thought. It couldn't be possible. Splodge and Poppy must have got the coach to Wales for the festival on Thursday night. But I couldn't shake my worries about the note. What if they hadn't made it to the coach station? What if Zoe had seen them first and bundled them into the back of her car, then broken in through Poppy's bedroom window and left the note? Could Zoe really have overpowered Splodge though? Big fat almost-six-foot-tall Splodge? Splodge who played piano in the orchestra. Splodge who had very nimble long white fingers. And hadn't he had a mole on one of them? I wished I could remember his hands more clearly. Damian had been knocked over last night too. Had that been Zoe as well? Or had it really just been an accident, some drunk driver?

All I knew was that I didn't know. But I did remember what Zoe had said when I'd asked her where she'd got the hands and organs from:

I had some spares lying around from when my father used to experiment.

And I remembered something else she had said earlier on the bus:

My sources are limited. I take what I can get.

Did that mean killing people if she couldn't find what she wanted in Daddy's spares box or in the hospital mort-yoo-ary? Was she really going to some medical school in London to get the head? Or had that been a lie? If I'd been in a film or one of those detective dramas, this would have been the bit where I started breaking into offices and stealing secret papers or hiding around corners with a camera, hoping to get proof, and it would have had this tinkly suspensey music in the background and I'd have been acting all shrewd and detectivey as I pieced the bits together. But I wasn't shrewd or detectivey and I had no idea how to begin piecing what little proof I had together.

One thing was for certain – I didn't really have a clue what Zoe Lutwyche was capable of.

Love Makes You Do Crazy Things

Another night, another truly cruddy night's sleep and it wasn't just because I kept knocking my nose. I had an even more cruddy dream. I dreamed that me and Louis were being chased by some hideous, tall, drooling blue-eyed monster and the monster got Louis and dragged him to the ground and he was screaming and being eaten alive. The only good bit in the dream was that hanging from the trees were millions and millions of cherry hair scrunchies, just like the one I'd lost. And when I woke up I missed it even more.

Me and Pee Wee walked to college for double Biology, eating our greasy bacon-and-sausage sandwich, and I saw

Louis standing outside the front entrance. I was a little relieved after what had happened to him in my dream. He was wearing a black basketball vest and shorts and he smiled when he saw me. My heart did a little pole vault thing. Definitely needed to go easy on the fried food.

'Has Splodge called you yet?' I said, unable to stop smiling myself for some weird reason.

'No,' he said. 'Walk with me? I'm late for practice.'

'I didn't know you did basketball so early,' I said as we walked side by side towards the sports block.

'It's an extra practice cos we've got a big inter-college championship coming up. I'm usually a sub but they've had a few guys off with injuries so . . .'

'What kind of injuries?!' I said, grabbing his arm. 'Did they say what happened?'

He frowned. 'Just hamstring pulls and stuff I think. But look, I'm getting really worried about Splodge.'

'Why?'

'I went round to his house and his mum told me about him just doing a bunk in the middle of the night with Poppy. She showed me this note he'd written. Something wasn't right though. It was a really neat note. It didn't look like Splodge's writing at all.'

'I had the exact same thing when I went round to Poppy's house! Her mum showed me this really messy note from her.'

'I guess they could have written each other's notes?' said Louis.

I had a think. 'Yeah, that would make sense I guess. What did his note say?'

'It said "I'm in love. Back soon." That was it.'

'That was it?'

'That was it,' he said, pulling his sports bag up his shoulder from where it had fallen down. 'Maybe Poppy was just in a hurry and neat handwriting was the last thing on her mind?'

'Yeah. I thought that too. Maybe Splodge just felt like writing it neatly cos . . .'

'. . . for once he cared what he was writing about?

Louis nodded. 'I guess that makes sense. I didn't know he wanted to go to the stupid festival so badly. Just wish he'd call. It still doesn't feel right.'

'What do you mean?' I said, as Pee Wee cocked a leg against the sign for the maths room. 'Good boy.'

'Well, Splodge has never even had a girlfriend before. Now suddenly he ups and leaves without a word to his two best mates? Me and Dame have known him since forever. I mean, okay, he hasn't always been the most reliable friend, but I've been there for him. I know him, Camille. He wouldn't have just gone off like this.'

I squinted and shrugged. Squgged, I guess. 'But have you ever known him in love before? Love makes you do crazy things.'

A couple of boys went past and their laughter floated over to us. They were looking at me and talking about freshers', I knew it. I heard the word 'sandwich'. They were laughing about my purple-tinged nose too. I didn't even care. I didn't even get the pang of hurt I always got when people laughed at me. I was tooooo tired.

Louis shook his head. 'I'm really worried about him,

Camille. I can't sleep, I can't concentrate . . .'

'Me neither!' I said.

'What if they've had a car crash and they're in some ditch?'

I rubbed my eye. 'No, Mrs Lamp said they took a bus to Abracadabra or something.'

'A bus crash then.'

'We would have heard about it.'

He stopped walking as we reached the double doors at the back of the gym and we moved to one side to let a small group of girls through. 'Well, the festival's over now, shouldn't they be on their way back?'

'I don't know. I just don't know.' Cue the tinkly suspenseful music. I couldn't say anything that would make him feel better. He looked like he was going to cry.

'Did you see the news last night?' he whispered. 'A young couple out hiking in the Welsh hills got mauled. They don't know who or what did it. How do we know that wasn't them?'

My mind went into free fall. Two bad nights' sleep and though my body was exhausted, my brain was a hamster on an endlessly-moving wheel. A bad mad hamster thinking bad mad thoughts.

'Oh Louis, don't!' I said, now proper crying myself. It came out of nowhere – I just started bawling.

'Camille, I didn't mean to upset you.' He leaned into me and wrapped his arms around my back and I sank into his shoulder. He was so warm and so comfortable and he smelled of that man shower gel that I liked sniffing in the supermarket. He rubbed my back. 'I'm sorry. I'm just way overtired. It's just me being paranoid.' *Rub rub rub.* I went limp against him. I was soooooo comfy.

Seconds later, he was standing before me, holding me at arm's length. 'Camille? You went to sleep!' He was laughing.

'I did?' I said, clearing my throat and blinking manically.

'Yeah. Look, do you want me to walk you home? I can skip basketball practice and Geography. I haven't got anything else until Media so I could be back for that.'

'No, I'll be okay,' I said, trying to stretch my eyes open where they kept falling closed. 'I have to go to Biology. I have to see if Zoe's back.'

'Well, let me walk you back home later then? I'll meet you out here at lunch.'

'No, I'll be fine.' I started walking away. A swaggering figure in the same black basketball kit as Louis was coming straight towards me. It was Damian.

'You seen the mess them hamsters made of reception? They've totalled it.'

'Yeah,' said Louis. 'It's out of bounds for the whole of this week.'

They were in full conversation about the hamsters – how the music room was all holey; how the cellos would have to be replaced. I started walking away but I was still looking at them, waiting for Louis to look back at me. And then he did and smiled and put his hand up to say goodbye.

And I walked straight into the side of the building.

*

I should have taken Louis' advice and gone home. Double

Biology was horrend. The lab smelled of fish, I got told off for yawning and Zoe was there but she completely blanked me. When the lesson ended, she was first to leave.

At lunchtime, after I'd walked Pee Wee, I really needed to sleep so we went to the least-visited corner of the Library, Large Print, and cuddled up for an hour. It didn't help. I was still yawning my head off by the time double English came around at three o'clock. Our tutor, Jill Price, made me read aloud the opening paragraph of the short story we were all supposed to have read. *Herbert West: Reanimator* by H.P. Lovecraft.

None of us had read it.

'*Of Herbert West, who was my friend in college and in after life, I can speak only with extreme terror,*' I began. '*While he was with me, the wonder and diabolism of his experiments fascinated me utterly, and I was his closest companion. Now that he is gone and the spell is broken, the actual fear is greater. Memories and possibilities are ever more hideous than realities.*'

'Thank you,' said Jill. 'Anyone like to have a stab at what the narrator is telling us there?' Everyone looked at everyone else. 'Come on, who has read this?'

A sea of blank faces. My mind went cloudy. Rain pitter-pattered on the darkening windows. The room was so warm. My eyelids went heavy.

Weird Alice's voice: 'He's talking about his friend's weird experiments and how at first he thought they were wonderful and boundary-pushing and then, as the scientist got more and more dangerous, he grew afraid of him. Terrified even. He's witnessed something really bad and he's going to tell us about it.'

Jill Price's voice: 'Yes, good. Well, I'm glad someone's read the set homework. So can anyone else tell me what these experiments were?'

My eyes started closing. Nobody was making eye contact with Jill. There was a very definite scratching sound in the pipes behind the wall. Hamsters, no doubt. We all got a little distracted. But Jill wasn't having any of it. She slammed her dry wipe marker down on the board ledge.

Weird Alice piped up again. 'They experimented on dead bodies,' she said.

My eyelids sprang open. 'What?'

Weird Alice looked at me and frowned, nodding. 'Yeah. This Herbert West was trying to bring them back to life and the narrator is explaining how they went about it, stealing the bodies and stuff.'

'Oh my God,' I gasped under my breath.

'Right,' said Jill. 'Since Alice is the only one who even bothered to look at this text, we'll waste the entire period reading it aloud so everyone else catches up, all right? You'll take turns. Philip, you carry on from where Camille finished, please.'

As Philip Always In Shorts read on, the story just got weirder and weirder. I wished I understood some of the really flowery bits and long words, but I didn't. I just highlighted them in my book with my pen that smelled of strawberries. I felt sick with every new passage I marked. Though it could have been the smell of strawberries.

In his experiments with various animating solutions, he had killed and treated immense numbers of rabbits, guinea pigs, cats, dogs and monkeys.

That was Zoe! That was Zoe's dad! Animating solutions, like the blue serum!

We followed the local death notices like ghouls, for our specimens demanded particular qualities.

Like we'd done with Luke the Lifeguard's body, read through the obituaries!

I saw him inject into the still veins the elixir which he thought would to some extent restore life's chemical and physical processes. It had ended horribly . . .

Oh my big fat God . . .

His slight form, yellow hair, spectacled blue eyes and soft voice gave no hint of the supernormal – almost diabolical – power of the cold brain within.

So Zoe wasn't slight or bespectacled and she didn't have yellow hair, but she did have blue eyes and a soft voice. And a cold brain. A cold, cold brain.

And the story got weirder and scarier. It was as though this writer bloke had time-travelled to our college, spied on me and Zoe and gone back to his black-and-white olde worlde time and written it all down, changing all the names so no one knew. *We* were the story. The story was us!

I looked at the skirting boards. The filled-in holes where the hamsters had gnawed through.

One thing . . . had risen violently, beaten us both to uncon-sciousness and run amuck in a shocking way before it could be placed behind asylum bars . . .

Holy focaccia bread. Asylum bars? I thought. Was my perfect boyfriend going to go mad? Was this what had already happened with the hamsters? And Pee Wee? I looked down at him in my bag, curled up cutely with his little eyes closed, twitching as he dreamed his little dreams. Dreaming goodness knows what little dreams. No, Pee Wee wasn't mad. He was odd, but he wasn't mad. To me he was perfect. But then, I saw nothing wrong in stealing body parts to make myself a boyfriend. What was wrong with *me*?

I looked around the room, my heart galloping, my cheeks so hot I thought they were going to burn right through. The guilt must have been written all over my face. Any second now, someone would stand up and shout, 'Jill! Jill! Camille and her mad friend are doing what Herbert West did, and they've killed Poppy Lamp and Splodge Hawkins. They've chopped them up! We've got to tell the police!' But they didn't. No one said a word. Everyone carried on looking bored and Monday afternoony.

But I was in a horror story. I wasn't making a boyfriend; I was making a nightmare. I couldn't concentrate on English any more after that. I just had to get out.

After the lesson, Jill Price asked me to go to her office for a 'little chat'. She had a room in the English block. She made me a cup of watery tea in a chipped mug and sat down on the end of her desk. Her skirt rode up to show the veins in her lumpy legs. Along the skirting board were holes where the hamsters had chewed. There was a hole in Jill's tights. I wondered if the hamsters had done that too.

Jill fed Pee Wee a ginger biscuit and he gobbled it up in a second and sat by my chair, gnawing the leg. 'I thought we should touch base,' she said. 'Talk about how things are going, if that's all right, Camille? You look tired.'

'Yeah, I've had a bit of trouble sleeping lately. I'll be okay.'

'How are you finding the work at the moment?'

'Yeah, I'm fine,' I said. 'The work's fine. Really fine, in fact. Splendido. Totally.' I realised I was over-egging the fine-ness and stopped talking.

'And you're also doing History and Sociology, that's right, isn't it?'

'No, History and Human Biology now,' I said. 'I swapped.'

'Oh right. And everything's okay at home? You're not worried about anything?'

I couldn't tell her about my real worry. There was no way she would understand. So I just said, 'No, I'm okay.'

'You seemed very absent in today's lesson, Camille.'

'No, I was definitely there, you saw me,' I said.

'Yes, I know you were there but you didn't seem to participate as readily as you normally do. Are you understanding the texts all right? Because you should say if you're not. Some people really grasp Lovecraft, others don't.'

'Oh I grasp him,' I said. 'I think I grasp him a lot.'

'Well, always ask if you're not sure about something. Do you think you'll cope with the assignment?'

'What assignment?'

Jill sighed. 'You really weren't listening, were you? The assignment to write a modern take on a Lovecraftian text.'

'I didn't hear that, I'm sorry,' I said, hanging my head. 'I'm sure I won't have a problem with it though.'

'Are you enjoying the set texts?' she asked. I nodded. I hadn't read any of them outside of the lessons.

'Have you read any of the non-compulsory texts on the syllabus? *Jane Eyre*? *Northanger Abbey*? *The Taming of the Shrew*?' I shook my head again. 'What do you read for fun?'

I leaned down and rummaged about in my bag for the two books I was currently reading. I handed them to her. I could tell she wasn't impressed.

'*Jake the Sheikh and the Mistress Unbound*,' she read, 'and *Yule Be Mine: Stories of Christmas Lovin' Under the Mistletoe*. Camille, you really shouldn't be reading this sort of . . . nonsense,' she said, handing them back to me.

'I like them,' I said, as again the blush taps in my cheeks went into flood mode. 'I just like nice books, no chopping off feet or sticking things up each other's bottoms or drowning kittens or anything like that. Just nice stories.'

'You're not enjoying the poetry texts then?' she said. 'Well, I suggest you borrow some classics from the library and get yourself a good night's sleep. And if you need to talk again, you know where I am. My door's always open.'

I wondered if I could tell Jill my worries about Poppy. *A problem shared is a problem halved*, as my dad always said, *cos if you keep them inside that's how you grow tumours*. I thought Jill would be as good a person as any to tell. Then I'd only have half a tumour to worry about. 'Can I come tomorrow and talk about it?'

'I'm not here tomorrow. TUC conference in Chester. Any other time though. Apart from half term obviously as college is closed then. Or when I'm at home. Can't have students on the beige carpets, not after last time. But any other time, I'll be right here.'

I nodded and tickled the top of Pee Wee's head. 'I'll be okay. Pee Wee needs a wee wee.'

Dead people can be so romantic

It was half past five by the time I left college. I didn't like leaving in the dark but at least I had Pee Wee with me. The traffic was still quite heavy on the main roads into town and I stuck to the pavements that had street lights on so I could be seen, like Dad had taught me. Pee Wee was a pretty good guard dog too. His weird little bark and him walking directly in front of me rather than beside me was a total turn off for anyone coming in the opposite direction – a couple of people actually crossed over to avoid him I was sure.

As I got to the traffic lights, I had to wait for Pee Wee to poo and then clear it up. Some men were walking into town on the opposite pavement. All I could see in my head were the bits of them that would look good on Sexy Dead Boy, the name I gave my future boyfriend. The one in the blue shirt – his hair. The black one in the yellow trainers – his face. The one in the tracksuit – his broad back.

Was this what Zoe thought about too? Had she seen Splodge's piano-player's hands? Had she seen nice clean-living Poppy and made a play for her organs? What about Luke the Lifeguard? Had it been Zoe who had planted the Snot Monster in the pool changing rooms? I just couldn't figure out what was true and what was just me and my overacting imagination.

As I made my way through the churchyard, a twig snapped. Pee Wee barked.

'Who's that?' I called out, brandishing the dog poo bag ready to defend myself.

'It's okay, Pee Wee. There's no one there. Let's go home.' Pee Wee trotted on, ears pricked up.

A little further along, I stopped again. I could feel someone behind me. I quickly whipped around but there was still nobody there. I carried on walking. Pee Wee barked and hopped up and down on his front paws.

What if Zoe was following me? Stalking me? Ready to pounce and chop something off? I waved the poo bag again and got out my thickest Biology textbook and held it in front of me like a shield.

I turned around. 'Right, that's it. Who are you? Show yourself, you weirdo!'

Someone stumbled out of the bushes, followed by someone else, their foot catching and making them fall forwards. 'Oomph!'

I caught my breath. 'Who are you?'

'Louis, it's Louis,' he said, getting to his feet with his hands up, like I was the police. He was laughing.

'Hahahaha,' cried the other person, whom I recognised instantly as Damian de Jager. He had paper stitches over one eyebrow, and from the way he was falling about I guessed he was drunk. Pee Wee was straining on his lead and barking.

I lowered the poo bag and sighed in relief but I still brandished my textbook. 'Louis? What are you doing here?'

'Sorry if we scared you, Camille,' he said, laughing as Damian fell over.

'Have you been following me?'

Louis scratched his head. 'Yeah, kind of,' he smiled. He was drunk too, I was sure of it. He was holding a can of Crunk Juice that kept spilling. He giggled at Damian, who was goading Pee Wee to attack him. 'We skipped Media and headed into town. Damian's got this sweet deal going with some of the lads from St Anthony's. He's getting them cheap sim cards and cigarettes and they're paying him through the nose.'

'Oh, nice,' I said, banging my eyes shut to show my disgust at them fleecing private school boys just because they could.

'We were just coming back when I saw you going up the road so we followed you then. Not in a weird way, just . . . sorry.'

'Come on then! Come on then!' Damian was teasing

Pee Wee, who was pulling even harder on his lead. 'You want my big hairy balls, you come and get 'em!'

'Stop teasing him,' I said. Pee Wee barked and strained harder, eyeing up his target: Damian's crotch. 'I see your head injury didn't make you any less of an idiot. I've got a good mind to let him off and teach you a lesson.'

Raaawwwwwrrrr raaawf raaaaawf raaaawf!

'Go on then, let him off. Let's see him do some damage!' Damian laughed, and with that, I bent down and unhooked Pee Wee's collar from the lead and Pee Wee pounced upon Damian with such force he knocked him back down on the grass.

'Ahhhhhh shiiiiiiiiiiit! Get this thing off me!' Damian yelled, jumping up and throwing Pee Wee off, only to have him leap back up to his hood and hang on by his teeth. Damian sprinted around the graveyard trying to flick him off. Louis was wetting himself. Not literally, but really, really laughing.

I laughed too, I couldn't help it, but I was still really cross with Louis for jumping out at me. Damian and Pee Wee disappeared into the darkness, just as I caught sight of a bin where I could sling the poo bag.

'I'm sorry,' said Louis, when I returned from making my deposit. 'I said I'd walk you home. I waited for you after Geography.'

I decided to get on my high horse, not least because he'd actually almost literally frightened me out of my wits and because I was still mucho mucho tired. 'I don't need walking home by a . . . drunk person, thanks very much.'

'Camille, listen. I know, okay? I know,' he said, as Damian's screams and Pee Wee's growls came floating over the gravestones in the distance.

'Know what?'

'I know about Luke Truss,' he said.

I wound the dog lead around my wrist. 'What do you mean?'

'Well, I don't know exactly.' Louis shivered, folding his arms so his biceps went bulgy. He was wearing three-quarter-length jeans and a sleeveless checked shirt that was done up right to his neck. We were exactly the same height. 'But I know he wasn't your boyfriend. That's why you didn't go to his funeral.'

My brain wouldn't work properly. But then I remembered. 'Oh the lifeguard!' I said and sort of laughed. He looked at me and his eyes went all starey like Zoe's did. 'Luke . . . yeah, he died. I . . . couldn't face it, what with all the grief and everything. I had to mourn and stuff.'

'You went into History,' he said. 'Wes Carpenter told me you weren't there cos I asked him.' He swept his fringe out of his confused brown eyes. 'Just, say it. He wasn't your boyfriend, was he?'

'Uhhhh . . .' My 'uh' was going on for a long time and wasn't leading to any brilliant cover-up lie, so I just admitted it. 'No. I didn't know him.'

'Then why did you want to see his body at the funeral parlour that night if you didn't know him? Were you just breaking in?'

'No,' I said, folding my arms.

'Well, I don't know what to think, Camille,' he said. 'I just know . . . you're doing something you don't want people knowing about and it involves our funeral parlour. And when I saw you at the hospital that day . . .'

'I had a nosebleed, from when *you* opened a door in my face, remember?'

'Yeah, but why steal the bed? Why steal incineration bags? It's Zoe Lutwyche, isn't it? That psychopath's making you steal stuff. She's not . . . doing what her dad used to do, is she? Making Frankenstein's monsters?'

'No, of course not!' I shouted, louder than I meant to. 'And she's not a psychopath.'

'Camille, you can't . . .'

'AAAAAAaaaarrrghhhhh!' Damian screamed as he came pounding down the path. Pee Wee was still dangling off his hoodie. Louis grabbed Damian's arm to stop him and started unzipping his coat so he could scramble out of it. Pee Wee let go of the hoodie and started tearing into it on the ground.

'That thing wants putting down!' Damian puffed. 'It's a maniac!'

'He just doesn't like you,' I sneered, bending down to pick up Pee Wee and give him a cuddle. 'Pretty good judge of character, I'd say.'

'Ooh, look who's grown a bush,' said Damian. 'You've got more spunk than your mate Lynx. She don't stop pissing and whining.'

I scowled. 'Why don't you dump her then, if she's such a bad girlfriend?'

'Oh she passes the time.' He went to pet Pee Wee, who

immediately started gnashing his teeth at him again. 'I've had enough of this, I'm going down the pub. You coming, Mario? Princess Peach, can I tempt you?'

I shook my head as Damian's phone started ringing in his jacket pocket.

'Yeah, I'll meet you there,' said Louis as Damian grabbed his torn jacket, answered his phone and swaggered off down the path.

I turned to him. 'Go on then, I'm not stopping you,' I sniffed, well and truly on my high horse now.

Louis did that boy thing of adjusting his pants, the thing our Sociology teacher Mr Atwill used to do in class all the time, possibly because he wore trousers made of that really itchy stuff that sacks are made out of. 'You can tell me what Zoe's making you do,' he said. 'I can stand up to her if you don't want to. If you're . . . in trouble or anything like that.'

I kind of wanted to tell him then, but I knew I couldn't. I knew it would get me in trouble. Apart from anything else, we were doing this whole grave-robbing thing for my benefit. To find *me* a boyfriend. So I just snipped, 'It's none of your business!'

'Well, it kind of *is* my business, cos you were breaking into *my dad's* business,' he said. 'Trying to steal . . . I don't know what.'

'I can't tell you anything. I just can't. But no one is being hurt and I'm fine. That's all you need to know.'

'Damian said you wouldn't let on what you were doing,' he sighed.

'What does Damian know?' I cried.

'Only as much as I do. Which isn't much. He said if . . . if we could prove you two were doing something criminal or just something kinky you didn't want people knowing about, he could blackmail Zoe into going out with him.'

'What? Why?'

Louis shrugged. 'He really fancies her.'

'Damian fancies everyone,' I said. Pee Wee wanted to get down so I let him and he scampered off. 'Why do you have to be drunk at all hours of the day?'

'I don't. And stop changing the subject . . .'

'Then why are you always drinking? You're drinking now,' I said, looking down at the can in his hand. 'Is it to make you look cool? Because if so it really doesn't.' A fly flew into my open mouth and I coughed.

'I'm not drunk,' he said. 'This is just an energy drink.'

'Yeah, right,' I said.

'I'm not.'

'You were that night on the Pier when you . . .'

'Yeah maybe I'd had a couple then but . . .'

'So why do you do it?'

'Why does anyone drink?' he said. 'To feel better about themselves. To have the courage to do or say things they wouldn't normally.'

'What, act like a total idiot?' I snorted.

'None of that matters anyway,' he said. 'So are you going to tell me what you've been doing with Zoe Lutwyche or not?'

Pee Wee was going nuts, trying to dig up one of the graves. Behind him, near the top of the churchyard, I saw lights. Coloured lights, beaming up into the sky.

'What's that?' I said, pointing to the haze of pinks and greens and blues.

'What's what?' he sighed, looking to where my finger was pointing. I ran up the path towards it, stopping when I came to the kissing gate. And all at once I saw the most beautiful sight: lots of graves literally glowing in the dark.

'Oh my goodness! This is amazing!' I cried, squeezing through the kissing gate to get a closer look at them.

There was a metal squeaking behind me as Louis followed me through the gate, closely followed by Pee Wee.

'Yeah, pretty weird, isn't it?' he said. 'Glow-in-the-dark graves. It's one of our new lines at the funeral parlour. It's these stones.' He bent down and picked up a handful of yellow ones from a plot. 'People buy them thinking they're magical. That somehow they are the person's soul going up to heaven. Stupid really.'

'I think that's a nice thing to believe,' I said.

'You do?'

We walked further up the path. It was a bit like that scene in that film about the blue things when the girl blue thing is walking with the boy blue thing through that little glow-in-the-dark forest and all those little jellyfish things are coming down and it all looks so pretty. We didn't have little jellyfish things around us, we just had lighty-up graves but it was still quite pretty to walk through.

Louis binned his so-not-an energy drink as we passed a bin. 'It's a cynical money-making scheme if you ask me. My dad jumps on every afterlife bandwagon. He's now thinking about selling these phones which you can bury your loved one with. They're programmed to text you from beyond the grave, with things like *Wish you were here* or *Happy birthday, son.* How sick is that?'

'Yeah, that's creepy,' I said. 'I like the stones though. They make the churchyard look pretty.'

'They're warm too,' said Louis. 'Lie down on some.'

'What?'

'Lie down on some. They soak up the sun during the day, which makes them glow at night and when they glow, they're warm. I always lie on Edward Kendall Sheridan. You can lie on his wife, Edwina.'

'Isn't that a bit disrespectful?' I was one to talk about disrespect, especially since a few days ago I'd been to a dead boy's foot chopping ceremony.

'Not really,' said Louis. 'They've been dead about five years. I remember when Dad did the funerals. They died within hours of each other. She had a heart attack. And Dad said his heart just broke. They'd been together for like sixty years. Isn't that amazing?'

My own heart did a little pulse thing when I heard that. 'Aw yeah. Like in that film where they're in the nursing home and the man's telling his wife the story of their life together but she keeps forgetting and he says he'll never leave her and then they die in each other's arms.'

'Well, it wasn't quite like that but yeah, they'd been together for a long time.'

'You talk more when Damian's not around,' I said. 'You're different, actually.'

'Am I?' he said, sitting down first on Edward. I followed

him, lying on Edwina. The stones *were* warm, just like he'd said they would be.

'Yeah,' I said. 'You don't talk in History either.'

He sort of laughed and lay back. 'The glow only lasts a couple of years. Some relatives have paid us to come up here and refresh them every now and again, so they always glow.'

Louis was so nice without Damian around. We were having a nice time, even though we were lying on graves, talking about old people dying of broken hearts and his dad making money out of the bereaved. I liked him. I really liked him.

'Do you know what you're going to do after college?' I asked the stars.

Louis answered me. 'Nope. I thought about doing something with fish. Or basketball. Or maybe I could write horror movies or something. I'll probably end up just staying at the funeral parlour until I know. You?'

'No,' I replied. 'I thought I was the only one who didn't know. Like, everyone else I know knows, you know?'

'I know,' he said, scratching his wrist beneath his friend-ship bracelets and then putting his arms behind his head. I couldn't help noticing how soft his armpit hair looked. 'Damian wants to direct porn films and race Ferraris. He's wanted to do that since he was about twelve.'

'You'd be better off without Damian,' I said. 'He's a bad influence.'

'He's my mate. I'd rather him than that psychopath you hang out with,' he scoffed.

'Don't call her that,' I said. 'Zoe's my friend.'

'She's a psycho.'

I harrumphed. 'And what evidence are you basing your opinion on?'

'On her face?' Louis sniggered. 'That and the stories.' He turned on his grave and leant his head on his hand to look at me. 'That's why I need to know what Zoe's up to. Why she's got you stealing medical equipment, cos if she's doing what her dad used to do . . . you must have heard about her dad.'

'I've heard things. But they're just stories.'

His eyebrows rose. 'You heard how he died?'

'He's not dead. He's in some asylum somewhere, being looked after. Or . . . possibly living in the woods by their house.'

'No, he's definitely dead,' said Louis. 'We did his funeral. It was just before college started. She's supposed to be organising a headstone.'

'Prof Lutwyche . . . died? In the asylum?' I asked him. 'Are you sure?'

'My dad picked up the body. I didn't see it but I've heard all sorts.'

'Yeah, so have I.'

'He was only there a few weeks. Do you want to see where he's buried?'

I nodded and we both stood up. He started walking across the glowing blue red green and yellow churchyard, and led me to the exact spot under the willow tree where I'd seen Zoe digging on freshers' night. When she was just Digging Girl.

There was the mound she had been digging. The long,

body-shaped mound of earth, stamped down flat.

'Right here,' said Louis. 'There's no headstone because the council were afraid of people coming to the site to chip pieces off it. People do that, you know, when someone infamous has died.'

Why hadn't Zoe told me her dad had died? And so recently?

'Professor Lutwyche is buried here? Right on this spot?' I said.

'Professor Lunatic, more like,' said Louis, folding his arms. 'I've heard some truly nuts stuff about him. Running around the hills naked and cutting off his own head and, yeah, major lunatic.'

I didn't like hearing him talk about Zoe's dad like that. 'You don't know if any of that stuff's true. And lunatics don't invent stuff that brings animals back to life, do they? That's what he did though. You inject a dead thing with this blue stuff and then you electrocute it and it comes back to life.'

'No, it's all lies. That didn't happen.'

'It did happen!' I shouted. Pee Wee trotted over from the pet cemetery with a little pink plastic poodle ornament dangling from his jaws. 'I've seen it, Louis! I watched fifteen dead hamsters come back to life. Fifteen hamsters that had been gutted ten minutes earlier! Zoe did it, with the serum. The serum that *he* invented.'

Louis shook his head. 'Your teacher didn't chloroform them properly,' he said. 'That's what our Geography teacher said. Dead things can't come back to life.'

'But Zoe *can* do it. I've seen it! I'm telling you the

truth about this. Where do you think Pee Wee came from?'

He shrugged. 'I don't know. I thought he was yours.'

'No, Zoe reanimated him. He was cut in two pieces last week and now look at him. You wouldn't have known any different, would you?'

Pee Wee sat down between us, chewing his poodle.

'Camille, I've seen hundreds of dead bodies. Hundreds. There is no life in them whatsoever. No chance of it. Dead is dead, trust me.'

'Do you know for a fact that Professor Lutwyche cut off his own head? Or that he lived in the woods or have you *seen* any of his reanimations?'

'No, but . . .'

'Right, well I know one thing for sure. I *saw* Pee Wee come back to life. I saw Zoe inject the serum into his veins. And now she's going to do it on a . . . bigger animal and I'm going to help her.'

His eyes went starey, like Michael Jackson's in the *Thriller* video. 'What do you mean, a bigger animal? What is she doing?'

'A . . . sheep. She's going to do it on a sheep. And I'm going to help her.'

'A sheep?' he said. I could see he wasn't convinced. 'I don't buy it.'

'Well, it's true' I said.

'If I were you I'd steer well clear of Zoe Lutwyche,' he warned me.

'No, I won't,' I told him. 'And do you know why I'm not going to steer clear of her? Cos she's the only friend I've got, so excuse me if I completely ignore you.'

I walked off. 'Pee Wee!' I called back and within seconds I felt him by my side. Pee Wee that is, not Louis. Louis was still in the same spot as when I'd left him, probably laughing at me, like everyone else did.

Everyone but Zoe.

Nerves

I was way too antsy and emotional and sleep-deprived to go into college the next day and I really didn't want to see Louis in double History so I got my dad to call in sick for me. I tried to ignore what Louis had said, I really did. But somehow it had gotten into my brain, like a little worm, and met up with the little worm of doubt I had put there myself and they had made lots of babies and filled my head with worry worms.

She's a psycho. Zoe is a psycho.

The worry worms niggled all the next day. I Googled the word *psychopath*.

So when I first met Zoe, she was digging in her father's grave. Digging him up? Putting him back? Borrowing something? Burying something? What part of Professor

Lutwyche had she stolen for the project? Maybe that's where the hands had come from? Maybe it had been *his* organs she had taken.

There were lots of different types of psychopath on the Internet and all sorts of mega-complicated detail about them. Primary psychopaths. Secondary psychopaths. Distempered psychopaths. Charismatic psychopaths. And then there were sociopaths, a whole other bag of bunnies. I didn't understand any of it and there were all these quotes from scientists and psychologists, and footnotes and references that I couldn't force my brain to read. However, some words jumped out at me and left the rest to rot:

Psychopaths convey no emotions.

They are very intelligent.

They are good liars.

They are antisocial.

They are insane.

And they have something called 'parasitic tendencies'. I almost ignored this one until I read the line describing it. 'A reliance on others to do things for them.'

That was *me*! That was the reason she wanted me involved! I was Herbert West's assistant in that story! And Zoe was Herbert West. She was a psychopath who got me to do all her donkey-work for her. And if we *did* get caught, she would blame it all on me and I'd go to prison and it would probably kill my mum and dad off altogether. They couldn't take stress at the best of times. My dad went into shock if the postman was late.

I played ball with Pee Wee in my room. I taught him to roll over and stay. I gave him treats when he did it right.

It took my mind off what was in my mind, for a while. But taking your mind off your own mind isn't easy. Thoughts kept knocking. One thought was this: I had to stop her. Zoe Lutwyche, my best friend, was a bed-wetting, mother-abandoned, head-chopping psychopath. Louis was right. Who was next on her hit list? I couldn't let her finish making me a boyfriend, not if he was made out of people I knew. That just wasn't right. I had to go to the police and tell them everything and put an end to it.

But more thoughts started knocking: if Zoe *did* finish Sexy Dead Boy, I'd have a date. And I'd have a friend again. And maybe Splodge and Poppy really *were* at a festival in Wales and they would be back soon. And maybe if you stayed on the right side of a psychopath, it would be okay. Maybe I'd be okay.

At lunchtime, I went downstairs. Mum was in the sitting room, reading one of her crime novels with a bar of chocolate between her knees. The TV was on mute in the corner. *Prime Minister's Questions*. My mum fancied the prime minister. Apparently he'd been in some pop group when Mum was my age and she used to follow them around the country and write rude things in the dirt on the back of their tour bus.

'Mum?' I said, coming in quietly, because she'd jump about a foot in the air if I disturbed her reading.

'All right, love? Feeling any better?'

I nodded.

'You going to be all right for Biology this afternoon?'

I shook my head and sat down next to her. 'No, I'm still a bit hot.'

'Do you want some chocolate?'

'No, thanks. Mum, can I ask you something?'

'Hang on,' she said, reaching for the remote and turning the volume back up. 'He's getting all angry, look. He's ever so dishy when he's being heckled.'

'And I ask my learned friend to remember who it is who WON two elections in a row and whose job it is to clean up the mess left behind by the previous government.'

'Hear, hear,' said my mum, then muted it again and went back to her book.

'Mum, I need to ask you something,' I said again, now I had at least half her attention.

Her face fell. 'It's not that dog of yours, is it? He's not done a whoopsie on the new hallway carpet, has he? Because if he has, Camille, I'm telling you . . .'

'No, Pee Wee's fine. He's having his lunch in the back yard. I just wanted to ask you if you know anything about psychopaths, that was all.'

She laughed, obviously relieved. 'There's one of them in here, funnily enough.' She folded her book over. 'Serial killer he is. Right vicious swine he is too but he still wets the bed. You might like it. There's lots of dead bodies in it.'

'No, I've kind of gone off dead bodies a little bit,' I said, trying to smile.

'It's a good story,' said Mum. 'He's got this vicar's daughter tied to a radiator and he beats her with this big wet fish.'

'A *vicar's daughter*?' I cried, thinking immediately of Poppy tied to a radiator and being beaten with a big wet fish. 'Oh shizz!'

'It's not real, love. Clever though, because then he cooks and eats the murder weapon. The psychologist is trying to pin it all on his mother who abandoned him at birth, cos he only kills women called Yvonne, and that was her name. I'll lend it to you after . . .'

'NO, I don't want it! Thanks.'

'All right, calm down,' she said, laughing.

I came and sat down next to her, doing the same face I used to do as a toddler so she'd twiddle with my hair. She didn't though, just carried on reading her book. I leaned my cheek against her shoulder.

'Mind your make-up on my top, love. This is clean on,' she said, checking her sleeve.

'Sorry,' I said, moving away.

Dad came in with his coffee and set it down on a mat on the coffee table.

'All right, duck?' he said.

'Yeah,' I said.

'Those bin men still haven't come, Francine,' he said, picking up the remote and finding the news on one of the Sky channels. He sat down next to me and Mum so I was squashed in comfortably between them.

Police are asking for help in locating a young male model from South London who was last seen at an Underground station yesterday lunchtime. Eighteen-year-old Alex Rathbone . . .

I finally felt safe. I went to sleep on Dad's arm.

I had my dream again about the horse on the beach, the wind blowing through my endless blonde crinkly hair. Holding tight to a strong man as the stallion thundered on.

Crashing through the dazzling waters, his hair blowing behind him in the wind, his strong hands on the reins.

'Hya hya!' he shouted. But every time he yelled 'Hya!' something fell off: a clump of hair, an arm, an eye. All I could do was watch it bounce along behind me on the sand. Piece by piece, he disappeared before my eyes and soon I was riding along with just a set of teeth on the saddle in front of me. And every tooth was rotten.

The doorbell woke me up with a start, like my heart had exploded.

. . . last seen at the entrance to the Covent Garden Underground station. Anyone who believes they saw Alex on Saturday 11 October is being asked to call this number with any information that might help police track him down.

'No rest for the wicked,' said Dad, heaving himself up off the sofa.

'No, don't answer it, Dad,' I said, grabbing his arm. 'It won't be important.'

'It'll be guests, love. And guests equal money.'

I still clung on to him, my heart pulsing so hard I could feel it in my neck, my wrists, the tops of my thighs and everywhere else I had a pulse.

. . . that number again, if you have any information on the whereabouts of Alex Rathbone, is as follows: 0845 645 . . .

'Camille, love, I've got to get that,' said Dad.

I stared at the TV screen. *Missing model from South London.* Wasn't that where Zoe had been going yesterday? Hadn't she gone to London to get the head? Wasn't that what I'd said I wanted for Sexy Dead Boy – the head of a model or something? A square jaw. Soft thick hair. I looked at the photograph above the phone number on the screen. He was *exactly* what I wanted. Exactly what I had described! It was going to be the police at the door. The police looking for Zoe the murderer! *Oh no, oh no, oh no . . .*

The doorbell went again. Dad prised my fingers from his sleeve and gave me a funny look as he left the room, like he couldn't work me out. Like he couldn't possibly imagine the sheer horror of what was about to happen when he opened that door. It was going to be Zoe, with an axe, ready to chop off his head on the doorstep! And then she'd steal his brain before coming in here and hacking my mum to pieces too.

I ran into the hall, ready to unhook the fire extinguisher. But it wasn't Zoe. It was the old couple, Mr and Mrs Sangster from room one. They'd forgotten their door key, like they always did. I panted at the foot of the stairs as Dad joked with them and asked about their morning and they told him about the marvellous sand sculptures they had seen on the beach. I took my hand off the fire extinguisher.

I was afraid, for the first time, properly hand-shakingly afraid. I was afraid of Zoe.

And I knew my first thought had been right: I had to stop her.

So I totes have to catch a murderer

Bugger triple Biology – I had a murderer to catch.

I had to go to Zoe's house and she wasn't going to like what I had to say, so I thought I should take a weapon, just to protect myself. Halloween party date or no Halloween party date, she couldn't go around killing male models and my best friends and that was that. The problem was we didn't have a single useful weapon in our house. Even all our knives were blunt. Dad had a very old pellet gun out in the shed, which he used to shoot the starlings off the roof with, but I could barely lift it, let alone take aim and fire. And besides which, we didn't have any ammo.

So me and Pee Wee made the long trek up to Clairmont

House with the only weapons I could find – a birthday-candle lighter and a small bottle of peach shampoo. It always stung my eyes when I washed my hair so I thought it might be useful to blind Zoe with if I had to make a quick getaway. I held both of them in my coat pockets as I came closer to the turning for the driveway. The gates were locked.

'Pee Wee, no!' I cried as my naughty dog forced himself flat, crawled under the gates and then galloped up the driveway without me. He probably still had a whiff of that poodle he'd been chomping on a few nights ago.

'Brilliant,' I said, 'just brilliant,' and looked along the wall for a way I could get over and in. There was an overhanging tree branch a little further down and I made for it. I yanked it a few times and it seemed pretty sturdy. I used it to pull myself up the wall until I was just far enough up to hold on to the top while I swung my legs over and on to it. Then I jumped down to the other side.

There was no Pee Wee, no sight and no sound.

'Pee Wee,' I whispered, as loudly as I could. Nothing.

I ran round to the side of the house, keeping low in case of machine gun fire from an upstairs window. I really didn't know what to expect. But I could still be seen from every ground-floor window. I peered in through the kitchen window. Everything was still. I could hear the old grandfather clock on the landing chiming four o'clock. I could see the tap over the white sink *drip drip dripping*. Hear the buzzing of the freezer. But there were no signs of life or death anywhere else. I walked on round to the back door. I tried the rusty black handle. Locked.

'Pee Wee?' I saw his bottom disappearing through the cat flap. I was too late to grab him. I knelt down on the doorstep and lifted the flap to shout in. 'Pee Wee, you come out of there this minute or I'll . . .'

I could see that in the kitchen there was a small window above the sink that was slightly open. I was sure I could squeeze through it, so I crept round and shoved my hand inside to loosen the catch. It was stiff but it gave me just enough room. Pee Wee did a little jump on the spot when he saw me, as if to say, '*Yay, Camille's here, now we can play!*'

'Naughty boy!' I whisper-shouted.

But he wasn't listening. He trotted out to the hall and up the stairs.

'No, not upstairs! Pee Wee, here boy, here!' I said, slapping my thighs as if in some way this would prove irresistible and he'd have to come back. But Pee Wee was no ordinary dog and I was no dog trainer and he completely ignored me.

And it was at this point that I remembered Zoe's Aunt Gwen.

'Oh shizz!' I breathed as my skin prickled all over with sweat. 'Pee Wee, come here now!' I clutched the birthday-candle lighter in my pocket as he trotted off towards the bedrooms.

'Bad dog!' I whispered, running after him and knocking over a pile of letters on the hallway table. I stopped to pick them up and arrange them exactly as they had been but goodness knows if I'd done it right.

There were three doors on the landing. One was Zoe's

bedroom, door locked. The second had a painting of a fishing boat at sea on the wall beside it, door also locked. And the door to the right of that was slightly open. It creaked.

I had to come clean. If Aunt Gwen came out and saw me, she would think I had broken in, which I had. Or even worse, that I had come to do her harm, which I definitely hadn't. If anything, I had come to save her life. But what if it was too late?

'Uh . . . Mrs Lutwyche?' I called out, shattering the silence of the dusty old house. 'Mrs Lutwyche? Auntie Gwen?' No reply. 'My name's Camille Mabb. I'm Zoe's friend from college. I've come to see Zoe.'

I pushed the door open wider to see in. A neat and tidy bedroom with chintz curtains and a beautiful pink silk bedspread. Untouched. There was no one there.

Except a woman stood by the window in a big white hat, looking right at me.

'AAAAAAAAAAArrrrrgggggggggggggghhhhhhhh!' I cried as Pee Wee bounded in and raced over to the woman, jumping up to her outstretched arm and tearing it clean off. He then attacked it on the floor, shredding it into tiny pieces. Puffs of white polystyrene flew up into the air like a snowstorm.

'No, Pee Wee!'

It took me a moment to realise that the polystyrene and the lack of blood meant she was not actually a woman, but a shop dummy. A shop dummy with strings of beads around its neck and, of course, the big white hat. My pounding heart slowed to a more relaxed jog as I sat down on the edge of the bed, willing my hands to stop shaking. It was okay. It was all okay.

There was a chest of drawers next to the dummy. On it stood a stuffed squirrel in a tiny rocking chair smoking a pipe, some photos in frames and a blue lizard ornament. One of the photographs was of a woman with black hair, wearing the same large white hat. She was on a beach and there was a little girl with blonde hair and the biggest blue eyes, playing with a spade. The woman was so beautiful. She looked exactly like Zoe, but happy. I went to look at them more closely.

In another photo, the woman and the blonde girl were petting rabbits. In another, the girl was clutching Easter eggs and smiling. I picked it up. The little girl had to be Zoe, though I'd never seen her smile so widely, her starey blue eyes so sparkly. In another picture, the girl, aged about ten, was holding a large blue lizard, just like the stuffed one in the case in the hall. She was standing in front of a man with wild blue eyes who wasn't in any of the other photos. He wasn't smiling either. He was staring at the girl like he was afraid she was going to drop the lizard.

That had been Zoe's family. Now it was just Zoe. That was why she was doing all this. She was building herself a friend. Zoe was lonely.

But she would kill me if she found me in her house.

I pulled what was left of the dummy's arm away from Pee Wee and picked him up. He licked my face and snuggled comfortably into the crook of my arm. I looked out of the filthy window. A movement. The nail art van was coming up the drive.

Zoe was back.

'Shizzles. We'd better go,' I said, heading for the door.

It's at times like these when the last thing you want to hear is the sound of your phone belting out a Rihanna song in your pocket, but that was exactly what happened when I was cowering on the landing.

'Oh no no no!' I gasped, fumbling it out of my pocket with one hand and turning it totally off. Pee Wee gave me a look that said, '*Well done, you've totes just blown our cover; now the psycho's going to chop us up and wear our heads as shoes.*' But it was okay. Below us, the front door was only just being unlocked. It opened. It shut. It was locked. Keys were thrown onto a table. I put my hand gently over Pee Wee's nose, feeling like he was gearing up for a bark. I heard footsteps disappearing across the hall. The footsteps of a murderess, I thought. Stairs or kitchen, which way would she go? The footsteps went towards the kitchen.

'Thank God,' I breathed. Maybe we could make it down the stairs and out the front door. I started down, knowing full well that any noise I made might be heard by a person who wouldn't hesitate to tie me to a chair and torture me then kill me stone dead. The kitchen tap was running. Something clanked. I made it to the bottom step. A door closed. Tinkles of water. She was in the downstairs toilet. I was an arm's length away from the front door, when I looked towards the kitchen and saw it on the table. The cool bag.

She'd gone and done it again.

Something was in that bag. Or part of some*one*.

This was proof that I could take to the police. Actual bodily evidence. I sprinted towards the kitchen, just as I heard the flush go in the bathroom. I ducked into the pantry, pulling the door to as quietly as I could.

Through the crack in the door, I could see Zoe walking across the kitchen. She got herself a glass of water and stared out of the window. She put down the glass. I lost her for a second as she rounded the side of the table, so I crouched down to get a better look through the larger part of the crack at the bottom of the door. She was at the cool bag. She pulled the zip around the top. I almost didn't dare look. Slowly, she pulled on the little plastic tuft that was sticking up. A large bag of ice came up with it, and pretty soon she had pulled it out completely. In the middle of the ice bag sat something brown and red. The bag looked heavy. Bowling-ball heavy.

It was the head. My possible dead future boyfriend's head. And she was going to take it out of the bag and look at it.

I didn't quite know how I was going to react when I saw the severed head. Would a horrible face appear with bulging eyes and saggy mouth and all these bloody entrails dangling from the stump? Would I be disgusted? Shocked? Appalled? Would I cry? Would I faint? Or would it be amazingly handsome, the dream face she had promised me, the dream head of the boy I would eventually fall in love with and marry? I tend to fancy guys I shouldn't. My best friend's dad. Mug shots on *Crime Solvers*. Our Year Ten French supply teacher, Monsieur Ecorche. And now, possibly, a decapitated head.

I prepared myself, as much as I could prepare myself when I was stuck in a pantry with a flimsy door and a fidgety puppy. I took a big stomach-deep breath and readied myself for the sight.

Zoe put the plastic bag on the table and moved the cool bag out of the way. She twizzled the tie around the tuft. It came loose and the top of the bag opened. She slowly lowered both her hands into it. She pulled the head out, hands either side of it. And there he was. His skin was as white as a hard-boiled egg and his hair was blonde and slightly wet. The male model's hair had been blonde too. Oh. My. God. His neck stump was covered with an ice pack. He was shaking – Zoe's hands were shaking as she held him. Was she scared?

No, she wasn't scared. She was smiling. She was excited.

I felt a stinging in my throat. How could she be so calm? So cold?

Because she's a psychopath.

A loud *CLANG CLANG* sounded from the hallway and made me jump. Zoe quickly put the head back into the plastic bag and tied it up. Then she placed it back into the cool bag, zipped it round and disappeared as the doorbell rang again. *CLANG CLANG.*

This was my chance to escape without being seen. I could easily get to the back door and unlock it before she came back. I picked up Pee Wee and eased my way out of the pantry. I tiptoed to the back door and gently unlocked it. I was about to leave when I looked back and saw the cool bag on the table. Just waiting there. I went over to the table. Zoe's purse was lying open next to the cool bag. It bulged with coins and receipts. And there was a tube ticket sticking out of it. I took a closer look. She'd been on the Underground that Saturday she went up to London. So had that missing male model. She had been in London when he went missing.

This was proof. Proof that she had been in London when the model disappeared and proof that she had a human head in a bag. I took them both, pocketing the ticket and grasping the straps of the cool bag. Then I legged it, through the back door and out into the gardens, darting and weaving through the trees so I couldn't easily be seen. I put down Pee Wee and we ran together through the open gates and down the sloping streets until we had reached the town and the safety of numbers. Of witnesses. Lots and lots of witnesses who would save me if Zoe started running after me with an axe. I'd never been so happy to see people in my life.

Me and a head
that's dead

Out of breath and sweating even worse than at our last
school sports day when I'd gone against Lynx in the
800 metres, I sauntered around the shops, trying to
get my head straight and decide what my next plan of
action would be. I checked my phone. There was a text
from Louis. *Hi Camille. Just checking u r OK. Did u hear
n e thing yet? I'm working 2day at da fun parlour if u want
2 tlk. LB.* I didn't text back.

I knew I was in a mood with Louis about something,
but I couldn't remember what at that moment, and I had
more pressing matters on my mind. I really needed to get
to the police station and hand in the dead head. I put Pee
Wee on his lead and we went into Marks & Spencer – we

could cut through the store onto King Street, where the police station was. We were nearly there. Safety. There would be big burly policemen with big bulgy biceps to protect me and say things like, 'You'll be all right now, miss. No one can harm you here.' Like in that film where the woman with a perm goes to the police station and hides under the policeman's desk cos the man in the leather jacket and sunglasses is coming after her. Even though the man ended up killing all the policeman and burning down the police station, she was still safe for a bit under the desk.

'Camille?' said a voice as I was passing by the cold meats and deli.

'Lynx!' I said, trying to appear breezy and carefree even though I was in the biggest ever fluster. She was in her usual red-and-navy tracksuit and her hair was in an exceedingly ragged ponytail. 'What are you doing in here?'

'Dad's getting me some new spikes. Not in here. The ones we saw in Bracht Sports with the silver bits on?'

'Oh right,' I said, wiping my forehead in the crook of my arm. 'He finally cracked then?' My eyes darted towards the back doors. I was so close to King Street. So close now.

Lynx nodded sadly. 'He wanted to get me out of the house. He's had enough of me moping . . .' Her eyes started to tear up. 'Oh Mills!'

Before I knew it, Lynx was crying into my shoulder.

'What's wrong?' I said. Pee Wee was nipping at Lynx's ankles and the dead head was getting so heavy in the cool bag that my upper arm was killing me. I was also still sweating full-on beads. I tried to comfort her as best I could under these circumstances but it was all sorts of awks.

'Damian's dumped meeeheeeee!' she wailed.

My left hand had to take the full strain of Pee Wee's lead *and* the cool bag now, as I used my other hand to *there there* Lynx. It wasn't a nice *there there* though. Lynx was so bony and muscly and she grabbed on to me like you'd grab onto a rock ledge, not a friend.

'What did I do to deserve it, Mills?' she sniffed, pulling back from me and folding her arms.

I shrugged. 'Damian's not really the relationship type, is he? Louis says he's a right slut. And he's his best friend.'

She crossed her feet over as well as her arms. 'But we were getting on so well! The sex was good . . .'

'Oh you shouldn't have had sex with him,' I said, a bit too loudly, as an old woman reached past me for some corned beef and scowled at us. I moved us along until we were in the next aisle, the quieter aisle for dog and cat food. 'Damian's all about the sex. I realise that now.'

'He told me I was good at it, too,' she continued. 'And then . . . he texted me. He said he had to move on.'

'Oh, Lynx . . .'

'He said that he wasn't a one-man woman or something. And something about a rolling stone gathering moss. I didn't even understand it and when I texted him back he rang me and just said, "You're dumped, you stupid cow," and hung up! Can you believe it?'

'Well, yeah, I can actually,' I said. Lynx started wailing again.

Lynx's dad appeared behind us with his basket.

'Hullo, Camille,' he said jovially, pushing his little glasses back up his nose from where they were sliding down. He rolled his eyes. 'We've had this for days now, tears and tantrums.' He picked some tins of Pretty Kitty cat food off the shelf and carried on past us. Lynx flicked him the finger as he went.

'Hi, Mr Sutherland,' I called after him. I turned back to Lynx. 'Have you heard from Poppy recently?'

She shook her head. 'I've texted her loads. Last time I saw her was at college last week. She was in the cafe with Splodge talking about this stupid festival her parents wouldn't let her go to. Think they've gone to that.'

'West Fest?' I said.

'I don't know,' she snapped and started walking away. I walked with her. 'I don't even care. Some friend she's turned out to be. Hey, why don't you come down to the athletics track and watch me train tonight? We haven't done that for ages. Then we could rent a DVD and have a girly night in. Dad and Urni are going out so we'll have the house to ourselves.'

'Uh . . . well,' I began, moving the cool bag over to my right hand so it could take the strain for a bit. We joined up with Mr Sutherland again in the queue for the checkout. 'I'm a bit busy tonight.'

'Come on, you can do your homework at mine if you want. I've got nothing else to do.' The queues for the checkouts went all the way back into the aisles. Bored looking people and squawking toddlers shuffled past displays of Halloween decorations, cakes in the shape of pumpkins and cauldron shaped cookies. Mr Sutherland got fed up with waiting and dipped out into the self-service checkout line and we followed him.

'Do you mean if you had something better to do you wouldn't be asking me round?' I said to Lynx.

Lynx flicked her blonde-and-black-streaked ponytail back from her shoulder and helped her dad pack up the shopping. 'No, don't be silly. But since we're both at a loose end . . .'

My chest hurt but I kept talking. I couldn't stop my mouth. 'I said I was busy. What makes you think I'm at a loose end?' I snipped, yanking Pee Wee away from the assistant's ankle, which he was sniffing around.

'Well, you're never busy, are you?' she laughed. 'You're either reading your trashy romance novels or hanging out with your parents.'

She was right, I was never busy, and I also never usually passed up the opportunity to go round to Lynx's house. She lived in Plainpalais, the posh part of town, even posher than Clairmont Hills, and her step mum, Urni, was this beautiful Indian lady who made the most yummiest chicken Dhansak in the whole wide land. I never refused to go round. Until now.

'Well, I'm busy today, I'm sorry,' I said. 'Biology home-work. I've got tons to do.'

'I can help. I'm not great at Biology but I could try,' she said. 'Come on, Mills.'

'You didn't want to know me a couple of weeks ago,' I said. 'All you wanted was Damian.'

'Yeah, and look how that turned out,' she scoffed. 'Has Louis Burnett asked you to the Halloween party yet? I'll ask him if all else fails. He's single, isn't he? Quite cute too . . .'

'Don't you dare!' I cried, though I hadn't meant to say

it so loudly. 'Look, Lynx, you can't just pick people up and put them down whenever you want. Louis is worth more than that. And so am I. I think.'

This was me being assertive. This was me stating my case. This was me unpicking another stitch.

Mr Sutherland started beeping through the shopping. 'Try and do upstairs and downstairs bags, Lynsey,' he said to her as he fumbled in his wallet.

'I know,' she snapped at him. Pee Wee started snapping at her ankles again. We were all snapping at each other now, like a little gang of turtles. 'God, Camille, you've got so weird lately. I saw you hanging around Death Watch at college. You want to steer clear of her.'

My eyes flooded with tears. I was so angry. 'Why? Because she might actually be a good friend who doesn't drop me like a hot rock the second a boy comes along?'

'Oh don't be ridic,' said Lynx crossly, stopping her packing for a second.

'I'm not being ridic, actually, I'm being honest,' I found myself saying. I was on a roll now and my mouth was running ahead before my brain sent it the words to say. 'You and Poppy are as bad as each other. You both dropped me the second Damian and Splodge showed any interest. Even at freshers' you both let me make a complete idiot of myself. You just stood there and laughed. You've both been the worst friends ever!'

I suddenly realised that an electronic voice was going off behind me.

Unexpected item in bagging area.

I'd put the cool bag down in the bagging area.

'Oh my god god god!' I said, heaving it off quick and putting it down by my feet. Pee Wee immediately started sniffing it and tugging at the zip. 'It's fine, it's fine,' I sang, leaning across Mr Sutherland and jabbing the *Skip bagging* button on the screen again and again as hard as I could.

Unexpected item in bagging area.

'Oh come on,' I said, stabbing every single button trying to make it go away.

Please wait for assistance.

'Oh no no no!' I gasped.

Lynx just stood there, her arms folded, glaring at me like I'd just ruined her chances for the Olympics. 'That was way harsh, Camille.'

Mr Sutherland was a bit more understanding. 'It's all right, Camille, there's an assistant coming over now. She'll have it fixed.'

'Oh God, oh no please stop. Stop! Sssssshhhhhh!'

I became breathless and stared down at the cool bag, the Marks & Spencer cool bag with the definitely NOT shopping in it, hoping and praying that what I thought was going to happen wouldn't actually happen or that, if it did, I would soon wake up in bed and it would be morning again and I'd have just had a very bad dream.

A short blonde M&S woman with a bandage on her wrist and belt loop full of keys came bustling over. She swiped a card across the machine and tapped in a few numbers. 'Try running that last thing through again, the guacamole.'

Mr Sutherland did as he was told.

Please wait for assistance said the voice.

The woman looked at me. 'Hmm, it doesn't like it, does it?' she laughed, looking down at the cool bag. 'I'll have to cancel the transaction and run it all through again, sorry.' She bent down to take the bag and I moved it away with my foot.

'Um . . . no, this is my shopping, not theirs.'

'Okay, do you have your receipt? I just need to check what you've got.'

At that second, some God that someone believed in decided to totally do me the biggest favour and make a small child throw up all over the floor at the end of the aisle. The lemon drizzle cakes on the bottom shelf were splattered with a hot soup of chewed-up chicken nuggets and curdled milk.

'Oh blimey,' said the woman. 'I'll have to deal with that. Sorry. I've cancelled the transaction. If you go over to customer services, they'll scan it all through again for you.'

Lynx and her dad started putting all their bits back into the basket, both sighing and snippy with each other. I saw my chance to leg it. I darted back out of the food hall and into women's lingerie. I hid behind a bank of massive bras and watched as the Sutherlands noticed I was gone, looked around for me for a bit, and went back to their shopping.

I just ran as fast as I could, *wee wee wee wee* all the way home and when I got there, I stuffed the head bag at the bottom of the chest freezer in our shed and did the bravest thing I could think of doing. I dashed up to my bedroom, closed the door and hid under my duvet.

Zoe Goes Spare

I love my bedroom. If a room could give you a cuddle, my room would. It's pink and everything's squashy and comfortable and warm, and there're lots of cushions and my dolls' house and cute toys. And that was where I stayed for the rest of the day and night.

In the morning, Mum appeared in my doorway with a bacon sandwich and a glass of orange juice. She set them down on my bedside table and put it on top of two twenty pound notes, a ten and a five. 'There's your wages too, from Dad.'

'Cool, thanks,' I said.

'No college today?'

'No, I've got a free,' I lied, knowing full well I was missing double English. She went over to the windowsill and grabbed the crumby plate and coffee mug that I couldn't even remember leaving there. I watched her.

Mum. Help me. I'm in trouble. Please don't leave me.

I couldn't say it, but I thought it. I thought it until she disappeared back out onto the landing and back downstairs. I didn't feel like eating anything, but I made a start on my sandwich and fed Pee Wee a square of it too. I picked up my TV remote and flicked on the DVD that was in the DVD player. It was *The Little Mermaid*. We snuggled in to watch it together. I had such a pain in my chest though. It was like the feeling I used to have when I saw Damian in the corridor at college. But this wasn't love. No, this was fear. Love and fear were such samey feelings, I realised. I wished I'd been brainy enough to know why.

'Camille! Your friend's here,' Dad called upstairs.

'Huh?' I said. An elevator dropped in my chest. I hoped against all hope that maybe it was Lynx, come to apologise, or even Poppy, alive and well and all in one piece and maybe even having dumped Splodge at some service station on the way back from Wales and come to say that she was sorry for ignoring my texts and that she realised now that friends were worth way more than boyfriends.

But no.

It was a tall girl with messy black hair and eyes like icicles, dressed all in black. And I knew exactly why she had come.

I gasped as she walked in my room. My lovely cuddly pink room that suddenly looked as though someone had chucked black paint over it. 'Zoe . . .'

'I haven't got time to explain,' she said, closing the door behind her. 'I just need the head.'

I scrambled up the bed towards the headboard as my plate launched off the bed onto the floor, sending my sandwich all over the carpet. Pee Wee made short work of what was left of it. 'What head?'

'You know what head. Now where is it?' she said, coming further inside the room and frowning as she knocked her head against the hammock full toys suspended from the ceiling.

'Um, um,' I said, pressing my head back into the headboard. I wanted to melt into the wall where she couldn't see me. Couldn't get to me. My chest clenched.

'You were in my house yesterday afternoon, Camille. You were fairly obvious.'

'Uh . . .'

'And Pee Wee's drool was all over my chewed-up mannequin.'

'Your Aunt Gwen, you mean?' I said, trying to breathe in through my nose and out through my mouth like the dentist always told me.

'Yes – a cunning ruse to keep Social Services off my back,' she explained, coming closer to the bed. 'Gwen has her own bank account, her own signature. The dummy can be very effective. Sometimes I even get it to wave at visitors from the upstairs window. You know, for show. I have to pay a homeless woman when they actually want to meet her. That woman in the shopping precinct who eats chips off the floor?'

I cuddled into my duvet. 'Okay. I was at your house. I

came to tell you something.'

'And to take something,' she said. 'The head. May I have it back now, please?'

I rubbed the silk edge of my pillow for comfort. 'What do you mean, I did you a favour?' I tried sending a telepathic message to Pee Wee to bite Zoe on the ankle so I could make my escape but he was too busy golloping my bacon sandwich.

'I had an impromptu visit from a solicitor and a man from the building society. We've defaulted on some payments and there's a court bailiff coming to the house on Saturday morning to take formal possession of our house.'

'What? You have to leave the house?'

'Yes.'

'But where will you go?'

'I don't know,' she replied. 'But our conversation could have been very awkward if they'd seen the bag on the table.'

I frowned, remembering how I'd been hidden in the pantry when the doorbell rang and Zoe went to answer it.

'That was why you took it, wasn't it? To stop me getting into trouble?' she said.

'Yeah, that's why I took it,' I said, looking anxiously round for a weapon.

Pee Wee, my guard dog, had trotted off to the rug to watch the end of *The Little Mermaid*.

'So where is it?'

'At the bottom of our chest freezer in the shed.'

'Good, good. I knew you wouldn't let me down, that's great,' she said, breathing out. 'Excellent.'

And I took th . . . this,' I said, scrabbling round in my pockets for the tube ticket. 'This proves you were in London when that male model went missing. This links you to him.'

'What male model? I went to King's College, Camille, where my father used to lecture,' she said calmly. 'I got the head from their cold storage. I'm sorry you couldn't be there to pick one out, but I did my best, from what was in the freezer. Or rather, who. And now I need it back. I simply have to attach the head and insert the brain tonight. Time is of the absolute essence. You can still help me, if you want to.'

Okay, I thought. The thing about her visiting King's College would add up. Maybe she hadn't killed the model after all. I wanted to believe her. But . . .

'I thought you hated me. The way you spoke . . . on the bus . . . at college . . . you were in such a bad mood. You were acting really . . . psycho.'

'I wasn't,' said Zoe, flapping her hand and sitting down on the blanket box at the end of my bed. 'You've never seen me in a bad mood.'

'But . . . why?' I said. 'I thought . . . we were friends.'

'So did I,' she said on an out-breath. 'But then I realised perhaps this experiment didn't mean as much to you as it did to me and I became frustrated. Your mind is on other things, as it probably should be. And the way you looked at me in Biology the other day, it was the way everyone else looks at me. Like I am some kind of monster. And I thought, perhaps you'd gone cool on the idea. You seemed to be taking more of an interest in the living than the currently dead.'

'What?' I said, still not quite understanding her.

'Your friend Poppy?'

'Yeah,' I said, 'I'm worried about her. I don't know where she is, no one does.'

'She's gone to some festival, hasn't she? That's what I keep hearing around the college.'

'From who? Who do you keep hearing it from?' I demanded.

Zoe's face finally showed some kind of emotion. She looked startled. Her huge blue eyes had gone wider. 'I don't know who they are, just people at college,' she said. 'Why are you looking at me like that? What have I done? You're acting as though this is anathema to you. I thought you wanted to be involved.'

'No,' I blurted out.

'No?' she said, eyebrows up.

'No.' I got up out of bed and looked round for my hockey stick to hit her with if she made a lunge for me. I couldn't find it, then I realised it must be in the wardrobe so I shuffled my way over to it. 'You're m-m-murdering people, Zoe, and I'm going to the police with the head to tell them what you've done.' I was trying so hard to keep my voice steady but it just came out in one long wobble. 'I can't concentrate on college. I can't sleep. I can't . . . well, I can eat, but only just. It's definitely affected my appetite. You're a murderer and a psychopath and I don't want anything more to do with this. It's wrong. It's just all wrong.'

I didn't know what she would do or say. She didn't make a move for me though. She just sat on my blanket box, feet crossed over at the ankles. 'Finished?'

I nodded, not making eye contact with her, my hand on the wardrobe knob.

'I haven't murdered anyone,' she said calmly, like a lawyer or something, though she seemed to be telling the truth. I really looked into her eyes. I thought about the photos of the little girl which I'd seen at her house. The little girl on the beach with her mother. 'Everything I have for the project was already dead when I took it. Leftover from my father's work, whatever he had not used and the police didn't confiscate. The feet are from the hospital mortuary, as you well know. The head is from King's College, where my father stored it in a separate freezing chamber. I haven't killed anyone. You've just been listening to the town grapevine.'

'No I haven't,' I said, probably too quickly.

'You're being paranoid, Camille. I'm not a murderer.'

I twiddled the wonky wardrobe knob. 'So where are my friends then?'

She shrugged. 'How should I know?'

'But you . . . you ran Damian over that night, didn't you? When he and Louis were walking back from the Chinese. Admit it, that was you, wasn't it? You wanted some part of him for the experiment.'

She frowned. 'What night? When did he get run over?'

I sighed. 'The night we stole Luke the Lifeguard from the funeral parlour. When we saw Louis at the hospital the next day, he was there with Damian. Damian had been run over.'

'I didn't know that,' she said, serene, calm, collected.

She gave nothing away. 'Why would I want any part of that idiot for this experiment?'

I didn't have an answer. 'What about the hands then?' I blurted. 'Where did you get them from? And the organs?'

'Spares, as I've told you already.'

'Yeah, but *whose* spares? Huh? They looked fresh when I saw them. You can't tell me they've been in some freezing chamber for months.'

'Not exactly a freezing chamber but an ice house,' she said. 'When my father got sacked, he set up a makeshift lab at our house, so he could continue his work. He harvested some materials from the University, anatomy specimens that were mostly due for incineration anyway. Some busy bodies poked their noses in and the police came and ransacked the house, taking most of the specimens away.'

'Most of them?' I said.

'Yes. I salvaged what I could and took it down to the bottom of the garden where there is an old ice house, buried beneath the overgrown grass. I created a small freezing chamber down there using a cryostat filled with liquid nitrogen and stored the organs and hands in parcels of frozen blood. They had thawed when you saw them. That is why they looked fresh. You can come and see it if you don't believe me . . . '

'What about the brain?'

She sighed. 'If you must know . . .'

'Yes, yes I must.'

'It's my father's brain,' she said.

'Your dad's?' I cried.

'You saw me digging on the night of the party when you got bathed in cow manure, if you remember? I was digging up my father. He was always going to be the brain for this experiment. I was just waiting for the right time to . . . retrieve him.'

A jigsaw piece finally floated into place.

'That's what this has really been about,' she told me. 'Reactivating my father's brain in a new body. So that he may live again. He wasn't a mad man, Camille. He was madly in love with his work, with improving methods of anabiosis and organ transplantation. And I won't let that brain die, it's too important. The other bits and pieces . . . are immaterial. I wouldn't go to the trouble of murdering people at the expense of my own freedom, when I could obtain free specimens from graves or medical schools, would I?'

'I suppose not,' I said, eyeing her up and down. 'But is the brain going to work if it's been in the ground for months?'

'I visited his body in the funeral parlour. I believe it was Louis' father who allowed me some time with him. On my own. I injected his brain with the serum there and then, to preserve it until I could come back and claim it.'

'Oh right,' I said.

'I just want him back, Camille. I want my family back.'

'I still don't understand,' I said.

'No,' she said. 'Why would you? You've got your family. Your perfect parents. Your grandparents who come and see you whenever they get the chance. Who pinch your cheeks and tell you you're beautiful . . .'

This was well weird. 'How did you know about my grandma pinching my cheeks?'

'I see things. Things other people take for granted. I watch families.'

'But why?' I said.

Without another word, she shrugged herself out of her coat and it dropped to the floor. Then she wriggled out of her black jumper so that she was stood there in just her bra and trousers.

'Oh no, no, what are you doing?' I cried as she unbuttoned her trousers and stood before me in just her shabby grey underwear.

'Come here,' she said, holding out her milky white arm.

I shook my head so violently my ponytail whacked me in the face. Zoe walked towards me instead and I backed up against the wardrobe and snapped my eyes shut, waiting for certain death or forced lesbian sex. But when I opened my eyes she was just standing there, eyes boring into me, her arm held out before her. She was just showing me her arm. There was a deep red scar on her elbow crease.

'There's something I haven't told you about me, because you didn't need to know. You probably should know now,' she said.

I looked at the scar. 'You're an emo?' I cried.

'No, I'm a partial,' she said. 'I'm a partial reanimate.'

A what?

'My mother and I were in a car accident when I was six. She walked away from it. But my right arm and leg were both trapped. When my mother saw me, after the operation to remove them, she couldn't live with what she had caused. She'd been drinking, which was why we crashed. She couldn't bring herself to look at me, much less be around me. So she left. And I never saw her again. My father vowed to find me new limbs. And he did. Against all the odds, he stitched me together again, made me almost as good as new. I was the first experiment, Camille. His first human experiment.'

'You were?'

'Yes. I never knew where the new arm or leg came from. But as far as I'm concerned, they've always belonged to me. There are some things I can't quite achieve. I can't throw a ball to any great distance and I can't run very fast but I don't feel any different. I just am.'

'Wow,' I said, hushed and staring at her arm scar and the one she was showing me near the top of her pale white leg. They both encircled the limbs, right the way around, but were no thicker than a red pencil line.

'When my father died a few months ago, I had no one left,' she explained. 'I'd always been home schooled so I didn't know how to integrate with people my age. It was just me. I enrolled at the college to try and ingratiate myself with "normal" society. But I discovered that because of who my father was, what other people *thought* he was, normal society didn't want me. So I vowed to do the next best thing: bring him back. Bring back the only person in the world who saw me as just Zoe. Not a freak. Then I met a girl in a graveyard who looked at me like I was extraordinary. Someone who didn't just think, "There's that mad professor's daughter." Who didn't scurry by. And who helped me dig. And I thought she could help me with my experiment.'

'And that was me?'

'And that was you,' she said.

'Why didn't you tell me your dad had . . . died?'

'Because in my mind, he isn't dead. At least, he *won't* be for much longer. Not if I have my way. And he didn't cut off his own head off or get eaten by one of his "Frankenstein creations" if that's what you've been told. He had a heart attack, shortly after he was sectioned. A massive heart attack. He had worked himself very hard and

I think it broke his heart when he had to give it up so suddenly. He loved his work. Lived for it.'

'So how did all the rumours start?' I asked her.

She shrugged. 'How do any rumours start? Half-truth plus fear plus paranoia plus hyperbole. He grew to be a little . . . eccentric, my father. Obsessive. Fixated. A little overwrought. But a freak? No. Insane?' She shook her head. 'Not a chance.'

'I got called a freak in primary school,' I said, trying to pop the large bubble of silence that we were suddenly inside. 'It doesn't matter now though, does it? It doesn't matter when you've got a friend.' She moved her mouth like she was going to smile, but it wasn't quite a smile. It was like she was afraid to make her face do one. 'So . . .' I said, trying to get up to speed. 'What about your experiment? What about Sexy Dead Boy?'

'What about him?'

'Is he still going to be my boyfriend?'

'Yes. If you still want him,' she said, buttoning up her black pedal pushers. 'He's almost ready now. He has all his organs and his blood. I just need to attach the head and give him the brain.'

I made a face. 'But won't it be weird? Me having a boyfriend with your dad's brain?'

'That will be immaterial to you though, won't it?' she said. 'He will still look like one of your poster boys.' She nodded at the tatty magazine pictures on my wardrobe door. 'He'll have the outward appearance of your perfect man, but the brain of a once very sweet and loving, kind and intelligent . . . gentleman. That is all.'

A gentleman, I thought. A gentleman would open doors for me. Kiss my hand. Offer me his coat when I'm cold. It could still happen. My dream. But she was talking about a STOLEN gentleman. With a MAD brain. And limbs taken from DEAD BOYS. 'I still don't know about this anymore, Zoe,' I said.

She moved closer to me. I had flashes in my brain of moments from my serial killer documentaries. The last thing the victims saw before their necks were tied or their throats were cut or their noses were full of chlorophyll.

'I just need you to do one last thing for me. Give me back the head so I can attach it and the brain today. Then help me move him to the college on Friday night so I can reanimate him there.'

'You're going to reanimate him at college?' I cried.

'I have to. I have to get him out of the house. At some point they're going to send a locksmith to change all the locks and barricade the gates ready for repossession. I have to leave.'

'It'll be much riskier at college, surely, with all the students and teachers are stuff, won't it?'

'No, because it's empty at weekends, isn't it? There isn't a soul about then. You don't have to stay and watch if you don't want to. All I ask is that you give me back the head and help me move it to the college on Friday night. Then, if you wanted to, perhaps you could come and see him when he's finished. If you still feel the same way and want nothing to do with him after that, fine. I'm on my own. Again.'

I looked at her. 'You *promise* me you haven't killed anyone.'

'Camille, you seem to take a shine to every other male face you see. It really wouldn't have been worth the effort.'

I still wasn't sure. I still didn't quite trust her. But if all I had to do was see him when he was finished, maybe I could just do that. 'You promise me I don't have to go along with it if I still don't want to?'

'Yes,' she said. 'You can walk away and we need never speak to one another again.'

'And you won't . . . try and . . . hurt me. Or my family?' I stuttered.

She frowned. 'Why would I want to do that?'

I shrugged, going a little red. 'I don't know. I don't think I really know anything at all.' My heart thumped in my ears.

'Camille, I don't want your family. I don't want to sever any piece of your anatomy. I just want you to help me complete my experiment. So will you? Will you help me complete it?'

I thought about the little girl in those photos, little Zoe with no mummy or daddy, and now no house either. She had nothing. And I had all of that *and* a little dog. I thought of her scars, which didn't look drawn on so I guessed she must be telling the truth, and I looked into her eyes. I was wrong about lots of things – maths, map reading, the ending of that movie when there's all these blokes and one of them turns out to be this really evil bloke though you'd never know it because he's got a limp – but when I looked into Zoe's blue eyes at that moment, all I saw was my friend shining back at me. And I just didn't want to not believe her anymore.

'I'll help you,' I said.

Call 999 for
Mr DeLISH

There comes a point in a girl's life when nothing, absolutely nothing is more important than knowing what her brand new sexy dead boyfriend looks like. I just couldn't concentrate on anything all day Thursday and, by Friday, I was desperate to see how Zoe was getting on.

Knock knock knock. Tap tap tappity tap tap. Knock knock KNOCK.

'I can't wait anymore. I'm on my way into college for triple History so I really can't stay too long but I just couldn't wait to hear from you . . .'

'He's finished,' she said, stepping back from the front door to let me in.

'He is?' I said.

Zoe nodded, looking as pleased as a pie chart and wiping her hands on a bloody tea towel and beckoning me from the front door. Pee Wee trotted in after me.

This was the moment, I thought. But what would that moment bring? I didn't dare even wonder as I followed Zoe into the freezing-cold kitchen where she had been working most of yesterday and all of last night, judging by the bags under her eyes.

On one of my Disney DVDs, there's this bit when Snow White is supposedly dead in a glass coffin and the prince comes to see her and is just flabberdoodled by how gorge she looks dead and then he kisses her and she wakes up not dead. I'd dreamed about my own Prince Charming kissing me awake tons of times and the thought of it actually happening had never been more real than at that moment. I'd had to settle for Prince Chest Freezer when the moment came but I wasn't complaining.

When I first saw Sexy Dead Boy as a whole human being and not just bits of dead ones, I was awe-struck by how fine he looked.

Film star fine. Airbrush fine. Prince Charming fine.

In a word, he looked totally AY-MAY-ZING!

'Oh my goodness, Zoe!' I said. 'He's deLISH!'

Zoe wiped her brow with her forearm. 'I'm glad you said that because he's been absolutely tedious to complete.'

'He's beautiful,' I whispered, creeping closer.

He really was beautiful, like a prince in any one of my romance novels. Or at least, the hot junior doctor who gets the registrar pregnant in *Call 999 for Doctor Delicious*. There were no more open wounds or stumps. His skin was smooth like a marble statue and every join was made with the neatest stitches that were, even before my eyes, disappearing, melting into perfect pink skin. His feet were beautifully shaped and clean and the toenails short and white. The toes were the right length too. His legs were long and quite hairy, but finely muscled at the tops. Then came his hands, strong and square, the nails neat and clean. No mole on any of the fingers either. I must have imagined it before. Maybe they really hadn't been Splodge's hands. Maybe Zoe *had* got them from her stash in the ice house, like she'd said. His strong-looking arms were attached to a v-shaped torso with the cutest inny belly button. His shoulders were pale and smooth like the span of a seagull's wings. And at the top of it all was the most gorgerini face I'd ever seen. He had a jaw that looked like it had been carved from soap. His hair was like golden thread. His lashes were soft and brown, as they should be.

I wasn't all that sure I wanted to kiss him on the lips though. He was, after all, pretty dead still. And one look at his winky made me go red in the cheeks. That bit wasn't a fairy tale. I poked his man boob (which wasn't really a boob as it was very toned). It was solid.

'You've done an amazing job, Zoe,' I told her. 'What colour are his eyes?'

'Uh, blue I think, yes, blue.'

I really wanted to believe she hadn't killed people. I really wanted to believe those weren't Poppy's organs inside that wondrous chest. That those weren't Splodge's piano-player's hands. That it wasn't that missing model's head sitting on those soft-as-a-seagull's-wing shoulders.

I wondered how blue was the blue under those soft pink lids. Pee Wee's lead was yanking and when I looked, he was snarfing about inside the carrier bag under the kitchen table – the bag containing the rotten feet and hands. I pulled him away.

'What are you going to do with those?' I asked her as she washed up a couple of knives in the sink.

'I'll take them to the garden incinerator at college. I saw there's one at the back of the tennis courts.'

'And tell me about the brain again,' I said, stroking my hand over his toes.

'It's from the outstanding anatomist of the twenty-first century. Two PhDs. Over twenty years' experience in the field. On his way to being a Nobel Prize winner. As a human being, he was polite, gentle, kind, studied poetry, read widely and loved his family.'

'Perfect,' I said. 'He'll look great in a tuxedo too.'

This was the finest boy who'd ever lived. This boy would be a living god. And he was all ours. I felt quite squidgily excited by this time.

'Incipit Vita Nova,' said Zoe.

'Huh?' I said, my eyes locked on his face.

'"Thus begins a new life." It's the college motto.'

'Oh is it?' I said, eyes still locked. 'Can we go and get him some clothes?'

She looked at me. 'Yes.'

'And can I pick them out for him?'

'Yes,' said Zoe. 'That side of things is all down to you.'

We covered him up, closed the kitchen and hallway curtains, and walked down into the town together. Zoe went to her triple Physics class while I went to triple History. Louis Burnett tried to talk to me afterwards while I was waiting for her class to come out, but I blanked him. I actually blanked him. I felt awful after he'd walked off, but I just couldn't face talking to him at that exact moment. I didn't want to hear any more 'Sorry's or 'I was just worried about you's. And besides, we were on a mission now. A mission to go shopping for the most boring things anyone could possibly buy: men's clothes.

'He looks too good for me,' I said, as I thumbed through a shelf of t-shirts. I put three in the basket: green, blue and pink. Pretty random, but I liked them.

'Well, you wanted perfect, didn't you?' said Zoe, trundling along behind me. 'I thought you wanted a suit for him? Suits are at the other end.' She pointed out the part of the store we needed to go to next.

I did want perfection, for deffs, and Sexy Dead Boy was as close to perfect as I could imagine. But something just didn't feel right.

On the way to the suits department, I aired another worry with Zoe. 'What can we do about his . . . you know. His . . .'

'Underpants?' she said as we passed a whole display of them. She found his size and threw three packets of white briefs into the basket.

I didn't want to say it. I went all red. 'No, his, you know . . . his . . . his winky.'

'His penis, you mean. I find it hard to discuss the male organ of procreation by referring to it as a "winky".'

We reached the suits. 'It looks scary.'

'That's only because you've never seen one before.'

'I have. I've seen loads. God.' I blushed. 'Well, I think I saw my dad's once when he was changing under a beach towel. But it might have been his thumb.'

I didn't like the look of any of the suits. They were all either black, grey or navy blue. No colour or kilts or anything. I turned back and went into the sock department.

Zoe followed. 'All male animals have penises, Camille. There's nothing scary about them. They're not designed to be on display so it hardly matters, does it?'

I thought about Damian. *He* had one of those. Louis had one too. 'Do they all look like that?'

'I haven't seen all of them, but I imagine they're all much of a muchness.'

'It's not very pretty,' I said, trying to find some socks that weren't black or black with a tiny bit of colour on the heel. 'Can't we find another winky for him?'

'No,' said Zoe. 'I draw the line at that.'

The queue was about thirty people long when we got there and looking into our basket I did some rubbish mental maths and found that I'd spent pretty much all my month's wages. I was quietly pleased with my little haul though, especially seeing as I'd never bought clothes for a man before. It felt good. I'd got t-shirts, pants, some socks with Bart Simpson on, a shaving kit, some manly shower gel and shampoo the type that Louis smelled of, two pairs of jeans and some long shorts like Louis wears. I'd have to do this all the time before long. That's what girlfriends did.

Buy aftershave and golf balls for birthdays. Valentine's cards and big teddies with hearts on for Valentine's Day. Christmas cards with 'For My Boyfriend' on. I couldn't wait. I still hadn't got him anything posh to wear for the Halloween party though.

'What's his birthday?' I asked Zoe as we shuffled forward in the line.

'You decide,' she said.

'Um . . . how about the day he wakes up?'

'Yes, that fits I suppose.'

We shuffled forward another place.

'And will he be able to, you know, do everything other boys do?'

'Yes, he should be able to engage in intercourse with some assistance,' she said, fiddling with some Halloween socks with ghosts on them. The woman in front of us on her mobility scooter whipped her head round and looked at us like we had bras on our heads.

'Well actually, I meant playing football and driving and stuff.'

'He wouldn't be able to procreate though. My father's research on goats and pigs proved that. I'm sorry.'

'Oh,' I said. 'Edward in *Twilight* could. And he'd been dead for a hundred years.'

'Who?' said Zoe.

'Never mind,' I said, sagging. I was too young for babies anyway. But the thought of never having them was sad. I liked the idea of little mees. Little mees I could teach and cuddle and love. I guess we'd have to adopt or have artificial insinuation. That would be okay, I guessed.

The queue was moving quite well so we shuffled forward a few more places.

'Do you think he might love me when he wakes up?' I asked. 'Do you think he'll get that love at first sight thing that baby chicks do?'

'Of course. You're a nice person,' said Zoe, as the bells went off again at the checkout cos Mobility Scooter Woman had picked up a flannel with no price on it.

'Aw thanks.' My tummy went bubbly. 'But do you think he'll fall in love with me? Like, the sort of love where you always want to be around someone? I don't know. I haven't really thought that far ahead. I'd have to see how we got on at the party. It would be more awful if he came to life but didn't love me back.' We moved forward again.

'I can't manipulate his feelings to ensure he falls in love with you, I'm afraid,' said Zoe.

'But you said monkeys and dogs had been reanimated and had their memories wiped.' Silence. 'How about a love potion or something?'

She looked at me. 'My father and I haven't spent our lives finding cures for hiccups or analysing what turns pigeons homosexual, you know. We have actually been doing rather important work. Love potions are bunkum.' She picked up a pair of pumpkin deely boppers and flicked a little switch so they glowed orange.

We shuffled forward. 'What if he wakes up and thinks I'm odd, like most people do? I'm not as pretty as he is, or as clever. What if he thinks I'm thick?'

'You're not thick. And just because you don't have a surgeon's brain doesn't mean you won't fulfil his dreams.

Opposites can attract, you know.'

'Mum says opposites don't always attract. You have to find someone who's like you or it never lasts. That's why she chose Dad, cos they're both into gardening and canal boats and crosswords and the war. Mum really likes the prime minister and that bloke from *CSI* but says she could never marry anyone like that because they're too perfect.'

'That's her opinion,' said Zoe, putting down the deely boppers and picking up a chocolate vampire bat. 'There isn't one romance formula for all. Human beings make up their own minds. It's one of the many things that differentiate us from the leafcutter ant.'

'But he doesn't *have* his own mind, does he?' I said. 'He's got your dad's.'

'True,' she said. 'In that case, I don't know.'

'But you know everything.'

'Not when it comes to matters of the human heart I don't. I can restart one so that is all that matters to me.' It was nearly our turn at the tills. 'Are you having doubts again, Camille?'

'No, no, I was just thinking. In the graveyard there's this couple who died within hours of each other. The lady died and then the man died of a broken heart. Louis Burnett showed me. They died still in love. Just made me think. That's what I want. Love that's felt by someone else. Everlasting. Like, beyond death.'

She shook her head. 'That, I'm afraid, is all a big myth conjured up by people who write garden centre bookmarks. Anyone who tells you otherwise is either a fantasist or grossly misinformed.'

'You could have it,' I said, waiting for a reaction. 'If you could like someone back. Louis says Damian fancies you.'

'What?'

'Damian de Jager. He fancies you for deffs.'

'How preposterous,' Zoe scoffed, chucking the chocolate bat back on the shelf. I could have sworn her brilliant white cheeks were glowing.

'It's true. Louis said he really fancies you. I think he wants to ask you out.'

'Huh,' she huffed. 'Well, he's got his work cut out with me then, hasn't he? Or his liver, whichever he prefers.'

I laughed. 'So you wouldn't want to go out with him then?'

'I'd rather inject the Ebola virus into my eyeballs,' she said.

I didn't know what that was but I guessed no virus was a good virus to get, especially in your eyeballs. 'Louis is so different to Damian, isn't he? It amazes me that they're friends. Do you think Sexy Dead Boy could be their friend?'

'Possibly,' she said as we reached the till and started unloading the stuff onto the counter. She found the little pack of friendship bracelets I'd hidden under the pant packs. She looked at me.

'I like Louis' friendship bracelets and thought maybe SDB could wear some too. They're only cheapy ones.'

Zoe was still staring at me. She pulled a pen torch from the pocket of her pedal pushers. She clicked it on and shone it right in my eye. I jolted back. She clicked it off. 'You're in mydriasis,' she said. 'I noticed it when we came in.'

'Am I supposed to know what that means?' I laughed, blinking to get my eyesight back. The girl on the till was looking at us like we'd just sprouted antlers.

'It means your pupils are almost completely dilated,' she said. 'You've either been taking drugs or you've bumped your head.'

'I haven't, I haven't,' I interrupted, like she was accusing me.

'Or you're in love.'

'Really?' I said. 'You think I could be in love with Sexy Dead Boy already?'

'Hmm,' said Zoe, taking my wrist pulse. 'It certainly seems like you're in love with something.'

We took Pee Wee for a long walk on the beach, which he loved cos there were a couple of dead seagulls he could gnaw on and the tide was in so he could splash. Then we wasted some coins on the arcades at the pier and I played Electrocutie a few times. Zoe couldn't see the point. She couldn't see the point of a lot of the games on the pier actually. Guitar Hero. Air hockey. The haunted house. The go carts. But she went on everything with me, just cos I wanted to. It was great to have a friend again. I wasn't even thinking about the last time I'd been to the pier, when Louis had banged my nose on the door and Lynx and Poppy had gone off with Damian and Splodge. It didn't cross my mind that the last time I had gone there, I'd had Poppy and Lynx as my friends. None of that mattered any more. Well, I tried not to let it matter anyway.

We went back to mine and I gave Pee Wee a bath and

Mum cut us some of her homemade quiche and we went up to my room to watch *Snow White* cos I really fancied watching it. Zoe let me do her hair too so I gave it a trim to make all the ends the same length and straightened it. Zoe let me do whatever I wanted to her – she didn't care at all. Manicure. Pedicure. Blackhead popping. We did it all. It was awesies! I think she enjoyed herself, sort of. In her own Zoe way.

At teatime, I told my mum and dad I was staying at Zoe's house for the weekend to sleepover and they seemed okay with it. Especially as I didn't tell them who Zoe was, at least who her dad was. They weren't as liberated as I was and I didn't think they would understand. But I wasn't really going to Zoe's house for a sleepover of course. We were only going there to pick up my brand spanking new fully-assembled dead boyfriend and taking him to the Biology lab at college.

And we weren't coming back until he was alive.

Hooking Up

I had dressed all in black, like Zoe, so we both looked like ninjas. Except I wore my (now dyed black) bridesmaid dress and long-sleeved top, and tights and Union Jack Doc Martens underneath, and she still had on her normal black pedal-pushers-and-turtleneck combo. We did look very disappearable though, just right for breaking into college at night, except for my stupid blonde hair. I thought about dying it black like Zoe's so I'd be more camouflaged but she said there wasn't time to get any and do that.

My phone had been off since I turned it off at Zoe's house. I switched it on again when we'd got SDB in the back of the van and Zoe had gone back inside the house to get some things of hers that she didn't want the bailiffs to take the next morning. I had *five* messages and two voicemails. Oh my God, I thought. Poppy. Poppy's been trying to call me and my phone's been off! I listened to the voicemails.

Hi Camille, it's Louis again. I'm just checking you're okay. I'm sorry about . . . I'm just sorry we fell out. Can you give me a call or a text or something. Bye.

The second voicemail was also from Louis.

Camille, it's Louis again. I don't think you're a bad person at all and I do want to be friends with you. I understand why you didn't want to talk to me this morning but I just hate that we're not friends. I guess I just don't know Zoe yet. Maybe I shouldn't judge a book and all that. Okay. I'll speak to you soon. Bye.

And every single text message was from Louis too. And the texts were all just one big long message, basically saying what he had said in the voicemails.

'Okay, Louis, I get it, you're sorry,' I mumbled, turning my phone off again and looking out of my window towards the house.

'Pardon?' said Zoe, as she opened the driver's door and got inside, handing me a very small suitcase.

'Nothing,' I said. 'What's this?'

'Just some essentials,' she said, turning on the engine.

'But what about all your clothes and stuff?'

She looked at me and pulled the handbrake off. 'I have everything I need,' she said, and we moved off down the driveway.

Zoe somehow had keys to the Sciences block at college so getting inside was not going to be a problem. What *was* a problem was the fact that the Biology lab where we usually had lessons was locked by some key that Zoe didn't have. What was *another* problem was the fact that the cleaners were working when we got there, so we had to wait in the van for an hour until they'd left before we could even think about going inside. But once we were in, we were in.

'Okay,' I puffed, as we wheeled the body safely into the Chemistry lab, which we did have a key for. 'What now?'

Pee Wee walked in behind us, dragging the yellow incineration bag of rotting hands and feet, which he had clamped between his jaws.

'Electrics,' she said, jingling the van keys in her hand.

I'd never been very interested in electrical circuits. At school in Physics, we'd been forever fixing screws and switches into wooden boards and hooking up batteries and tiny light bulbs to switch on. It had been dead boring. But now that we were setting one up to reanimate my future husband, it was actually quite interesting.

First Zoe made me go and grab a rubber mat from the store cupboard in the gym and then we placed it on the workbench in the Biology lab. She then told me to get the big coil of wire from the lab store and a first aid kit, which I did. She popped out with the van keys without saying where she was going and I waited with Sexy Dead Boy and Pee Wee. Ten minutes later, there were three slow knocks on the door. I opened it and Zoe was there, carrying a heavy-looking grey brick.

'What's that?' I asked her, opening the door wider to let her in.

'Battery,' she said, heaving it over to the table at the end. 'From your mother's van.' She panted for air. 'Where's the wire?'

'Here,' I said, handing her the spool. 'That's the battery from Mum's van?'

'Yes,' she puffed, prising Pee Wee's teeth apart and grabbing the carrier bag of rotten hands and feet. He really didn't look happy.

Raawwwwrffff!

'Where's the first aid kit?'

'Here,' I said, giving her the box, wondering how on earth a) how we were going to get the van home and b) how I would explain its battery-less-ness to Mum.

'Excellent,' Zoe said. 'But we may have a problem.'

I sagged. 'Oh what now?'

'I think we're being watched.'

'What? By who?'

'I don't know, but there was a definite movement in the bushes as I was getting the battery.'

Pee Wee was straining at the lead to get to the incineration bag which Zoe had put under the sink. I picked him up. 'Could have been a bird?'

'No, I don't think it was. I need you to do a sweep of the area with Pee Wee. Take the torch and just check the perimeters. When you come back inside, lock us in again and check all exterior doors are secure.'

'And what if someone's out there and they ask what I'm doing, or worse . . .'

She strapped on her headlight, to which she had added a magnifying glass on the end of an old television aerial so she could see things more clearly. 'Well if we shouldn't be on the premises, then they *definitely* shouldn't be on the premises, so we should stand the better chance in court.'

'But . . . what if it's a flasher or a stranger?'

She turned around and turned back and handed me a pair of surgical scissors. 'Threaten him with these. He'll soon take to his heels.'

'But . . .'

'. . . and when you come back, I'll have wired up the circuit and we'll be ready to electrocute. Off you go.' She shooed me and Pee Wee out of the room and closed the door, leaving us standing in the long, empty corridor, wondering what had just happened.

It was weird walking around college when no one was there. The place was silent except for the echo of my feet on the tiled floors. As we walked past the notice board, a draught ruffled the papers on it, advertising the bring-and-buy sale and the weekend exercise and cookery classes. I felt like a burglar ghost. A burglar ghost with a zombie dog.

Every now and again, I'd catch sight of a little thing scurrying along the wall and then disappearing into a classroom. I couldn't be sure as I was always too late with the torch but I think the pest controllers had missed a couple of the demon hamsters. Every room was empty and smelled of coffee and old meaty sandwiches. We walked past the Art room and saw the Halloween masks that had been designed for the party, pegged to a washing line. A little shiver ran through me. They'd done them already!

For the party! The party where I'd bring along my brand new boyfriend, who wouldn't be dead any more. I got a little bit excited. Pee Wee did too and had a little wee. I went to grab some tissue from the boys' toilets to mop it up and when I came back, I found him ripping one of the masks to pieces on the floor.

'Bad Peeps!' I said, picking up all the bits of paper. A little thought flashed through my mind. What if Sexy Dead Boy did that to his mask on the night of the party? What if he started gnawing through the walls like the hamsters? No, it was too ridiculous a thought to have. But I had it nevertheless.

'Come on, Peeps, come on,' I called him, clapping my thighs and bending down to hurry him up. He wouldn't. But eventually he followed me like the good boy he really truly was.

I went upstairs and across the glass bridge that led to the Humanities block rooms. I shone the torch down as we walked to see if there were signs of anyone outside, but there was nothing there. Everything was still and quiet and dark. I came upon our History classroom. All the chairs were pushed in neatly to the desks and there were still some markings on the whiteboard from the last lesson. Pee Wee found a half-eaten sandwich tucked behind the teacher's desk and he was right on it. I walked to the back of the room and sat down on the chair where Louis Burnett usually sat. I ran my finger over the pen markings on the desktop. He scratched them with his Biro in the lessons. I put my head on my arms on the desk and looked at them. Letters and symbols everywhere. A wolf's face with gnashing teeth with drips coming off them. A devil with little horns and a fork. Flames, like the ones on his skateboard. A heart with stitches running through the middle of it. The letter C.

Voices.

I heard definite proper actual voices, coming from outside.

Without a second's thought, I scrambled up from the chair, knocking it backwards and ran to the window. I couldn't see anything outside. I clicked on the torch. The hedge. Something in the hedge.

I saw it, I saw it! A leg. A definite person's leg as it darted back into the hedge.

Somebody *was* out there. Zoe was right!

'Come *on*, Peeps,' I said, picking up his lead and we raced back down the corridor and down the stairs. My heart was way too racey to even consider going outside so I just checked all the external doors like Zoe had told me to. All locked. All safe. No one could get in. And if they were going to, then we had to make sure Sexy Dead Boy was alive before they did. Otherwise . . . well, otherwise didn't bear thinking about.

I didn't tell Zoe what I'd seen when I got back to the Chemistry lab. Truth was, I forgot all about it. Because Sexy Dead Boy was ready. Zoe had hooked up the copper wire to the battery and to six points along the body – his feet, his hands and each side of his head – taping them in place with plasters from the first aid kit.

We got ready too. Apart from the scopey thing around

her neck, Zoe had me to dress exactly like her, in some white rubber wellies, rubber gloves, white coats and goggles that she'd found in the Food and Nutrition department. I closed the door. It was moment of truth time.

'Go to the head end and watch,' Zoe told me, and I settled Pee Wee on my coat under the sink and tied his lead to a Bunsen burner pipe so I could do as she asked. She stayed at the feet end with one hand on the switch on the battery.

Zoe smiled, but there was fear in her eyes. I felt it too. If this didn't work, we had nothing and the last few weeks had been a complete waste of time and limbs. But if it did work, we'd both have everything we ever wanted. She – her dad back (in some way) and proof of the importance of his work; me – a date for the Halloween party. It was all or nothing. Like on *Deal or No Deal?* Except this was *Dead or Not Dead?* I suppose.

'Ready?'

I put my goggles over my eyes. 'Ready.'

Zoe slowly turned the switch on the battery, but what happened next happened fast. The body juddered into life, his legs shuddering and shaking. The wire at the feet end was alive with purple lightning.

Fizzzzzzzzzaaaaaa juddddddddda fizzzzzzzzzzzzzzzzzzz crack a judddda.

His bottom half, his legs and feet, was flipping and juddering away like crazy; his top half was completely still.

Zoe switched off the battery. Her hand was shaking.

'Did it work?' I asked, looking at Sexy Dead Boy's face. He didn't open his eyes. 'The wire was all purple.'

'No,' she said. 'The current's not getting through to the wire at that end at all. Must be a break in the circuit.'

'So what can we do?' I asked. Pee Wee was straining at his lead, just not settling at all. 'I think I need to take him out,' I said.

Zoe didn't answer. She began removing all the wires and putting them all in again. 'We'll try it again.'

Once the wires had all been replaced and the connections to the battery checked, Zoe flicked the switch again, and this time, Sexy Dead Boy's chest rattled and juddered and bashed against the table, his arms flapping about like fish. But his bottom half stayed still.

'For God's sake!' Zoe shouted, but instead of flicking the switch off, she turned it higher so the juddering got even more violent and soon Sexy Dead Boy's top half was shuddering so powerfully, his whole back left the table.

'ZOE, NO!'

Fizzzzzzzzzaaaaaa judddddddddda fizzzzzzzzzzzzzzzzzzz crack a judddda.

An eye opened.

'Did you see that?' she cried, flicking the switch right off so Sexy Dead Boy was still again. Still and smoking hot. Literally.

Pee Wee was barking under the sink. 'Shut that dog up!' she yelled at me and I went over to him and gave him a cuddle. Zoe put her scopey thing in her ears and placed the round bit over his heart to listen. Her face lit up. 'Three beats! I heard three beats!'

'Oh my God!' I cried, leaving Pee Wee and scurrying around to the other side of SDB's chest. 'Are you sure?'

'No question,' said Zoe.

'Let me listen, let me listen!'

Zoe tore off her scopey thing and handed it to me, placing two fingers on Sexy Dead Boy's wrist. I listened to his chest. It was as still as a grave.

I handed the scopey thing back to her. 'I can't hear anything, Zoe.'

'There were three heartbeats, Camille! We're nearly there. Just a bit more . . .'

'You're going to shock him again?' I said.

Her hand was back on the battery. 'The serum has reached every part of him so there are electrical pulses at all the key points now. It's just a matter of time. There's enough electricity here to get a dead elephant to its feet. COME ON!'

Fizzzzzzzzzaaaaaa juddddddddddda fizzzzzzzzzzzzzzzzzzzz crack a juddddda.

'But he's not an elephant, he's a man,' I tried telling her, but she was like a concrete block. There was no getting through to her. And Pee Wee was still barking so loudly, I thought maybe she hadn't heard me.

I ran back up to the feet end and in an instant the body jolted again, harder and faster, and this time, the wire at the leg end was a force field of purple lightning.

Sizzzzzzzzzzzzzzzzzzzajudddddddddddddddda juddddddda juddddddda fizzzzz.

The circuit was alive and the whole body was charged again, this time his arms and feet thrashing about all over the table, and the room echoed with the crackling noise.

Fizzzzzzzzzzzzzzzzzzzzzcracka cracka crack cracka fizzzzzzzzzzzzzzzzzzzzzzzzzzzzzzzzzzzz . . .

Zoe turned up the battery again.

'Just a bit longer!' she cried, her eyes widening with every second the battery pumped him full of electricity.

His legs spasmed. There were sparks coming out of his feet.

'Zoe!' I cried. 'Stop! His toenails are going black! His hands are fizzing!' I could smell burning too. 'Zoe, his hair's smoking. Zoe, stop, stop, STOP!!!'

'No! It's working! His toes twitched!'

I had to physically switch the battery off myself and pin Zoe against the store cupboard door to stop her from shocking him any more.

'Camille, let me go, let me go!' she shouted, trying to squirm away from me, but I held her there with every ounce of strength I had. It wasn't enough. She wriggled free and darted back over to Sexy Dead Boy and listened to his heart again. The air around us was filled with the smell of burnt meat.

She whipped her head round and snapped, 'It's *your* fault it didn't work that time, Camille. You shouldn't have stopped me!'

'Zoe, it wasn't working. He wasn't coming to life; he was burning.'

'It *was* working!' she cried, scraping her hands through her hair. 'I heard his heart beat three times,' she said and her voice was going all wobbly. I joined her at the table and stood by her side.

'It could have been your mind playing tricks on you,

Zoe,' I said to her. I watched as she rested her hand on Sexy Dead Boy's still chest. 'When you want something so much, your brain starts imagining it's really happening.'

'His. Heart. Was. Beating!' she said slowly through her teeth.

'Okay,' I said. 'If you say so.'

'Don't patronize me, Camille. I heard it, I know I did.'

I nodded. Zoe looked at Sexy Dead Boy's smoking hair and slumped down beside the table with her head on her knees. When I joined her on the floor, there was water trickling down her cheeks.

She sniffed. 'His heart was beating. For a short time.'

'Yeah,' I said.

She wiped her cheeks with her rubber-gloved hands. 'Maybe I incorrectly hooked up the circuit . . .'

'You didn't, Zoe,' I said gently. 'You don't make mistakes like that.'

'Yes, well, you think I can work wonders and shit miracles,' she sniffed. 'And I can't. Much as I've always thought I could, I can't. What would he do?' she muttered. 'What. Would. He. Do?'

'What would who do?' I said, but she didn't answer me. Sexy Dead Boy's hair was still smoking. 'Look,' I said, trying to perk her up. 'We've come this far. We've gone to all the trouble of stealing a body and sawing off feet and sticking him together, so we'll just keep trying. We have to find another way, that's all. Okay, it worked on Pee Wee and the hamsters and all those other animals your dad tried, but maybe for a human it has to be slightly different?'

'In what way, slightly different?' she said, clearing her throat.

I shrugged. 'I don't know. If it's not something we've done, maybe it's something we *haven't* done. What have we missed?'

'I don't know,' she said sadly. 'If I knew that, we would have done it by now.'

'Can we look it up? On the Net? Or in one of your books?'

'No. I don't have *Corpse Reanimation for Dummies* I'm afraid.'

'Is there one?' I said. 'Maybe they have it in the library; I'll go and check . . .'

'Camille,' she said, holding me back. 'I have no Plan B.'

I put a hand on her arm. She didn't look like she wanted it there but she didn't shrug me away either. I shuffled up next to her. I couldn't quite get the angle right to hug her so I moved my hand away and sat down cross-legged, and when I felt the time was right, I rested my head on her shoulder instead. She didn't move.

'Why do you care so much?' Zoe muttered.

''Cos you really want this. You need this to work. And I'm your friend.'

'But why?'

'That's what friends do. They help each other out. They stick together.'

'You know I used you, don't you?' she sniffed. 'I used you because you were the only one who even bothered with me.'

I shrugged. 'Yeah. I kind of used you too though. I

needed a friend. And I wanted a boyfriend.'

Zoe's huge blue eyes stared at me in their usual starey way. There were tears in them again. 'I'm not friend material.'

'But we kind of work well together, don't we?' I said.

'We don't have a single thing in common,' she sniffed.

'Neither does he,' I said, looking over at Sexy Dead Boy. And she laughed. I actually heard Zoe laugh for the first time ever. It made her whole face totally change. I still had so many questions I wanted to ask her, so much I still didn't know, but one thing I did know for absolute certain at that moment was that Zoe Lutwyche wasn't a psycho. She was odd, she was starey, she was stupefyingly intelligent, but she wasn't mad. She was just lonely. And desperately in love with the idea of bringing her beloved dad back to life.

I felt her head rest against mine. I heard her take a tiny in-breath, but she didn't let it out. She was looking at the door. Her mouth was open. So was the door.

'You locked it,' she said, though I didn't know if it was a question or a statement of fact.

'Yeah,' I said. 'I thought I did.' I couldn't remember though. I really couldn't. 'I definitely pushed it to. I know I did.'

'Where's Pee Wee?' she said, getting to her feet and peering out into the corridor.

'He's under the sink,' I said, looking over for him. But he wasn't there. His lead was still dangling from the Bunsen burner pipe. He'd slipped right out of it.

I got to my feet. There was no sign of him. 'He was

right there,' I said, pointing to the little cubby-hole under-neath the workbench where my coat was. The yellow incineration bag of hands was there too. The bag had been chewed open.

And one of the rotting hands had gone.

So Pee Wee
had run off

The sky outside was full on black as night. If it hadn't been for Zoe's torch I would have fallen over oodles of times. The air smelled musty and damp and owls overhead twooted to remind me to be scared. Every now and again, in the distance, came a yelping kind of scream. I looked at Zoe. 'It's just a fox,' she said but the sound only strained my already shredded nerves.

We had spotted Pee Wee as he scampered across the rugby pitches and seen him dart into the woods that separated the college from the town park. Zoe had chopped a couple of fingers off the other rotten hand as a lure and was beckoning him with them, just in case he had finished the hand and wanted seconds. I just prayed that he wouldn't go out of the grounds because if anyone found him with the hand, we'd never be able to explain it away. I mean, what would we say?

'What do we say, Zoe, if someone finds him with the hand? What if the police find him? Or someone hands him in and they put him in the pound.'

'My dog has a taste for rotting human flesh, Sergeant. Don't they all?' said Zoe. 'And it's not the 1930s. They don't have dog pounds any more. If you hadn't left the door unlocked, he wouldn't have got out; ergo we would not be here on this hopeless wild goose chase.'

I was agog. 'I forgot, okay? And anyway I didn't know he was going to chew through that bag, did I?'

'He's no ordinary dog though, is he? I knew we should have been more careful. Should have known not to let that thing into the lab in the first place. He's obviously been waiting to get his teeth into those limbs.' She stamped her foot on the hard earth.

'Is your leg on the blink?' I asked her.

'No, it is not,' she snipped.

I rubbed the hem of my dress. 'Why did you stamp it like that?'

'Because I'm annoyed, Camille, and it's the only way I can project my annoyance without resorting to physical violence. This is yet another obstacle we don't need and which we do not have time for.'

We came to a large dip in the earth, which I'd seen boys riding their bikes in and out of and doing their skateboard jumps in, like a natural half pipe in the ground. Zoe shone the torch into the trees on the other side. 'He's not here, is he?' she sighed. 'But I can smell it. I can smell the hand.'

'Can you?' I said, marvelling at how Zoe's body always seemed to be doing things mine couldn't. I wondered if that was one of the powers you got when you had some-one else's limbs. 'You're like a detective. I wish I could smell it. So, what now?'

'I don't know,' she huffed and her breath cloud seemed never ending. 'Wait.' She held out her hand and shone the torch higher up. 'I saw white.'

We both ran down the hollow and back up the other side and looked up into the branches of the enormalous tree. A flash of white caught the light.

'What was that?' I whispered. 'Is it Pee Wee?'

She squinted up the torch beam. 'Yes, looks like it. You'll have to get up there and coax him down with the fingers.'

'Me?' I squawked. 'I can't climb trees.'

'Well, I can't. People with reanimated limbs aren't supposed to climb. It can damage us irrevocably if we fall.'

'Really?' I said, thinking that was the worst excuse ever and even I wasn't going to fall for it. 'We're stuck then, aren't we?'

Zoe's jaw clenched. 'Camille, will you please climb the tree and retrieve that flesh-eating puppy of yours. Pretty please?'

'I can't climb trees, Zoe,' I said again, much more slowly. 'Seriously, I actually probably literally will shit myself. I fell out of one when I was seven, right onto my grandma's pavlova when we were having a picnic. I swore, from that day forth, I would never climb trees again.'

Zoe ran the torch all along the branch to the other end and back again. 'He looks quite at home up there.'

'I didn't think dogs could climb trees,' I said.

'Normal dogs don't have a penchant for killing and eating other dogs or munching rotting human body parts either but yours does. Who knows what else it likes doing?' She looked up towards Pee Wee. 'I'll wait here. You go to the caretaker's shed and find the retractable ladder, and then you can climb up and get him, can't you?'

'Get what?' said a voice behind us.

I flipped around to see two figures standing on the edge of the hollow. It was Damian's trainers I saw first. The brightest white trainers I'd ever seen. They matched his teeth. He also had on his tightest black shirt and jeans. Next to him was Louis in a sleeveless yellow *Zombie Apocalypse* t-shirt, long shorts and scruffy pink-and-yellow Nikes.

'Oh go away,' said Zoe, putting all her emphasis on the 'way' part of 'go away' as though she really was quite irritated by the sight of them.

Damian walked down into the hollow and swaggered towards us. 'Hello, Blue Eyes. Princess Peach. Now what would you two be doing in the woods on a Friday night, eh? Waiting for us, was ya?'

Zoe threw me a look. I threw Zoe a look.

'You're sticking your noses into a particularly angry bee hive here,' Zoe warned him.

Damian laughed. 'Come on. You know this is where Damie likes to hang with his women, don't you? Don't tell me this is a coincidence.'

'Ugh,' said Zoe. 'Just when I thought I couldn't hate you more.'

Damian laughed and scratched the tip of his nose.

I glared at Louis. 'It was you who Zoe saw hiding in the trees at the front of college, wasn't it? And who I saw in the hedge outside the Humanities block. Have you been following us?' I glanced up into the tree in case Pee Wee truly let the hand out of the bag.

'Uh . . .' said Louis, flicking his hair out of his eyes. It was wet; I guessed he'd showered recently.

'Yeah it was us,' said Damian. 'We went up to Spook Central to see what was going on and when we saw the van leave, we followed you down here. Then we waited. And we watched. Ate a couple of burgers. And . . .'

'. . . and we wondered if you needed any help or anything,' Louis cut in.

'Well we don't,' said Zoe. 'So you can go now.'

'Can't,' said Damian. 'Loser was worried about the Princess here. Thought you were chopping her up or something,' he sniffed.

'What?' I snipped.

'You didn't answer my texts,' said Louis. 'I was think-ing all sorts.'

'He thinks you're a psycho,' Damian told Zoe.

'Most people do,' she replied, looking up into the tree. She didn't even look angry. Then I realised, she wasn't. She got called a psycho or a freak every day of the week. It was water off a duck's beak.

'Course, I don't,' said Damian, folding his arms.

'Actually, I think you're pretty sexy, for a goth.'

'Zoe's not a goth, she's a . . . scientist,' I said, 'and I told you what we were doing, Louis. It's a sheep, okay? We're seeing if the reanimation serum works on a dead sheep.' I looked up into the tree again.

Damian caught me. 'Why do you keep looking up there? Lost your cat, have you?'

'No, it's my dog,' I told him and Zoe shot me an angry glance. 'He went up the tree and now he won't come down.'

'That little maniac what attacked me? I'd let him rot,' said Damian.

'Dame,' said Louis. He looked up into the tree where the torch shone. 'What's in his mouth?' I said nothing.

'I ain't risking my neck for that one. Go on, Loser, you go up and grab him.'

'Me?'

'Yeah. Do it for your girlfriend.' Damian looked at me.

'Don't be stupid,' Louis scoffed.

'Go on,' said Damian, pointing up at Pee Wee. 'You can jump up to that one, hook your leg over and you'll be away. Sweet.'

'I'm not doing it.' They were arguing just like me and Zoe had done earlier.

'All right, I'll go then,' said Damian, preparing to take a running jump at the trunk.

'No, wait!' said Louis, pulling him back. 'I'll go.' He jumped up and hung on to the branch.

'Ha ha, knew you couldn't resist. Anything to impress her.'

Louis jumped down. 'Leave it, Dame. Not now.' He brushed his hands off.

'No, I think it's about time. Camille, this loser's got a raging chub on for you but he ain't got the balls to say it. Right, there, I said it. Now you can jump her bones, can't you? No more fannying around.'

'Damian, for f . . .'

'Tell her where her scrunchie is, Lou.'

'Shut it, Damian!' said Louis, squaring up to him. 'Just shut your hole, right now!' It looked like a lion cub trying to stand up to the head of the pride.

'What's a chub on?' I said. 'And what about my scrunchie? Have you seen it?'

Zoe headed towards me and hooked her arm through mine. 'We have to get out of here.' We turned together and began to walk away.

'Why?' I whispered.

'Because that dog is going to drop that hand any second and the moment it does, Laurel and Hardy are going to want answers.'

I stopped. 'But I want to know where my scrunchie is,' I said, looking back at them. It was all I could think about.

'Damian, please don't, please, let me do it . . .'

'He loves you to death,' Damian shouted at me.

'You bastard!' Louis launched at Damian with such power, he knocked him clean off his feet. I grabbed the torch from Zoe and shone it at them as they rolled around on the ground, trying to get a grip on each other and flinging insults back and forward. I looked at Zoe for an answer to how to stop them, but she was halfway across the field, walking back in the direction we had come.

Damian's forearms were up, covering Louis' blows. 'Just tell her for God's sake! Stop being such a pussy!'

Damian had him pinned to the ground by this time, and Louis was glaring up at him with a face full of hate. It was the same look I gave salad.

'Oh for goodness' sake,' I said, marching over to the fighting boys. 'What are you doing? Get up, get up now!'

Damian got to his feet. He held a hand out for Louis to help him up, but Louis smacked it away and got up without it. 'Here,' he said and held something out to show me. 'Here's your scrunchie.'

I took it and looked at Louis. He looked like he was going to say something, but he turned away. I looked down at my cherry scrunchie. At least, it *looked* like my cherry scrunchie. I picked it up and sniffed it. It smelled of boy sweat.

'He picked it up after you ran off on freshers' night,' said Damian, panting. 'He wears it on his wrist and smells it. Now it's all out in the open, Loser, and you ain't gotta pussyfoot around her anymore, 'ave you?'

'What?' I said. 'Why did he have it?'

'Why do you think?' Damian cried. 'He's head over heels for you, you dozy cow. Only he's too scared to do anything about it. That day on the pier, when he smashed your face on the door, that was because he had that thing on his wrist and he didn't want you to see. That's why you ended up clanging your schnoz.'

'Huh?' My brain was a train on its way to a station

everyone else in the world had arrived at. I just didn't understand anything anymore. Why would Louis Burnett have my scrunchie? I couldn't work out what the game was. If it was a joke, it wasn't funny at all. You don't mess with a girl's scrunchie.

'I mean, personally I can't see the appeal,' Damian sniffed. 'Seen bigger tits on an ironing board. But you try telling his dick that. I can't get him out the bathroom some days.' I shone the torch at him. There was a bit of blood inside his nose. He wiped it away. 'But he saw you on open day and remembered you from kindergarten or something and that was his thunderbolt moment. He was all geared up to tell you at freshers' but the snakebite bit him on the arse.'

Louis walked away, hands up over his head like he was trying to crush his own skull. Louis loved me?

I still couldn't make sense of it all. I wanted to cry. I remembered the open day, but I didn't remember Louis. Or did I? I remembered seeing Damian, lying across some chairs by the wall in the gym, his top buttons undone, chatting to three girls in maxi dresses about freshers'. Someone else had been there. He'd held one of the double doors open for me. Had it been Louis? He hadn't said anything. I'd noticed everything about Damian: his t-shirt saying 'Porn Olympics 1969', his blue jeans with the chain on the pocket, his brand-new Nikes with the silver tick up the side. He'd been peeling an orange in one long strip. I hadn't noticed Louis at all.

'Dozy as arseholes, the pair of ya. Tell you what, you deserve each other,' said Damian, striding out of the hollow and ducking under the branches of the tree. 'I'll leave you two to it. I'm gonna have another crack at Professor Pinch Pussy.'

Louis was sitting against Pee Wee's tree, his arms on his knees and his head resting on them. I looked up into the branches to see if Pee Wee was still there. But there was no sign. I walked over to Louis and knelt down on the ground beside him.

He didn't look at me. He just said, 'I'm sorry,' like he always did. All he ever said to me was sorry. Sorry about banging the door in my face. Sorry about startling me that night in the graveyard. Sorry about . . . this. And that was the moment I realised that every time he said 'sorry', what he was really saying was 'I love you.'

I didn't realise I was shaking until I saw the torchlight flickering on the ground. I held it steady with both hands. 'This isn't a joke, is it? I mean, I don't think it's a joke but you have tricked me before . . .'

I didn't mean for him to answer. I was just saying it to reassure myself, but he shouted, 'I never tricked you before! That was an accident on the pier. I never meant to smash your face in!'

'Don't shout at me,' I said. 'I was just checking.'

'I can't do it, okay? I can't say it. It'll come out wrong,' he said.

'What will?' I said, sitting down next to him on the ground.

'The stuff in my head,' he replied. 'The stuff I want to say . . . about you . . . You never should have found out from Damian.'

I couldn't catch my breath. Was I excited? Was I scared? I didn't know. I just wanted him to tell me what was going on. 'Tell me. I won't laugh or anything.'

He sighed. 'It's so stupid.'

'What is?'

'This.'

'This?'

'Yeah, this,' he said. 'Spending all your time knowing that the best thing that could ever happen to you probably won't because you haven't got the balls to grab it. You wake up and there's a pain because they're not there. Then there's a pain when they *are* there. You drink to give you the courage to say it, but you never say it cos it's too hard. You don't offer them your coat when they're cold. You see them upset but you don't hug them. You don't stop them making a fool of themselves. Because then they might find out. And you don't want that because if they didn't feel the same way . . . it would just be the worst.'

'Am I *they*? Are you talking about me?'

'YES. Who do you think I'm talking about?'

'There's no need to snap.'

'There's every need to snap at you, because you . . . you . . . oh, forget it. Just go, all right.' He stood up.

'No.' I stood up too. 'You don't own the woods. I can stand here if I want.'

He crossed his arms. This was too weird. I laughed.

'What's funny?' he whispered.

'I don't know.' I really didn't know, I wasn't just saying that. 'I don't quite believe that someone's fallen in love with me. No one's ever done that before. I mean, I do it all the time and boys never do it back. It's a bit scary.'

He nodded like he completely understood. 'It's not like a thunderbolt. I tried to explain it to Damian but he didn't really take it in. It's more like a spark. A spark on a bomb. It fizzes and crackles and just keeps getting nearer and nearer until, one day, you're in full-blown you-know-what. And you didn't even see it coming. And then there's nothing you can do about it.'

My heart was going berserk. 'So you actually like . . . love me?' He nodded.

I frowned. 'Like Splodge loves Poppy love me?' He nodded again. 'Like Jack loves Rose? Like Peeta loves Katniss? Like Edward loves Bella?'

'Yes,' he said. 'I can't believe you didn't get the hint.'

In the past, boys had only ever said this kind of thing to me before they pushed me off something or into something, or before just telling me they were joking. But Louis wasn't joking. 'But why me out of all the girls at college?'

He shrugged. 'When I saw you on open day, you were wearing your lemon bridesmaid dress thing and leggings, same as the night on the pier when I . . . smashed your face in. These girls laughed at you when they saw you but you didn't take any notice. I just thought you looked . . . kind of . . . like me. It reminded me of before, at St Raph's, when you found me in the toilets and gave me the peppermint. And I thought you were beautiful and stuff then too. I just couldn't tell you cos every time I saw you, I froze. I thought it had gone away when I saw you on open day, but it hadn't at all. I still felt the same. But you were all about Damian.'

'I'm not all about Damian,' I scoffed.

'You really like him. It's okay, I get it. Everyone likes him. I know my place in the pecking order. After Damian, before Splodge. Maybe.'

'You really think I'm beautiful?' I said.

'Well, yeah.'

And in a heartbeat Louis Burnett became the most attractive guy I had ever seen, heard or read about. He was every hero in my romance novels, every leading man in every rom-com I'd watched, every hot boy who'd blanked me in the corridors at school, every soap actor or rock star who I'd stuck posters of on my wardrobe. But none of them were really anything like him, because none of them had ever liked me back or told me I was beautiful, and at that moment nothing could have meant more in the world. My chest felt like it was going to burst.

I got the biggest urge to touch him. So I did. I dropped the torch and lifted my hand to touch his cheek. My hand was freezing. His cheek was boiling. I'd known it would be.

'I knew you'd be blushing.' I put my hand down again.

He laughed. 'Worst ever. I'm glad it's dark.'

I finally understood it. It had taken me so long, but I got it now. That feeling. Full-blown you-know-what. That volcano kind of feeling when you think you're going to explode if you don't kiss someone. Like when Rose runs down below deck to save Jack and break his handcuffs with an axe, even though the boat's going down and they're going to die for sures. That's how I felt about Louis right at that moment. Like I'd wade through icy water for him and cut him free with an axe. If I ever had to.

'Did you really sniff my scrunchie?' I said, smiling. I hadn't told my face to smile, it just did it. 'Was it so you could pretend you were smelling my hair?'

He nodded. 'I was going to give it back but . . .' He shook his head again and took a really deep breath. 'I didn't want to.'

I sniffed the scrunchie again. 'You haven't . . . done anything to it, have you?'

'No,' he said. 'I just liked to smell it, you know. It didn't smell of funeral parlours and disinfectant. It smelled of a faraway place. It made me happy. I liked it.'

'Okay, you're starting to sound a bit stalky now.'

'Oh God, sorry.'

'It's okay.' I smiled. 'Makes me feel wanted. You are weird though.'

'So are you,' he said. I shone the torch into his face and he shied away from it. 'You still wear your bridesmaid dress.'

'So? You wear a kilt!'

'You steal from hospitals!' he came back.

'You work with dead people!' I came back.

He smiled. 'You're friends with a psychopath.'

I smiled. 'You're friends with a twat.'

I laughed. He laughed. It was a dead strange feeling. Still scary. Like something really bad or really good was about to happen. I reached out my hand towards him again, and put my fingertips over his heart. It was going bananacakes.

'What are you doing now?' he whispered.

'I'm seeing if your heart's beating as fast as mine. Then I'll know, for sure.'

He waited while I shone the torch over his face. I looked at his lips. I imagined how they would feel on mine. 'Do you believe it now?' he said.

I nodded. His heart was a heavyweight champion. His hand was on my cheek.

'I'm trying to believe it too,' he said. Slowly I felt him getting closer and closer and closer to my face. It was just his breath against my mouth for the longest time, and in my ears were whooshing noises. I couldn't believe what was happening. His lips touched mine and we pressed our heads together and we kissed, slowly at first, until our lips moved and our mouths were opening and closing around each other's. And though my nose still hurt a little bit as it smushed against Louis', it was the most fantastic moment of my whole life ever. Because his lips weren't a poster or my pillow. They were real live boy lips. I shuffled closer to him so we were completely touching, and he wrapped his arms around me. It felt like we were melded together forever and nothing could come between us, like my Barbie and Ken when I left them by the fire. His hands were on my head. My hands were on his back. His damp hair smelled of grass and boy shampoo. Our tummies touched. I felt a surge I had never felt before, running right the way through me from my mouth to my feet. It was electrical. I didn't ever want to stop kissing him, ever ever ever.

But I had to cos something heavy dropped down from the tree and smacked him hard right on his head.

'Ahhhhhhhhh!' *Flllllll-uhhhmmmp.*

'Louis?'

Louis had totally and automatically passed out flat on his back.

And the hand had landed.

Shizz

Pee Wee had appeared around the same time as the hand, looking at me like a rotten hand wouldn't melt in his mouth.

'Bad, bad Pee Wee!' I whispered sternly at him. He panted, smiling at me like he'd done something brilliant.

I picked up the torch and shone it over Louis' still body. 'Louis?' I said quietly, nudging him in the ribs. I bent over him and put my ear to his warm, t-shirted chest and listened to his heart. There were beats, thank goodness. He was okay.

'Louis, please wake up,' I said, shaking him by his shoulders. Pee Wee trotted over and started licking his hand. No, not his hand. *The* hand.

I heard a groan in Louis' neck. He was coming round.

'Oh Louis, thank goodness,' I cried and stroked his hair

away from his eyes.

He levered himself up. 'Camille? What the hell was . . . what is that?' He was looking directly at the hand Pee Wee was licking.

I didn't think. There were no more excuses now. This wasn't a science experiment with a dead sheep anymore. This wasn't any old drama prop that I could just explain away. Louis knew a dead hand when he saw one. And he had seen one. I grabbed it, scrambled up out of the hollow and started running back towards college as fast as I could before Louis had even got to his feet. I had to get back to the lab, double fast. I sprinted back across the rugby pitches with that naughty Pee Wee yapping at my heels all the way like it was all a big funny game.

At the back of the Science block I flung open the door and we raced down the echoey corridor all the way to the end where the lab was. It was dark inside the college but the closer I got, the better I could see the lab door. Someone was standing outside it. Damian. I slowed, hiding the hand behind my back, dangling by its middle finger like a stinky designer handbag.

Pee Wee pounced on Damian the second he saw him but this time, Damian was having none of it. He picked him up by the collar and flung him straight into one of the metal lockers opposite the lab, slamming it shut.

'Hey!' I puffed. 'That's mean! Let him out, now!'

'What's she doing in there?' he demanded, pointing at the lab door. 'She's locked it. She's got someone in there.'

'Who?' I panted as Pee Wee barked and banged inside the metal locker.

Raaaaawwwwwrrrrrffff raaawwwffff raaaaawwwff!

'Zoe,' he shouted over the racket. 'She's got someone in there. A bloke. I saw his feet through the window before she pulled down the blind. What's she up to?'

I shrugged, still panting for air. 'I don't know. It might be perfectly innocent.'

'Pull the other one. You and her are thick as thieves. That's why she doesn't want to go out with me, isn't it? Cos of this bloke she's got Fritzled up in there.'

'Um . . .'

'Come on, out with it.'

I shook my head. 'I don't know anything.'

Raaaaawwwwwrrrrrffff raaawwwffff raaaaawwwff!

Damian glared at me. 'What's she doing, Camille? And where's Lou?'

'He's . . . he's in the woods.'

'Aw you haven't dumped him already have you? I tell you, you could do a lot worse. All right, so he dresses like a tramp but his heart's in the right place . . .'

'I know it is.' I stood firm, still clutching the hand behind me. 'You've got the wrong end of the twig.'

Raaawrrrrrffff raaaaawwwff!

'Bit of extracurricular Human Biology, is it? What is he, a teacher? That one who takes the girls for netball and does the knicker checks? I always thought there was something wrong with him.' He glanced downwards and frowned. 'What you got behind your back?'

'Nothing. Just my bag,' I said, lifting my arm ever so slightly so he just caught a glimpse of the hand, just a glimpse, not a full-on close-up.

His eyebrows raised in a 'Tell-me-or-die' kind of way.

'We're . . . we are . . .' I noticed the notice board and a pinned up flyer for the bring and buy sale, the cake stall. 'We're making a cake,' I blurted out, 'for the bring and buy.'

'A cake?' He frowned. 'What, and he's helping you, is he? Lying on his back on a table? Cobblers.'

'No, he *is* the cake,' I said, only just knowing where my mouth was taking this particular lie. 'It's a . . . man cake. A cake in the shape of a man.'

'What?'

'It's true. Yeah, it's in the shape of a man because the headmaster wanted us to do it, so we thought it should look like him. It's made of sponge and soft pink icing and there's jam and cream. And we're going to paint on a suit . . . with grey food colouring. It's ginormalous.' My mouth was watering at the thought of jam and cream, until I remembered it didn't actually exist.

'What's that smell?' Damian frowned again.

'Bins,' I said, without thinking. The nearest bin was right the way up the other end of the corridor by the gym. I was gripping the rotten hand so hard behind my back that my fingers were starting to sink into its soft flesh. He said nothing. I said nothing. He didn't know what to believe and I didn't know what more I could say to make him believe me. A door *clunked* at the far end of the corridor and a figure dashed through it. It started running towards us, panting.

'Dame! Damian!' it called out.

'What?' Damian called back.

Louis pointed at me as he slowed down, his Nikes

pounding the floor, his fringe stuck to his forehead with sweat. 'They've got body parts. They've cut off someone's hand!'

Damian looked at me. 'Cake?'

Louis turned to me, sweat glistening on his cheeks. 'There is no sheep, is there? It's body parts. It's human, the thing you're bringing to life. Isn't it?' He rubbed the top of his head. I looked from Louis to Damian and back again. 'That's what you've been doing. That's why you were at the hospital and the funeral parlour that night. It all fits now. It's not a sheep, is it? You are doing what her dad did. You're Frankensteining, aren't you?!'

'What the hell . . . ?' said Damian.

'Louis, please don't hate me. Please!' I begged, seeing no other way to go. 'Just give me a chance to explain.'

The boys were looking down at something. I was begging with three hands.

Raaaaawwwwwrrrrrffff raaawwwffff raaaaawwwff!

'Oh my God!' Louis cried.

'Oh my God,' I said.

'WHA . . . ?' Damian slammed his hand over his mouth.

'It's a boy!' I cried. 'We've built a boy!'

Zoe was standing in the open doorway. 'Well done, Camille. Do you want to take an advert out in the *The Herald* while you're at it?'

I was crying by this time. I thought maybe Louis might realise his tone was making me upset and put his arm around me or kiss away the tears that were rolling down my cheeks, or just be kind to me like he had been outside the funeral parlour that night. But he didn't. He was looking mad. And Damian was looking confused. And Zoe was looking at me with snake eyes.

'I had to, Zoe,' I pleaded. 'The hand . . .' I waved it in the air to show her. 'It fell out of the tree. What else was I supposed to say?' She walked forward and I handed the hand to her and went to rescue Pee Wee from the locker. He was shivering with fright and immediately licked my chin in thanks.

'You had all better come in, hadn't you?' said Zoe and held open the door as the three of us scuffed inside – me first, followed by Louis, and eventually Damian.

Zoe had cleaned him up from earlier when he had been burnt by the electric shocks. She must have serummed him up again. I had no idea how the boys were going to react. They were seeing what I'd seen when I first saw Sexy Dead Boy in one piece – a dead man. Just a dead man. Except I had known what was coming.

The second Damian saw Sexy Dead Boy, he cried out. 'He's dead! He's a dead man!' He flinched and flung himself towards the store cupboard with such force, it was like a giant finger had poked him sharply in the ribs. He gripped the cupboard. 'What the Christ is going on here? Oh Jeez, oh man that's disgusting, that's . . . Ugh, I'm gonna be sick. I'm gonna be sick.' He retched and ran to the back of the room to actually be sick into the sink.

'Oh yeah, he hates dead bodies, doesn't he?' I said with a nervous laugh, but Louis didn't answer me. He just walked, dead slowly, over to the workbench.

'Why is this here?' he said, not taking his eyes off Sexy Dead Boy.

'It's perfectly simple,' said Zoe, standing beside him. 'We stole the headless body of Luke Truss from your funeral parlour.'

Louis looked at me. 'You lied to me? You STOLE Luke Truss?'

'Well, we stole his body, yes,' said Zoe.

'His whole body? No, you can't have.' Louis shook his head and laughed, even though nothing was funny. 'We cremated him.'

'Uh, no, you didn't,' said Zoe, tidying away her empty syringes. 'You cremated his head. And a water-cooler bottle. And two large sacks of potatoes.'

Louis looked like he had been turned to stone. 'No.'

Zoe sighed. 'What do you want, diagrams?'

Louis shook his head again. 'This isn't real. This is a joke.'

Zoe adjusted her headlight and began injecting even more serum into the parts of Sexy Dead Boy she had singed earlier. 'I don't joke when it comes to science. We took a headless body, we found a new head and a brain and we connected them. We didn't plan on replacing the hands and feet but they had begun to decompose.'

By the look on Louis' face, I could see a penny had dropped. He looked at me. I nodded. He looked down at Sexy Dead Boy's arm. He picked it up and rubbed along the hand. 'This isn't his hand?'

I shook my head. 'No, we added the hands. Well, Zoe did. And the feet. And the head. And some of the organs. Cos they'd been donated.'

Louis went to the head end of the bench and rubbed along the side of Sexy Dead Boy's marble white neck with the very tip of his finger. 'There's no join.'

'The serum,' I said, pointing to the empty syringes. 'That's what it can do. That's what I tried to tell you about in the graveyard.'

Zoe explained to him about serum 651 and the battery and Pee Wee and the hamsters. She pointed at Pee Wee, who was washing himself under the workbench, having just polished off the rotten hand. 'That dog was dead a fortnight ago. It now sits there, blood pulsing through its veins, synapses firing in its cranium. The serum accelerates tissue repair, you see. Add in a significant electrical surge and the only outcome is anabiosis. New life.'

'Aw man that's sick!' cried Damian. 'That's sick! I've got to get out of here.'

He made for the door but Louis stopped him and held his wrists. 'Damian, calm down, you're not locked in. Nothing's going to hurt you, all right? Just . . . be quiet for a minute, please.' Damian shut up. I didn't think that was possible.

I pointed to a hole in the skirting board. 'The hamsters really were all dead, I told you. Zoe really did bring them all back to life in Biology. I didn't lie about that.'

Louis sat Damian down on a chair by the wall and made him put his head between his knees. Then he turned and glared at me. 'Why are you doing this?'

'Why?' said Zoe, putting down her syringe. 'Because science has progressed and if we don't progress with it we may as well all be living in caves and chewing on mammoth femurs. And Camille wanted to be a part of that, didn't you?'

I nodded. Well, I half-nodded. 'I really just wanted a date for the Halloween party,' I said. 'Zoe had the idea and I . . . went along with it.'

'Bodysnatching for the sake of having a date for a party is not an excuse, Camille. How COULD you do this?'

I frowned at him, not knowing whether I was on the verge of shouting back or crying my eyes out.

'I made her do it,' Zoe said suddenly.

'Zoe, you didn't,' I said.

'She was vulnerable. She'd done everything to impress this . . . person,' she said, nodding at Damian's hunched over back, 'to no avail. She wanted a friend, a companion. Someone she could trust. Someone who wouldn't just use her for their own entertainment. I struck while the humiliation was hot.'

'That's so warped,' said Louis, clasping his hands behind his head and pacing the room. I felt sick with embarrassment. He'd fallen out of love with me, I knew it. I'd had it so good for, what, ten minutes? And now he hated me. Now he thought I was disgusting like all the other boys did. Tears came again.

Damian jibbered as he felt his way along to the sink like he was going to be sick. 'Nothing's gonna hurt me,' he was muttering. 'Nothing's gonna hurt me. I hate dead people. I hate 'em. But they're not gonna hurt me.'

Zoe ignored him and continued firing at Louis. 'If someone in your family lost their legs but *you* could give them new ones *and* ensure they could walk again, would you stand aside and just say, "Well, it's just one of those things that happens"?

'Would you let something beautiful, something you love, die, even though you knew there was a chance it could live again in some other form?'

He looked at me. He looked back at Zoe. 'People die,' he said. 'If nothing died, the planet would be overrun. Death is just . . . nature. It's horrible when it happens but it's got to happen. That's just how it has to be.'

'That's what your A level Philosophy teaches you, is it?' Zoe snorted.

Louis bit his lip. 'No, it's what I think. What's the point in living if we don't die? We're put on this earth to make the most of the time we've got and then we have to leave and let the next generation come along.'

'Come along and do what?' Zoe snapped.

He shrugged. 'See if they can do any better than we did, I guess.'

'Exactly,' she hissed, her finger in the air. 'Exactly what I'm doing. Improving on my father's methods. I'm not insane. I'm not creating monsters. I'm giving a second chance of life!'

'Your father was a psycho!' Louis shouted.

'He wasn't, Louis!' I shouted back.

'He was! Everyone in this town knows he was killing people to make his . . . freaks. Monkeys with human arms. Fish with human feet. Dogs with fins . . .'

'That never happened, Louis. He didn't *do* any of that!' I cried. 'I've been to their house. I've seen the stuffed animals in the hallway. They're animal mash-ups, that's all. There's nothing human about them. You've just heard rumours, that's all.'

But Louis wasn't quite finished. He said slowly, 'I warned you, Camille. And if this serum stuff is proven to work on humans, I'm telling you, it won't be a good thing. Everyone will want a piece of it . . . a piece of *that*.' He pointed to Sexy Dead Boy. 'They'll all want their loved ones brought back to life.'

'I'm not talking about everyone!' Zoe snapped. 'I'm just talking about HIM!'

Damian's face was deathly white as he launched himself over to the sink again and retched. We all looked at Sexy Dead Boy in silence.

'Well, you are talking about everyone, Zoe, aren't you?' I said.

Zoe stared at me. 'What?'

I gulped. 'You want everyone to know about this and the serum and your dad's research so he'll be syndicated a thousand times over. It'll prove all his research was worth it and that he wasn't mad.'

'Vindicated,' she said quietly.

'Yes,' I said. 'So, then everyone *will* know about it. Everyone will know what an amazing scientist he was and they'll want to try it then, won't they?'

'Yes,' she said sadly, sitting down on the teacher's chair behind her.

Louis looked at me, then back to Zoe. 'You hadn't even thought of that, had you? You'd be giving the world a walk-ing talking reason to believe they can live forever. And we can't. We get old and we die; that's just how it's supposed to be.'

I suddenly became extremely cross with Louis. Even

though less than an hour ago we had been in love with each other now I just wanted to shout at him. Louis stood in silence. I stomped over to the teacher's table and tore two rubber gloves out of the box on the end. 'Fine. This isn't about anybody else anymore. This is just about Zoe now. And we're going to finish him, whether you like it or not . . .'

Damian squeaked over by the sink.

Louis walked over to me. 'I helped you,' he said. 'I let you in the funeral parlour while you were . . . crying over that body . . . I worried about you . . . at the hospital when you were taking . . . God knows what else. I thought it was my fault you were there, because of what I did to your nose.' He stepped back from me. 'I'm going to the police,' he said. 'You can't do this, it's not right. I've seen all the Frankenstein movies, Camille, it never ever ends well.'

'Go away,' I said, snapping on the gloves and not looking at him. I couldn't believe how harsh I was being. I turned away and heard him walk towards the door. There was a second's pause and then the lab door slammed. Footsteps from the sink area. Damian scuttled out behind him.

I turned back to Sexy Dead Boy and picked up the teacher's desk lamp, unwrapping the lead from round its stem. I switched it on.

Zoe looked at me. 'We can't tell anyone about this, can we?'

She was asking *me*? I thought. I shook my head. 'No, he's right. It would probably be pandemonium.'

'I didn't even think of that,' she said softly. 'All I could think of was proving them all wrong. And bringing him back.'

'So come on,' I said, 'what does it matter? Let's just bring him to life. Forget everyone else. This is just for you now. Come on. What are you waiting for? Crank up the battery, Zoe.'

'That means my father's reputation will always be as a mad man.'

I shrugged. 'Not to me it won't. And now Louis and Damian know too,' I said. 'You can finish this, Zoe. And if you do, you can have your dad back. In a way. Won't that be better than anything? And who knows what he might turn out to be?'

Zoe smiled at me. 'You're a very bright person, Camille. You might hide it, but sometimes it just bursts out of you.'

A tear had escaped from my eye. I hadn't even known I was crying, I was so pumped full of that thing that athletes get. I only ever got it when I was cross or about to throw the discus.

'So we can finish him?' I said.

'*I* can finish him,' she said, checking the wires on her side of the body. 'You go after Louis. You're wobbling that light too much to be of any help here.'

A pain gripped the middle of my body. I set the light down. 'No. Not after what he said. Not after how he said it. And what he said about your dad.'

Zoe picked up the light and shone it on the arm, injecting Sexy Dead Boy with the other hand.

'Did he look sad when he left?' I asked her as a pain

stabbed my throat.

'Yes,' she said.

'Did he look back at me?' I said, as a tear fell down into Sexy Dead Boy's hair.

'Yes,' she said.

'No,' I said, as determined as I could, wiping away my tear track. 'We need to finish Sexy Dead Boy. If only to make him jealous, we have to finish him.' I was firm. I knew what we had to do. I did the deep breath thing to blow out the pain, but it didn't do any good. It still hurt. Zoe had stopped again and was staring at me.

'What?' I said, unable to catch my breath.

'Go. After. Him.'

'No,' I said. 'I want to finish Sexy Dead Boy.'

'You don't want to lose him. Louis is the one who's made for you, not this one,' she said, looking down. 'I can see that now. I can see it when you look at each other. You shine.' She nodded towards the door. 'Now go. And don't come back until you've made things better.'

My head still didn't agree, but my feet did the thinking for me, and before I knew it I was heading towards the door and out the door and running down the empty banana-skin-stinking corridor and out onto the concrete at the front of college.

And Louis was sitting there on the wall right outside the Science block.

'I thought you were going to the police,' I sniffed.

He stood up and walked towards me. 'Yeah, well I can't, can I?' he said. 'You'd never speak to me again. And that would kill me . . .' He looked back at Damian who was

-264-

sitting right next to him, holding a cigarette with a shaking hand. I hadn't noticed him until that moment. 'Because I love you. I really, really love you. And I don't want to do anything to ruin that.'

I sort of squeaked and made an 'Oh' sound. It was all I could do. Once again my heart boomed into life.

'Think I'm gonna puke again,' Damian muttered, swaggering away blowing his smoke high up into the night air.

'If being with you means I have to go along with this, then I'll go along with this. I know it's crazy but I'll do it.'

I'd never heard anything so romantic in my whole actual life ever. I reached out to hug him and immediately felt his arms around me and we hugged for the longest time. I'd seen a couple in a garden centre hugging like this at Christmas last year and I'd watched them for ages, until they'd caught me looking and flicked me a V sign.

'I can't wait to go to a garden centre with you,' I sighed into his shoulder.

'What?' he said.

'Nothing,' I said, pulling back and kissing him smack on the lips. He started kissing me back like he was a starving orphan and I was the best burger in the world, but I had to pull away from him. It took some willpower but I knew what we had to do now. 'Come and watch us electrocute Sexy Dead Boy.' I took his hand like some little girl who wanted her dad to see some kittens.

Louis held open the door of the Sciences block. 'Are you coming or what?' he said to Damian.

'Else what?' he said.

'Else you'll have to go home. Or stay out here on your own.'

Damian gave a quick look round, threw down his cigarette and scuffed after us, hanging back like a stroppy kid. A stroppy kid who'd been told he had to play nicely with the dead bloke.

Shocks

It was broad daylight but the college was still empty so we had the place to ourselves. We tried shocking Sexy Dead Boy again.

Twice.

Fizzzzzzzzzaaaaaa juddddddddda fizzzzzzzzzzzzzzzzzzzzz crack a judddda.

Fizzzzzzzzzaaaaaa juddddddddda fizzzzzzzzzzzzzzzzzzzzz crack a judddda.

And each time, Zoe had her scopey thing at the ready to hear the heartbeats. But they never came. Louis held my hand. Pee Wee was asleep under the sink. Above him, Damian sat on the draining board and tried not to look. The sight of Sexy Dead Boy writhing and squirming had him totally freaked out but the alternative – being left on his own – was much worse. He was getting used to it though, I could tell. He'd stopped retching and had even looked over twice. The two electrocution attempts didn't singe Sexy Dead Boy, and the second time we all swore he'd taken a breath. The chest had definitely gone up and then down again. None of us could deny it.

She went for a third time.

Fizzzzzzzzzaaaaaa juddddddddda fizzzzzzzzzzzzzzzzzzzz crack a juddddda.

'Did you see that?' Damian shrieked, jumping down from the draining board and running over, still keeping a safe distance. 'He opened both his eyes, he did! Just for a second, he did!'

Zoe put her scopey thing on Sexy Dead Boy's chest. We all waited. Nothing.

Without any warning, Zoe went ballistic. She kicked over the tray of knives and empty syringes. Swept pots and beakers from the surfaces. Smashed test tubes and bottles against the walls. Sent everything banging and crashing and sliding across the floor. I felt awful. I put my arms around Louis and he cuddled me in.

'Well that ain't gonna help no one, is it?' said Damian as the contents of the shelving units rolled and clattered about the floor.

Zoe paced up and down the length of Sexy Dead Boy's body, tapping his knees, checking his chest, shining her tiny torch into his lifeless eyes. She leaned over his face, listening.

Sexy Dead Boy's eyes batted once.

'Did you see that?' she shouted. 'Did you see THAT?'

'I saw it, I totally did!' said Damian. 'You're unbeliev-able! You're a genius!' They fist bumped. Zoe and Damian actually fist bumped. I couldn't believe it.

'Could have been a muscle spasm?' said Louis. 'The ones we get at the funeral parlour do that sometimes. Freaks us out when they open their eyes or fart or some-thing but it's just a leftover reaction or escaping air. It doesn't mean anything.'

'It means there was life present and that there could be life present again,' said Zoe. 'What am I doing wrong?'

'I hate to say it but did you know there's a cookery course in the Food and Nutrition room at half nine?' said Louis, still holding my hand.

'What?' cried Zoe.

'Yeah,' said Damian, still looking away, 'and middle-aged women's aerobics in the gym at lunch. We're going to have to make ourselves scarce for the day.'

'Now you tell me,' she said, her head falling back in utter exasperation.

'We can come back later,' said Damian, which I thought was actually quite a helpful thing to say. For Damian.

'Yeah, we'll cover him up and you can lock the door, Zoe,' I suggested. 'He'll be okay until tonight.'

'And what about refrigeration?' she said, hands on hips.

'I'll whack up the air con,' said Louis, and I felt the ache of his hand leaving mine as he went to the wall and flicked down the plastic cover on the room temp box. He pressed a couple of the buttons and in seconds, I felt the room go as cold as a fridge.

Zoe nodded. She seemed happy. Unfulfilled, antsy and tired, but happy.

It was still only half past eight when we made it into town. Nothing was open so we basically walked the streets, sat in bus shelters, sat on the roundabout in the park, kicked pine cones and conkers around. (Zoe didn't.) Me and Louis kissed a lot. Damian and Zoe argued a lot. And Pee Wee chased wasps and did wees a lot. I had a good time. I really liked being with them. It was like having Lynx and Poppy back, but kind of better.

The seafront cafe Wonkies opened at ten and we were the first ones in.

'Who fancies a fry-up?' said Damian, rubbing his hands in glee. 'I'm having the full monty – double egg, bangers, five rashers, beans, black pudding, fried bread and mushies. Loser?'

'I'm not that hungry, Dame,' said Louis, getting out his wallet. 'I'll get this though if anyone else wants anything. Camille?'

'I'm not hungry either,' I said. Then I had a little think. 'We could share some toast though?' I never EVER shared food usually but at that moment, I didn't actually mind.

'Yeah, all right.' Louis smiled, offering Damian a ten pound note. 'And a hot chocolate. We could share that too.'

'You two are gonna be at it like rabbits, aren't you?' Damian laughed as Louis blushed full on in both cheeks. 'Put your cash away; this is on me. Blue Eyes, can I tempt you?' he said to Zoe.

Zoe shook her head and continued to stare out of the window.

'And a couple of sausages for Pee Wee,' I called after Damian when he'd gone up to the counter. 'You should eat something, Zoe,' I said. 'You haven't eaten anything for yonks.'

'I'm fine,' she said. She carried on staring out of the window.

Louis held my hand on the table and did this wind-screen-wiper thing with his thumb on my hand. I liked it a lot. If Zoe hadn't been there, I would have just kissed him on the mouth and stayed like that for however long, I wouldn't even have thought about time. But then I remembered. I remembered how much it had hurt me to see Lynx and Damian kissing all those times. How annoying Poppy and Splodge had been and how ignored I'd felt. That might be how Zoe was feeling, watching us hold hands. There would be tons of time to kiss him later. I dropped his hand. He frowned.

'Just for a bit,' I whispered. He nodded but he looked like Pee Wee did when I took his empty bowl away.

Damian came back to the table, order placed, pushing fifty pound notes back in his wallet. 'So what we doin' after this then? Fancy going dogging?'

'What?' said Louis.

'I heard about this lay-by on the outskirts of town where they do it at all hours. We could just watch if you want.'

I looked at him with complete disgust, and then he folded over with laughter. 'Your faces! Pulling your leg, aren't I? Christ, why's everyone so miz?'

'Why do you think, Dame?' said Louis, his eyes darting towards Zoe.

'Oh come on, beautiful,' said Damian, sitting next to Zoe and putting his arm round her. 'You just need a break from it, that's all. Tell you what, why don't we all go back to mine, I'll kick Dad up to the golf course for a couple of hours and we can chillax till tonight and maybe come up with a new plan to get your corpse working. There's loads we can do. PSP. Snooker. Dad's gym's up and running now too. I bench pressed 200 pounds last week, Lou.'

'Great,' said Louis, who'd probably been forced to watch him bench press lots of times before.

'Or we could sling some steaks on the BBQ and have a pool party if you like. You two could nip home and get your bikinis on.' He winked at me. 'It's October,' I said. 'Don't matter. Pool's heated. Still can't use the hot tub though.'

'He had an accident,' Louis told me.

'Had a couple of birds in there in the summer and the patio heater fell in and electrocuted 'em.' He sniggered and lay back until his chair tilted. 'They weren't best pleased,' he laughed. 'Even less when they found the vids on the Internet the next day.'

'You gave them second-degree burns!' said Louis as our food arrived. He ate a piece of toast, I went to drink the hot chocolate but it was nuclear so I put it down and tried panting to cool my scorched tongue tip. I broke up Pee Wee's sausages and put them on a napkin on the floor for him. He dived right in.

'Yeah, well, they were the ones who suggested filming it,' Damian said. He grabbed the ketchup bottle, flipped it over in the air and caught it at the neck, squirting it all over his food.

'Ugh. You tape girls when you have . . .'

Damian shrugged and tucked into his fried breakfast. 'Yeah. Dad still does a bit sometimes too. We got quite a library going.'

'You're joking,' I said, trying the hot chocolate again. Still scorchio.

'No, he's not joking,' said Louis.

Zoe was looking at Damian, equally disgusted. Then out of nowhere, as he was tucking into his beans and sausage, she grabbed hold of his chin and turned his face towards her. 'You electrocuted two girls in your hot tub?' she said slowly.

Damian chewed and then gulped. 'Yeah . . .'

The same thought seemed to dawn on him too. I looked at Louis, but we were still none the wiser.

'Are you thinking what I'm thinking?' Damian said to her.

Zoe nodded. 'Galvanic bath.'

'Huh?' I said.

'Water and electricity,' said Damian.

'Like, the worst combination ever,' said Louis.

Zoe looked like she was in pain. 'Oh how could I not have thought of this before? Water is a highly-efficient conductor of electricity.'

Louis chewed a corner of his toast. He'd caught on too. 'Yeah! In one of my favourite films, *The Son of*

Frankenstein's Daughter, the professor reanimates this dead boy by putting him in this water tank. Then he adds the electrodes.'

'And SALT!' cried Zoe, grabbing the salt cellar off Damian who was merrily shaking it all over his mushrooms. 'We have to put him in a salt bath and *then* we apply the electrical source. It's so obvious! Water combined with salt acts as the perfect electrical conductor. We put him in a salt bath, apply a low voltage direct current and the electromagnetic field will greatly improve the circulation of the blood and the serum!' She looked at Louis and Damian in turn. 'You are both geniuses!'

Louis smiled and his cheeks went to Volcano Town. Damian laughed and wiped his mouth with a serviette.

Now I had caught on. 'But where will we get a bath from?' I asked.

'DIY place on the roundabout?' said Damian. 'They do baths.'

'Yeah,' said Louis.

'Or the hot tub at my place?' said Damian.

'Can you lie down in it?' I said.

'No,' said Damian. 'But you could prop him up with summing.'

'A hot tub is no good,' said Zoe. 'The modern ones tend to have plastic or polymer bases. The charge would be too hot. It would melt. Keep thinking.'

'Can't you just chuck him in a swimming pool and sling a toaster in after him?' suggested Damian, slurping a curl of bacon fat over his bean-smeared lips.

Zoe looked at him. 'Do you want to be the test subject

then? No, the bath has to be sterilised, an insulated tank capable of withstanding a powerful surge of electricity, ideally transparent as well.'

'Fish tank,' said Louis.

'What?'

'A fish tank. You can get some that are capable of withstanding really powerful electrical surges. For electric eels and barbs.'

'How the hell we going to get him in a fish tank?' laughed Damian. 'You'd have to chop him up again and I ain't doin' that! Geezer's been through enough.'

'We could get a big one, like the one they've got at Fat Pang's in town.'

'Perfect!' said Zoe. 'Would it be easy to remove?'

'Oh you can't remove it,' said Louis. 'It's full of fish. I just meant you need something *like* the one at Fat Pang's, not actually that one.'

'It's Saturday today,' said Damian. 'Most of 'em will be eaten at the All You Can Eat Buffet tonight. It'll be near empty so if we go in after hours, we just take out what's left and El Dunno. Sweet as a nut.'

'But how?' I said. 'Even if we do manage to get it out of the restaurant, how are we going to get it back to the college? We can't use my mum's nail art van, the tank's way too big. And also, we're kinda using the battery out of it too.'

It was like a light bulb had exploded above Damian's head. 'We'll get one of the Stiffmobiles from your place, Lou, yeah? Be long enough, wouldn't it?'

'We can't steal a massive fish tank from a Chinese

restaurant!' Louis cried, lowering his voice in case the waitress heard. 'Oh, you're joking.'

Zoe's face was glowing. Damian was wired, bouncing around on his chair like he was ready for action. 'Let's do it,' she said, and Damian smiled at her, for all the world like a boy who wasn't a total slut bag but was actually quite liking a girl for once. If it had been any other boy, I'd have thought he had just fallen madly in love. But it was Damian after all.

After we'd finished, we left a tip for the waitress and walked in the sheeting rain to Brite Street and the front window of Fat Pang's Chinese Fish Restaurant. It was closed until midday but we could all see the large glowing blue fish tank at the back of the room.

'There it is,' Damian pointed through the glass. 'There's our baby.'

'It's gonna be so tricky. I don't think we can do it,' said Louis. 'I don't want any of the fish to die either.'

'It's a bit late to be concerned about them, Lou,' Damian laughed. 'Most of 'em will be in a pancake or a curry by closing time anyway.'

'I don't care. I can't kill fish,' he said.

I touched his arm. 'We can find some bowls to put them in. They'll be okay. That's all right, isn't it?' I asked Zoe.

'Definitely,' she said, more geared up than ever. I could have sworn that she and Damian exchanged a little smile too, but it could have been my eyes playing tricks on me.

'But how exactly will we remove it?' said Zoe. 'It must weigh a ton. It'll be too heavy for us to carry, won't it?'

Louis slapped Damian on the back. 'Not for someone who can bench press 200 pounds it's not, eh?'

All four of us took one last look in the window and turned to make our way back to college. We passed the television shop on the way. Sky News. I read the headline. *Missing model found safe in Paris.* I felt relief. I felt bad for ever doubting Zoe. And I felt Louis' hand as it took mine and held it tightly.

Four teenagers in a stolen hearse wearing stolen Halloween masks

'Pee Wee, anyone comes in, you bark at them, okay? Guard Sexy Dead Boy. And don't eat him,' I said and put the last of the rotten fingers down before him to keep him busy while I tied the end of his lead to the handle of the teacher's desk. Then we locked the lab doors and started the walk back into town in the dark.

We waited inside a hearse outside the funeral parlour, watching Fat Pang's across the street. We were all squished in the front seats, each wearing a Halloween mask that we had stolen from the Art department at college. We did our best not to look like four teenagers in a stolen hearse wearing stolen Halloween masks, but that's exactly what we were. We were a gang. A really weird gang, but still a gang.

When it had been me, Lynx and Poppy I'd always felt like the outsider. But here, I felt important. I was Zoe's best friend (whether she liked it or not). I was Damian's 'one who got away'. And I was Louis' own proper girlfriend. The gang didn't work without me and I liked sitting in the dark with them.

'Are you sure this is necessary?' Zoe complained, rubbing where the elastic cut into her ear. Her mask was a witch's face.

'Yeah,' said Damian, lifting up his black cat mask. 'I told you there's CCTV inside. I checked it out before.'

'Won't you get in trouble, Louis?' I said. 'People will know it's your hearse.' My mask was a pumpkin.

'No,' he said. 'Any passer by will just think the hearse is parked out front for the night. We leave them out for cleaning sometimes.' He was a pumpkin too.

All our voices were muffled and hollow-sounding behind the masks and my face was getting sweaty. I lifted mine up and saw a group of people coming out of the restaurant. They crossed the road towards us and waited at the bus stop. They lit cigarettes and chatted beneath the orange street light. They didn't see us. Another group came out just after them, all laughing and happy and full of spare ribs and fried rice, some carrying doggy bags and gift bags. There were two people at the back of the crowd I recognised, but before I could say a word, Louis and Damian both said what I was thinking.

'It's Splodge!'

'And Poppy!' I said, seeing the red-headed girl with her arm linking his. Her hair looked bouncy and clean and she looked like she'd put on some weight too. He had his arm around her and they looked really happy. It was so good to see her, but even if I could have done I wouldn't have thought of going over to say hi. I got the feeling I would be the one left feeling stupid if I told her how worried I'd been about her. It looked like she didn't have a care in the world.

'Splodge!' Louis said again, and made to get out of the hearse, before Damian reached across me and Zoe and pulled him back inside.

'What are you doing, you idiot? They'll see us!' He slammed the door shut.

'I want to know where he's been this last week,' said Louis.

'We can't be seen by anyone, Lou. Even them. Everyone's gonna know about this by tomorrow morning and I can't take the risk of anyone seeing me, not with my record,' said Damian.

'What a . . . dick,' spat Louis.

'Hold up, there's no need for that.'

'Not you. Splodge,' Louis sighed. 'He disappears for days, not a word to either of us, his two oldest mates, and then he just . . . comes back, like nothing's happened.' We watched them walk along the road. A fat woman who looked just like Splodge, but in a dress, was giving Poppy a thoroughly disapproving look as she kissed Splodge full on the lips. The woman was holding a big gold gift bag and a man who I assumed was Splodge's dad was holding a large blue-and-red balloon with HAPPY ANNIVERSARY spelled out in gold letters. He was giving them a filthy look as well.

'Doesn't look like his parents approve of the union much,' said Zoe.

'He's totally dropped us, Dame,' Louis mumbled.

'Probably couldn't carry the weight of that ego anymore,' Zoe muttered, nodding to Damian. I smiled.

'What?' said Damian. 'Oh who gives a toss about him anyway. He's moved on. Let him rot, we got bigger fish to fry, right?'

'Right,' said Zoe. I looked at her. Zoe and Damian in agreement again. Wow. Just, wow.

Louis still looked so wounded from seeing Splodge. I knew exactly how he felt. It was exactly how I'd felt seeing Lynx that day in Marks & Spencer, and how I felt now, seeing Poppy with Splodge's family. But I'd had more time to get used to the idea of losing them – to him it was still really raw.

'Poppy didn't tell me she was back either,' I said to him. 'And I've texted her loads of times.'

'She's got a new phone, ain't she?' said Damian. 'His dad got her a deal on it. He's bought himself one of them with the fold-out screens and direct line to NASA and all that.'

I remembered her showing it to me on the Pier the night of the smooshed nose. 'So she wasn't ignoring me,' I said. 'She must have changed her number and just . . . hasn't given me the new one.'

'Look, forget them, both of them,' said Damian. 'Let's stick to the plan, all right?'

We waited ages, at least another half an hour. I didn't mind the wait so much, but Zoe and Damian did. I softly pinched Louis' earlobe. I could do that now. It wasn't like being at a checkout and wanting to do it to a stranger who had cute earlobes and who would think I was odd for suddenly fiddling with them. I could fiddle with Louis' earlobes as much as I wanted. He liked it. His neck went all goosepimply and he smiled like a puppy having his ears tickled. I was glad that made him happy. A movement through the windscreen caught my eye. 'Someone's coming out.'

We watched as the waitresses left the restaurant. A light went off behind the bar inside. All four of us had tipped up our masks to get a better look. We watched as a figure moved towards the window and closed the slatted blinds. A man in a grey suit then another man in black stepped down from the doorstep and the first man put his key in the door to lock it. 'Is that Fat Pang?'

'Nah, that's just his sons,' said Damian. 'Fat Pang's about ninety stone and housebound. Might even be chop suey by now, I dunno.'

'They look like scary guys, like they do martial arts and stuff,' said Louis.

'I done a bit of ju-jitsu and aikido and all that in me time. Piece of piss. You just gotta front it out, blud. "The stance maketh the man," as my sensei once said.'

Louis scoffed. 'You did half an hour of karate in summer school when we were eleven and you didn't like it cos you had to take your Nikes off.'

'Whatevs. Anyway, here's the plan,' said Damian as we looked at him. 'Loser, you drive the stiff wagon round the back into Poe Street. I know the gate code . . . '

'How do you know the gate code?' asked Zoe.

'Does it matter? Point is, I do. It's 22468410. This disables the kitchen alarm too. Reverse in and wait for me to jimmy open the back door to the kitchens. Grab whatever container you can find, like them big buckets the fryer oil comes in, they'll be good. See if there's a few of them around. Then take them through to the dining room and start chucking in the fish. We got to get that water and them fish out of that tank as fast as we can. I reckon about twenty minutos should just about do it but if we can do it in fifteen, sweet. But we'll have to shimmy.'

'Have you done this before?' I asked him.

'Course,' said Damian. 'You don't think I'd lead an expedition without knowing my way round the mountain, do ya?'

Louis threw me a little look and I grinned at him. Zoe looked like it was all just a big fat boring waste of her time.

'All right, you animals,' said Damian, lowering his mask. 'Let's go hunting.'

Fish can be so romantic

The minute we got inside, we decided to ditch the masks to the backs of our heads – we just couldn't see anything properly. Damian found a way of switching the cameras off in the restaurant so it wasn't really necessary from then on.

It was bright inside Fat Pang's, thanks to the neon glow of the enormalous fish tank at the kitchen end of the dining room. I'd never been in there before but I'd seen it from the outside and it looked just magical. The floor was covered with an endless gold-and-red carpet and on the giant tables were gold tablecloths, cutlery and napkins and emerald encrusted chopsticks and little gold cat figurines with waving paws. Big green and blue dragons hung on every wall and there was a gorgeous smell of sticky fried pork and noodles.

I stood looking at it all for ages, gazing at how everything looked so beautiful glinting in the neon light. The huge 'specials' board on the wall was offering the most wonderful-sounding dishes – fugu fish platters with stir fried noodles; spicy Devil's fork squid with fresh chilli and ginger; tinker shark soup. I quite fancied the sound of the sweet and sour harlequin trout and the Szechuan style samurai carp or even the electrobarb satay on sticks. It all sounded so delish . . .

'Camille!'

. . . and I imagined the customers would pick what they wanted off the board, then they'd look in the fish tank and pick out the creature they wanted (maybe they'd seen a tasty-looking tinker fish or a squid giving them the eye), and then the chef would come out and catch the fish and cook it for them, right at their table. How grim? One minute this lovely little trout is swimming about, nibbling at reeds and thinking his biggest problem is if he'll be first to grab the fish flake, and the next, he's being rubbed with garlic and burned alive. No wonder Louis didn't eat fish.

'Camille!' whispered Zoe, who was standing behind me with a large blue plastic barrel and a length of rubber tubing. 'Will you come and take the end of this tube?' Zoe showed me what siphoning was. It involved sucking one end of a rubber tube and putting it in the fish-tank water, while dangling the other end over an empty blue plastic oil tub that we had found in the kitchen. She went a little further up the tank and did the same, until two oil barrels were full. She then went and got two more tubs from the kitchen and brought them in and we had to do the whole thing again. Then it was action stations.

'Hold that end.'

'Grab that eel.'

'Fetch another bucket.'

'Stop clowning.'

'There's a crab by your foot.'

'Get that fish in the ice bucket.'

The boys concentrated on bailing water and finding fishing nets so they could safely take out as many of the fish as possible before all the water went. Louis was getting soaked, mostly because Damian was soaking him. For ages, it was just Zoe barking orders and the boys messing around.

It didn't take long to free the tank once the water and fish were safely out. It began to shift on its shelf perch and though it was heavy, we'd be able to move it. The fish were everywhere though. Glitter guppies, laser fish and reef snakes in buckets all around us. A black-and-white samurai carp in the ice bucket on the bar. Jellyfish in the bathroom sinks. A few harlequin trout in one of the deep kitchen sinks and a whole shoal of electrobarbs in the other one. There were even tiny fishes in bowls on the tables.

'Wish we could set them all free,' Louis sighed when we'd all but finished. He came over to my barrel with his net full of yellow shrimp. 'Wish we could let them all go back into the ocean where they came from.'

'Why can't we?' I asked him. He was soaked to the skin, and his muscly bits clung to the material of his shirt. His arms were really toned and strong too, I supposed because of all the dead bodies and coffins he lugs about all the time.

'These are tropical fish,' he said. 'We can't set them free anywhere round here.'

'Oh right,' I said, doing the tube thing again, trying not to look at him. I'd never really understood before what women meant when they said they'd gone 'weak at the knees', but now I saw Louis in his wet t-shirt, I knew what it felt like. I was kind of thrilled and scared at the same time, because he was so close to me. About as far as the length of my long ruler.

Louis pinched at his clingy t-shirt, then all of a sudden put his hands behind his neck and pulled the thing clean off his body so his top half was naked. I didn't know where to look at first. Damian saw him do it and did the same, so suddenly both of them were standing there, half-naked, wringing out their t-shirts into the water-filled barrels, laughing away. Damian went into the kitchen and came back with two plastic parcels – new white Fat Pang's t-shirts, meant for Fat Pang's staff. He threw one across to Louis, who ripped into it.

'I can ask Zoe if we can save some of the fish if you like?' I suggested to him, trying not to look at his hard man-nipples.

'I think we've enough on our plates trying to get this thing out unnoticed,' said Zoe, struggling past with a heavy-looking barrel full of water and lobsters, 'without making a pit stop to release some guppies back into the wild. Damian?' she called.

Damian appeared behind her. 'M'lady?' he said, with a sweeping bow.

'There's a big bag of salt in the larder. Help me get it into the hearse.'

'As you wish,' he said, following her out to the kitchen. He turned back to Louis and whispered, 'I'm so gonna tap that,' pointing at Zoe.

'You're not,' Zoe called back and Damian seemed amazed she had heard him.

Louis walked over to one of the booth seats and picked something up. He came over to me and held up two little sandwich bags, tied at the top with a knot. The second the corners of the bags touched, a burst of blue light shot from one of them to the other. There were tiny little fish inside.

'I kept these two back, for us,' he said. 'Electrobarbs. They're cousins of the anchovy. One for you; one for me. Don't show Zoe and Damian, they'll make me put them back.' He handed me my fish bag.

'Why did you take them?' I asked.

He shrugged. 'I thought you'd like them. I know it's stealing. But there comes a point when you're in the process of stealing something so big and so wrong, that one more little wrong thing doesn't seem to matter.'

I smiled.

'I know you're not really interested in fish stuff but these fish are true romantics. See?' He gently tapped the side of the bag. 'That little flash of light means they're attracted to each other. They're letting each other know where they are. They court for ages by adjoining the suckers on their fins, almost like they're holding hands. How cool is that?'

'That is pretty cool,' I said, looking in the bags. The fish were tiny and pretty but not nearly as pretty as the glitter guppies or even the multicoloured reef snakes. And yet they both had a little line of electric blue running through their bodies, which looked gorgeous when it lit up. I untied the knot on the top of my fish bag. 'They should be in the same bag. It's not fair to keep them apart, is it?'

Louis smiled and opened his bag. I poured my fish in with it. Once the two fish had settled, we knotted the bag and watched as their fins locked. They were together.

'That's the most cutest thing I've ever seen,' I said, beaming from the tippy-most part of one ear to the other.

Louis beamed too. He had the deepest dimples. I leaned in to his face, stopping at his cheek, and I planted my lips there.

I pulled back. He looked at me. And then he took the plunge and went straight for my lips again. And we stayed there for a while like that, lips to lips, locked like the fish. I could have stayed there all night, my arms wrapped around his shoulders, touching his soggy hair ends.

Then Damian totally killed the moment.

'Come on, dickheads, stop fannying about and gis a hand with this tank.' He had a handful of greasy chips he'd found in one of the kitchen fryers and tipped his head back to down them all.

We got into position at one end of the fish tank and Louis rested the fish bag inside so it was safe.

Zoe eyeballed Damian in disgust. 'I'm actually amazed you don't have gills yourself,' she muttered, taking her position beside him.

One of us at each corner, on three we shifted the tank off its perch and heaved it down, carefully, slowly, heavily

– painfully heavily – through the kitchen, out into the yard and into the back of the hearse. We'd barely got the back door shut when there came the most deafening noise.

BrrrrrrrrrrRRRReeeeeeeeeeeeEEEEEaaaaEEEEaaaaEEEE aaaaEEEEaaaa.

I clamped my hands over my ears. 'What on earth is that?'

'Ah shit, we must have tripped a sensor!' yelled Damian as I clamped my hands over my ears.

'I thought the code you put in ensured we wouldn't set any alarms off,' Zoe shouted over the racket.

'I thought it would!' he shouted back. 'Must be a back up. Come on, let's motor!'

Louis dived into the driver's seat and started the engine as me and Zoe launched in through the passenger side. Damian opened the driver's door and started to shove Louis over.

'Oi!'

'You drive like a fat bird on downers, mate. Leave it to the master.'

Louis scooched over, without argument, putting our bag of fish in the glove box.

Then it was over to Damian.

He drove that hearse like he was back on the pier playing Zombie Road Rage 3. We all clung on for dear life. It still wasn't fast enough for him though. 'Shoulda brought Dad's Porsche,' he said, taking a sideways look at Zoe, as though trying to impress her. 'Dad can do 200 in that when it's been raining.'

'We wouldn't have had room for the tank though,

would we?' said Zoe, glaring at him but keeping hold of her seat and the holdy handle at the top of the door.

'Oh yeah,' said Damian, changing gear.

Me and Louis clung to each other and kept our masks down the whole way. Damian's was on the back of his head upside down. I didn't know where Zoe's had gone.

'Eat that, ya . . .' Damian spurted a load of swear words aimed at the drivers we passed. As we'd turned the corner of Poe Street, a police car started following.

'Will you slow down just the tiniest bit so we can all get out backsides back on our seats please, Damian,' Zoe yelled.

'Ooh I love it when you call me Damian,' he grinned.

'All right, moron, can you slow down, please?'

'You wanna get caught, do ya?' he laughed. 'You actually want to explain this to the feds?'

'Feds? What are you talking about, feds?'

'The old bill and that.'

'It's one police car with one local underpaid policeman behind the wheel. And he's probably half asleep.'

I could barely hear her for the screeching of our tyres. The few people on the road whizzed past us, so we were pretty sure they hadn't seen us for dust, or at least the spray off our wheels. We flew along the deserted roads, passed just-closing pubs and blurry late-night snack shacks – our big glass coffin sliding around in the back of the hearse like it was on ice. Louis put his arm behind me and grabbed on to one side of the coffin to try and keep it still. I put my hand on the other side and did the same.

'Move it, you little f . . .' Damian yelled at a cat who

was wandering aimlessly in the middle of the road by the Tesco roundabout, but he soon moved.

As a blur of orange street lights lit our way back towards college, there suddenly came a *WAW waw WAW waw WAW waw WAW waw* sound behind us. Quite a way behind us, but still very much behind us. Two police cars.

'Oh what now?' yelled Damian, craning his neck to look behind him. 'How the hell did they mobilise so quick?'

Damian took us down all sorts of little back alleys and lanes where a hearse had no business being, over speed bumps and rubbish bags and dustbin lids, but the police cars stayed locked on, until we got to the traffic lights by the pier and we realised we had lost them.

'I'll be amazed if that tank makes it back in one piece,' sighed Zoe as we rolled to a stop.

Damian pulled up the handbrake and we all looked behind. 'Where did they go? Anyone see them?'

'I don't know,' said Louis. The road behind was completely empty. Some fish and chip shop awnings flapped in the sea breeze. Some milkshake cartons clattered about the pavement. A street light flickered. Nothing else.

'Blimey oh crikey that was close,' I said, as the lights changed to green.

We rounded the bend to begin the steep climb up the winding streets of Clairmont Hill. The police car appeared again, way behind us but definitely locked on again and gaining on us.

'I don't believe it, he's back, he's back!' yelled Louis.

'I'm on it,' said Damian, putting his foot down again so our heads were thrust to the backs of our seats as the hearse roared up the hill, faster and faster. I didn't know hearses could go so fast. He floored it down the other side to the boulevard shops and Stoker Street, running parallel to the High Street. He hit the main road out of town and took the first right at the roundabout all the way onto Beach Road, where he spun the screeching hearse sharply left and onto the drive at the front of college. He parked it behind the bank of pine trees outside the Languages block and flicked off the engine. We waited, panting, wiping the windows clean of our breaths so we could see out, watching and listening and waiting and waiting and waiting. Eventually, the siren sound came closer and we saw the car speed past the entrance, a flash of blue-and-red and a scream of siren, and then it was gone. It hadn't seen us.

Damian turned on the engine again and slowly reversed the hearse back along the concrete towards the Science block. Home and dry.

Well, almost. There was just one tiny problem.

'You *are* joking,' said Zoe.

'Nope, that sucker ain't gonna go in there, no chance,' said Damian.

'Even if we tilt it? How about upending it?'

'Nah, too long and too wide.'

I could hear Pee Wee yapping for me inside the lab. 'What are we going to do then?'

We had got it into the building and as far as the door

to the Chemistry lab and there we had stopped. The fish tank wouldn't fit.

Damian shrugged. 'What do you want me to do about it? I can't take the wall down, can I?'

'Dudes, this is getting way heavy,' said Louis, straining to hold onto our end of the fish tank. I could hear Pee Wee barking inside the lab.

'It's okay, Peeps, I'm here,' I called to him and he woofed back as though he was happy to hear my voice.

At the other end of the tank, Zoe scowled at Damian. 'You could at least take the door off its hinges. Can't you even do that?'

'Nah, it still wouldn't go. That ain't gonna make no difference, taking it off its hinges.'

If we'd been anywhere else, doing anything else, they would have looked like an old married couple arguing about DIY.

Zoe looked exasperated. 'We HAVE to do this. We HAVE to get this done, before Monday. We've got no choice.'

'I hate to say this but it's now Sunday,' said Louis, grimacing with the pain of holding his corner of the tank, and nodding towards the clock. 'It's a quarter to four in the morning.'

'Sssshhh!' I said. I'd heard something.

And we all heard it then. Screaming sirens in the distance.

'Look, if we're gonna do this, we ain't got a lot of choice, have we?' said Damian.

'Meaning?' said Zoe, adjusting her grip on the tank.

'Meaning, there's no point standing here moaning because there's nothing we can do about it. The lab's a non-starter. We've got to find somewhere else. Somewhere with double doors or summing.'

At the other end of the corridor, after the two sets of double doors, was the gymnasium. 'The gym has double doors?' I suggested.

'We don't have the KEY,' said Zoe, the word 'key' sounding like it had a hammer attached to it.

'You don't need a key with me around, sweetheart,' Damian smirked. 'I can break your doors in for you, no bother.'

Zoe thinned her eyes and turned her face back to me. 'What about an electrical supply?'

'Um . . . well, there are ceiling lights, aren't there?'

'Yeah,' said Louis. 'There's a fuse box on the wall I think. If you've got a length of wire, you could hook him up to the fuse box. Or the electronic scoreboard in the—'

'Yes!' cried Zoe. 'I could re-route the electrical streams!' she interrupted. 'That's excellent, you two!'

I beamed. Louis beamed. Us two had figured it out together. My heart skipped a beat. And now it was all about getting Sexy Dead Boy's heart started. That was all that mattered.

Big fat trouble

The next ten minutes went by like Damian's driving: fast and furious. And, for me, flappy. Everyone else seemed to know exactly what they were doing. Zoe was in charge of Sexy Dead Boy, Louis was sent to find scouring pads and sterilising solution to clean the tank, Damian crowbarred our way into the gym with a crowbar he found in the Design and Technology room (I'd always thought crowbar was a verb – I didn't know they actually existed) and I went to see if Pee Wee was all right and then rushed back to join them.

'Camille, we need you,' Zoe called to me as I stood by the gym doors pretending to be some kind of lookout, not that there was anything to look out for – everything was dead quiet. I helped them carry the tank over to the far wall, in front of the back doors and directly underneath the pull-out electronic scoreboard where Zoe wanted it. Zoe then made us scrub the tank totally clean before Sexy Dead Boy went into it. The huge gym echoed as we worked, our shoes squeaking and thudding and scuffing loudly across the wooden floor. We used the gardener's hose from the tap just outside the back doors to get the fresh cold water Zoe wanted to fill the tank with and filled it with the salt from Fat Pang's. When we'd done all that it was ready for Sexy Dead Boy.

'On my count . . . one, two, three,' said Zoe, and on three, we gently lowered his freezing body into the water-filled tank. Even Damian was careful with him.

I hated to think what might happen if he didn't come to life this time. How Zoe might feel. What Zoe might do. This was our last chance and it *had* to work. For her sake, it had to work.

Once SDB was floating in the tank, everyone stopped talking and just looked at him. Then we all looked at each other. I reached for Louis' hand and he held it tightly. Then, much closer than before came the whining noise of police sirens.

'Oh my God!' I cried, my voice bouncing off the stone walls. 'It's them. They're coming for us!'

'Quick, get the copper wire from the Biology lab, Camille. Hurry!' Zoe called to me and I darted towards the exit. 'We need something to bar the doors,' I heard her shout as I ran.

'What can I do?' said Louis.

'Just don't let them in, don't let them in!' she shouted. 'Just stop them from coming in!'

The sirens sounded louder outside.

When I came back with the copper wire, Zoe snatched it from me and began tying it around Sexy Dead Boy's wrists and told Damian to do the same with his ankles.

'Camille, go and see how Louis is doing with the doors. Go!' Zoe barked at me and I immediately ran across the court to the main doors to help him. He was using a skipping rope to tie the door handles together.

'What are they doing?' I asked him, looking back at Zoe who was on Damian's shoulders and doing something at the back of the electronic scoreboard.

'They're creating a wire circuit between the scoreboard and the lighting panel,' he said, still winding the rope tightly around the handles, just as we heard movement out in the corridor.

'Can they do that?' I said.

Louis shrugged, coming to the end of his rope. 'They're both pretty good at Chemistry, aren't they? I don't know.' He tugged on the rope to check it was secure. 'I guess we'll find out now, won't we?'

Damian gave us the thumbs up and Zoe climbed down off his shoulders. She stood over by the light switches and Damian went and stood opposite her. Louis and I stayed exactly where we were and held hands.

There were sounds right outside the gym. Fists banged on the doors.

'Open up!' a voice called.

'They're here!' I shouted across the gym to Zoe.

'I'm going to flick the switches on three!' she shouted as she backed against the wall. 'One, two . . .'

'Three,' I whispered and all at once the switches went down and the ceiling lights exploded as *shooooooooooom* went the charge all along the wires, faster than lightning.

Sssszzzzzzzzzzzzzssssssssssssssssszzzzzzzzzzackackackackackackcackackack!

The glass sides of the tank lit up, a neon blue rectangle of fire with a shuddering man lying inside it.

FizzzzzZZZZZZZZZZZZZZZZZZZZZZZZZapssssssshhhhhpsssssshhhhhhh.

'Turn it off!' Louis shouted as water splashed out of the tank and all over the gym floor. The panel of switches was on fire.

'I can't, the switches are melting!' Zoe yelled back, trying to touch them but pulling her hands back because of the heat.

'It's too much charge, it'll blow up!' Damian shouted.

Louis turned and started undoing the ropes on the doors.

'No!' I cried.

'We've got to get out of here, Camille. This whole place could go up.'

'Up where?' I said.

'Up in smoke,' he said. 'Help me!'

Fire coursed along the ceiling as I started forcing open the ropes with him. Damian skidded over and helped until we had unravelled the ropes and freed the doors, wrenching them open and tumbing out of the burning room in one pile of legs and arms, only to be grabbed by two police officers on the other side.

'Come here, you three.'

'No, please, it's gonna blow up. The whole place is gonna go up!' Louis shouted as one of the policemen held his arms and a policewoman held mine. Damian escaped them both and bolted for the end of the corridor before either could stop him.

'Bloody hell,' said the policeman, looking back into the gym. He saw the scene. He saw Sexy Dead Boy in the tank. There was no hiding our secret any more. 'What the . . .'

'That sodding de Jager again!' the policewoman shouted. Then she saw it too. 'Jesus . . . they've got a body in there.'

Ceiling tiles were starting to fall and flames were licking up the climbing ropes on the side wall. That was when they started to pull us away.

'Zoe, we have to wait for Zoe!' I cried.

'She won't leave him, Camille. Come on, let them deal with it now!' Louis called as the policeman held his hands behind his back and guided him quickly along the corridor.

The policewoman talked into her radio. 'Yeah, one heading your way. Damian de Jager. One possible fatality. Male, by the looks. In some sort of fish tank . . . I've no idea what's been going on here . . . And a girl is still trapped but we can't get to her. We're bringing two more kids out . . . Yep, gymnasium.'

I saw Zoe as we were led away. She was standing close to the tank, gazing into it as Sexy Dead Boy juddered and shook and splashed in the water and the sparks got bigger and the tank was cracking and spewing and hissing water.

'Zoe, please!'

But she stayed where she was and just turned to look at me, in her shocking blue starey-eyed way. Through the flames and the noise and the falling ceiling tiles I could see that she was smiling.

And the last thing I saw was the ceiling as it collapsed in front of her.

Outside, the sound of sirens filled the air. Me, Louis and the police officers ran round to the front of the college where three police cars were parked in the driveway, red-and-blue lights flashing all over the place. Damian had been caught and was being frisked by a fat police officer with no neck. In the early morning sky, we could see flames beginning to shoot up at the back of the building. I heard one of the policemen on his walkie-talkie. From what I could gather, Fat Pang himself had called the police about the fish tank. So had Louis' dad about the missing hearse. And so had some woman across the road who'd seen us breaking into the college.

A fire engine wailed into view and pulled up sharply into the drive. Six firemen jumped out and started unreeling a long yellow hose from the back of the truck.

'Zoe's still in there. Please, she's my friend! She's in the gym!' I cried to one of them.

'Get back please, behind the cars,' he shouted at me just as two more fire engines arrived. I was so scared. I turned to Louis. 'She won't leave him in there. She won't leave him! She'll die for him, Louis.'

'It's okay, it's okay,' he said, hugging me into him.

'It'd be suicide going back in there, Camille,' said Damian, slouched hunched beside the police car. 'We can't help her.'

And it was then that I felt the plunge of dread in my stomach. 'Oh my God, Pee Wee!' I yanked away from Louis. 'Pee Wee!' I screamed. 'He's in the lab! I took him to the C-C-Chemistry lab. He's tied to one of the Bunsen burners! Oh my God, I forgot him!'

I made to run towards college, but Louis and a police-woman held me back.

'No one's going back in there. It's all right. We'll get your friends, don't worry.'

'My dog! My little dog's in there. He's only a baby, we have to get him! He's in the lab – it's just at the opposite end of the corridor to the gym. Please, if we're quick we can get to him, I know we can . . .'

'We can't, it's too dangerous,' said Louis. 'There're gas tanks in there, Camille.'

All around me the heavy black shoes of policemen clumped around, moving people back, stretching police tape all across the front of college. Fire hoses were pulled across the ground in every direction. I collapsed in a heap on the concrete, my head to the floor at Louis' feet. All I could see was his trainers and the rain puddles. Cigarette ends and splats of chewing gum. Flyers for freshers' night. Flyers for the Halloween party. All I could hear was the *plink* of glass breaking and the crackly roar of flames billowing out of the roof of the gym. The smells were of burning plastic and wood. All I could think about was my poor little dog, alone and burning inside the lab and I wept so hard. People shouted around me, telling people to, 'Get back. Come back!' I heard Damian yelling, 'It's not safe!' Then I realised I couldn't see Louis' trainers anymore. They'd disappeared. And so had he.

He'd gone back in. He'd gone back in for my little dog. Just as the building burst at the seams.

People who lived in the houses across the street were coming out in pyjamas and dressing gowns to have a look at what was going on.

I squirmed and wriggled with every muscle I had to get out of Damian's grip. 'No, Camille!' Damian yelled at me. 'Don't be stupid, it's suicide going in there.'

'Louis went in there! Louis went in there for Pee—'

'You're not going in there after him. Stupid . . . stop struggling. I'm trying to save your life, you dozy mare!'

I kicked and punched and burst out of Damian's grip and I ran my fastest ever around the side of the building. I could hear windows smashing in the distance and I felt the heat of the fire as it licked its way up the corridor. The Biology lab was already ablaze. I prayed the fire hadn't got as far as the Chemistry lab yet as I kept on running towards it.

'Louis!' I screamed, yanking back the door of the Science block and sprinting down the corridor. 'LOUIS!'

There was smoke already in the corridor, thick and black. It was boiling in there. The walls were sweating. A near-deafening squeal startled me as several frantic hamsters scuttled under the lockers outside the lab. The burning plastic stink was thick in my nose and it started catching in my throat. There was no actual way of getting to Zoe now.

Louis was untying Pee Wee when I got inside the lab. He saw me and his face looked angry. 'Camille! Get out of here, you stupid . . . What are you doing here?'

'I came to find you!' I cried, coughing all over him.

He tucked Pee Wee under his arm and grabbed hold of my hand. 'Come on, quick!' he coughed and we started running, as the windows all along the corridor began to explode, spraying glass outwards.

'The fire's getting closer!' I cried as we sprinted back down the corridor.

'I know, I know. Come on!'

'But Zoe . . .'

'We can't, Camille, we just can't get to her.'

As we darted out onto the concrete quad, there was another explosion and we just had time to sprint across to the Science block and dive behind the hearse. We huddled together over Pee Wee who was shaking in Louis' arms.

'It's all right, it's all right,' I whispered, out of breath and kissing Pee Wee's shivering little head, though everything around me seemed to be bursting or burning or crashing down. 'You went back for him,' I sobbed, nuzzling Pee Wee's warm head.

'You went back for me,' Louis laughed, as a shower of glass and stone and papers rained down on us, and I hugged them both tighter than I'd ever hugged anything ever.

Reani-mates

So we'd been at the hospital for three hours, waiting in a green-and-blue family room to hear news about Zoe and Sexy Dead Boy.

Our parentals had been called and they'd been all fine and dandy and offered to pay for all the damage and been actually quite pleased we had stolen a hearse and broken into the biggest Chinese restaurant in town and driven recklessly and blown up the college.

In. My. Dreams.

Once we'd got our story straight – that we needed the fish tank for our secret biochemistry experiment to reani-mate a dead sheep – they just had to deal with it. Louis had been grounded for three whole months and given the full hairdryer treatment from his dad and uncle, plus an actual clip round the ear from his mum. I hadn't actually realised a clip round the ear meant a whack; I'd always thought it was just some kind of clip.

My mum and dad had just kind of shouted at me for twenty minutes about stealing the nail art van, even though Mum hadn't used it in, like, a year, and for burgling and arson and all of that and I stood there and took it. I'd been glad Louis was holding my hand as I probably would have cried. With Louis there, I had been more worried about how embarrassing it was that my mum still had her rollers in, and that Dad had driven to the hospital in his slippers with the holes in.

'I can't believe how much you've lied to us, Camille,' Mum had said. 'And as for my van. Do you know how much batteries cost? You'll pay for that out of your wages. And you're grounded, indefinitely. And don't even THINK about going to that Halloween party you want to go to now, not a chance.'

I hadn't let on that this wasn't really a punishment because there was no longer a gym to have a Halloween party in, I had just stood there and taken my punishment. Truth was, I didn't actually care about the Halloween party at all anymore. I'd just as soon stay at home cuddled up on the sofa with Louis and Pee Wee, watching a film.

Damian's dad and his girlfriend, whom Damian had never met before, had thought it was all hilarious. I think they had just come from a party because they were dressed up and had both been quite drunk. His dad's first words to the cops had been, 'What's he done this time?' He'd offered to pay for all the damage cos he was loaded, knew

Fat Pang himself and had friends on the council. Damian was always getting into 'scrapes like these' apparently.

Zoe was okay, we were told by a doctor, burnt and injured but okay, and this had popped my anxiety bubble good and proper at least, but that had been all we were told about her for yonks. The saddest thing in the world was that nobody had come to the hospital for her. Nobody had come to tell her off or to give her a clip round the ear or to find out if she was okay. Nobody at all. Even Social Services hadn't sent someone.

The two police officers who had taken our statements were the same ones who'd got me and Louis out of the burning building. The policeman was called PC Kessler and he looked like that bloke in that film who goes out with this woman for one night and they end up having a baby together but really they're a total mismatch but in the end it's all okay because they've got a baby so it has to be. The policewoman was called PC Goodman and she looked like that blonde lady from that film about the woman in the yellow tracksuit. This is a brief snippet of our conversation with them:

'So who was the man in the tank?' said PC Kessler.
'What man in the tank?' said Damian.
'The man in the tank in the gym,' said PC Goodman.
A shrug from Louis. A shrug from me.
'We never saw no man in a tank. You must have been imagining it.'
'Yeah, it was just Zoe in the gym. And the sheep we'd been trying to bring back to life. The sheep we'd knocked down.

We were trying to do the right thing.'
'Honest.'
'Yeah, honest.'

Basically, we'd denied all knowledge of a man in a tank. As far as we were concerned, he'd never existed. We'd been so convincing, I'd started to believe it myself. As long as we all stuck to the story, it would be okay.

But ever since we'd shaken off our parentals and the cops and been shoved into the family room to wait for news on Zoe, Damian had been acting dead odd. He just paced and flicked through magazines and clacked the abacus thing on the kids' table. Silent. It wasn't like him at all. He'd never gone more than five minutes without making some comment or flirting at least.

Me and Louis were on the sofa having a cuddle session, my head resting on his warm chest. His heartbeat was so soothing and I was so tired. I'd read in my Biology text-book that the human heart beats an average of three billion times in a single lifetime. I thought mine would beat twice that now I'd met Louis. No, not since I'd met him. Since I'd realised what he meant to me. He wasn't just the spare boy any more. He was *my* boy. And that made him the best and most special boy ever.

I was as heavy as lead but I couldn't fall asleep, no matter how hard I tried. My mind was racing thinking about Zoe and SDB. We weren't being told anything about them. Pee Wee was sleep-twitching on Louis' lap. My poor baby was dramatized.

A male nurse finally came in after an entire ice age and

told us the latest on Zoe. Damian was ready for him.

'What do you mean, you don't know anything more? You've gotta know something more, you work here!'

'I've said she is stable. Now if you'd just like to take a seat . . .'

'That's all I've been doing for the last three hours, you dickhead, taking a frickin' seat.'

'Sir, if you're going to be abusive, I will have to ask you to—'

'Yeah, yeah, I get it, sit quietly and get ignored for another three hours, if I'm lucky and you might come and tell me she's dead. I get it, I hear you,' he shouted as the nurse left the room. Damian slammed the door behind him and slumped down in the purple armchair nearest the door and started leg jiggling.

'They'll come and tell us when they know anything, Dame. Chill,' said Louis, pouring some bottled water into the shallow pot plant tray on the coffee table. He set it down on the floor for Pee Wee who lapped at it eagerly.

'I can't chill; I gotta do something.' He bounced up and started pacing the room again. 'I've decided one thing though. I'm gonna get you three off the hook. I'll take the full wrap for this and I don't want any arguments.'

'What?' said Louis. 'We've given our statements already.'

'I'll say you both lied to protect me,' Damian sniffed, jumping around on the balls of his feet. 'I want it. I'll say I roped you all into it. I broke into the college and Fat Pang's. I forced you to help me with the tank. It was my idea. Everything. I'll say it was me. They'll believe it. They've been waiting to pin something big on me.'

'Damian, no,' I said. 'That's not fair.'

'Camille, I said I want it, end of. Cops are gonna keep asking them questions and they ain't gonna be satisfied till someone pays. What's the worst they can do? Dad'll pay for the damage and he has friends on the council so he'll be able to fast-track the college rebuild. I want this. I deserve it. Worst I'll get is community service. Hardly gonna blacken the glowing CV, is it?' He sat back down in the purple chair.

I looked at him. He didn't look right, he looked almost, well, humble. 'You're doing this for Zoe, aren't you?'

'No,' he said after a while of leg-jiggling and thumb-picking.

'You really like her, don't you?' I said.

Damian stood up and went to the window. 'I didn't go back in there to get her. Didn't even try. He went back in for a dog. I didn't do nothing.'

Louis stroked Pee Wee's tummy. Pee Wee looked like he was in a sleepy ecstasy. He loved Louis too, I could tell. 'There was no way you could have made it through the flames and saved her. She didn't want to be saved anyway.'

'I just legged it like always and saved my own skin. And now she's dying.'

'She's not dying,' I told him. 'The nurse said she was stable. That means not dying any more. They'll call for us when we can go and see her.'

Louis stroked my hair. He could do that now. I liked him doing that. It made my neck go goosepimply. I looked at Damian. It was the first time I'd ever felt sorry for him. How weird was that? And how weird was it that Zoe had been the one to make him so un-Damian-like? The words *Thus begins a new life* popped into my head. And I remembered Zoe saying it. And painful tears began to well up in my eyes.

A lady in blue pyjamas came in. She had a tag on. And then I realised she wasn't wearing pyjamas, she was wearing those scrubby things doctors wear. And she was a doctor.

'Camille Mabb?' she said.

'Yeah?' I said, standing up.

'Your friend is asking for you.'

I looked back at Louis. 'I'll wait in here,' he said.

'Can I see her n'all?' said Damian, jumping up.

'No,' said the doctor. 'She specifically said, "Just the blonde girl called Camille Mabb. Not the arrogant boyband reject." I can only assume she meant you.' By her sneer, I guessed she'd been talking to the male nurse Damian had shouted at.

Damian sat down next to Louis on the sofa. Louis squeezed his shoulder. Pee Wee woke up and growled.

Zoe was in a private room on the first floor. The doctor took me up in the lift.

'Was she badly hurt? Is she going to be okay?'

'She's got burns to her hands and arms and she's inhaled quite a bit of smoke from the fire. We'll need to keep her in for the time being.'

'Oh right.'

'She'll need a fair bit of TLC for a few months as there will be some tasks she can't do for herself. We haven't been able to get in touch with any of her family. Do you know where . . .'

'Uh, they're away,' I said. 'She's staying with us. My mum and dad are always there. And me. I'll be there too. We'll look after her.'

'That's good,' said the doctor. 'You're a good friend.'

Yeah, I wasn't sure what my mum and dad would have to say about it but I'd fought to keep Pee Wee so I would fight for Zoe as well, no problem. I suddenly couldn't wait to look after her, do things for her, make her meals and bring them to her on a tray, change her dressings. Make it all better. Make up for thinking she was doing all those terrible things. Murdering people and stealing their organs. Murdering my best friend. My ex-best friend. I was ready to nurse her back to health. And then I remembered who else might need looking after.

'And what about . . . the boy? Is he . . . ?'

The doctor tilted her head, like she hadn't quite heard me. 'Sorry, the boy?'

'Yeah, can I see him too? To say goodbye.' I owed him that at least.

'There was no boy brought in. It was just your friend. Was someone else in that building?'

'Um . . . oh no,' I replied, as the lift *binged* and opened onto a long beige corridor. 'I've probably got my wires crossed. It's been a long night.'

No SDB, huh? That didn't add up. Nothing ever did in my stupid little brain.

-312-

So what happened to Sexy Dead Boy?

Two doors down, in a hospital bed, lay my best friend Zoe. She looked just terrible. Her face was a sweaty, sooty black and both her hands were bandaged up. Her eyes were closed.

'She's on a lot of painkillers so you might not get much sense out of her,' said the doctor. 'I'll be just down the hall.' And she gave me an awkward smile and left.

I tiptoed over to the bed. 'Zoe? Zoe? It's me, Camille.'

'I am awake, you know, there's no need to creep around.' Her voice was croaky and she coughed when she'd finished speaking. She opened her eyes and they were still huge, blue and starey like before, unmistakeably Zoe amid all the soot. 'Might not get much sense out of her, huh,' she scoffed. 'I'd like to hear some sense coming out of her mouth once in a while instead of hearing what happened in the last instalment of *Celebrity Scrapheap*.'

I laughed. 'It's good sometimes, that. They have to dig around in some really bad rubbish and finds things to make . . .'

'I. Don't. Care,' she said tiredly but smiled at me at the same time.

'Sorry.'

I was so pleased to see her. I wanted to hug her and didn't care if she wouldn't hug back. I flung myself on her and she *oomphed* and laughed, coughing again. 'Sorry,' I said, pulling away. 'I told the doctor you could stay with us. Until you're better. I can help you.'

She stared at me.

'You can't say no. She said you will need help because of your hands.'

She still stared at me.

'It won't be a problem. My mum and dad will be cool. It'll be fine; don't worry. You could spend Christmas with us. Like . . . a sister or something, I don't know. I've always wanted to open my stocking with a sister.' I blushed, realising that had sounded better inside my brain where it probably should have stayed. *Damn you, brain.*

'A sister?' she said. 'You'd really want me to stay?'

'Yes!' I cried. 'Zoe, you've given me everything I ever wanted: a pet, a boyfriend – a true friend. I know we're not alike and I'm not as clever as you . . .'

'I'd like that,' she said. And she smiled and blinked away a little tear which I pretended not to see.

I got a little over-excited. 'We could even double-date if you got to like Damian. We could be, like, Z-amian and Cam-ouis.'

'Steady on now.' *Cough cough.*

I dragged a chair to the side of the bed and stroked her bandaged hand, doing the windscreen-wiper thing cos people did that in hospitals. And when they wanted to show people how much they meant to them. I don't think she could feel it through her bandages though.

'Ow,' she said, looking down at my stroking fingers.

I took them away. 'Oh sorry,' I said, biting my lip. 'So you're pretty burned then? How are you feeling? How did you get out of the gym before it blew? What happened? Did you try and get the tank out first? Is that why you wouldn't leave?'

'Which question would you like me to answer first?' she croaked with a cough.

'I don't know,' I laughed. 'How are you feeling?'

She coughed again. 'Burnt.'

'How did you get out of the gym?'

'I grabbed a crash mat from the store room and got the back doors open just in time. I rather think that crash mat saved my life.'

'Where's You-Know-Who?'

The fire was in her eyes again; the same fire that had been there at the start, when she'd been describing how we would collect up all the pieces and put him together. And then she was smiling. 'I have absolutely no idea.'

I frowned. 'What happened to him then? The doctor said there was no one else in the building. Did you get him out of the gym before it blew?'

'I didn't get him out, no. There was nothing left of him in that building.'

'Oh,' I said.

She stared across to the window. The sun had risen fully now and it was a clear blue sky outside. 'He's gone, Camille.'

I frowned. 'Gone where? You mean, he burned to d . . . ?' How can something that was never alive burn to death? He must have burned to no-chance-of-life-ever, I guessed. It was my turn to stare at her. I remembered the photos of her mum and dad at her house. Another person leaving for her to deal with. Another death. A re-death of her father. The little girl would always be alone now. A bubble of sadness popped in my neck. 'At least we tried. I can ask Louis if we could have some kind of funeral for him. A private one. Just us, yeah? We'll arrange everything.'

'Louis is . . . good for you, Camille,' she said, with a yawn. 'I knew it that day on the bus when I shouted at you. I knew how you felt about him before you did. You're tailor-made for each other. I was just afraid. Of losing my friend.'

I bit my lip. 'Best friend,' I said. 'I'll be a better friend to you than Sexy Dead Boy ever could have been. You'll see. I'll be your family now. Maybe it's a good thing that it didn't work.'

'Oh it did work,' she mumbled. She turned her head back towards me.

'What?'

'It did work. He's alive, Camille. Sexy Dead Boy is very

much *alive*.' Her grin went wide. She was making the exact opposite face to me.

'What? What do you mean, he's alive? You said he was dead.'

'No, I didn't. I said there was nothing left of him in that building. While you three were running for the hills, Sexy Dead Boy sat bolt upright in the tank. It took him a time to get his bearings but once I'd untied the wire around his feet and hands, he was off. He stood. And then he walked. And then he ran. Through the back doors, across the playing fields and far away.'

My chest hurt. My head throbbed. 'Are you sure? You're on a lot of painkillers, the doctor said . . .'

'Yes, to reduce my pain, not addle my mind. I know what I saw. It worked, Camille. It actually worked!' The tear that had been threatening to fall from her eye finally dropped onto the pillow beside her head.

This was unbelievable. I couldn't imagine Sexy Dead Boy up and about. Walking. Running. Breathing. 'Where did he go?'

'I don't know,' she said. 'And I'm powerless to go out and look for him in this state. I want you to go and find him.'

'Find him?'

'Yes. Find him and help him. He will be confused and afraid and he shouldn't be on his own at a time like this. I need you to find him and take him to my house and keep him there until I come out. You passed a locked room next to my Aunt Gwen's room when you were snooping, do you remember?'

'Yeah,' I said, remembering that day I'd stolen SDB's head from her house.

'Outside that room is a framed anatomical drawing of a lung. It's an original Castilho sketch; he was the Da Vinci of his day. On the top left-hand corner is a key. This key will unlock the locked room. He can go in there. I used to lock my father in there sometimes. On bad days. It's padded.'

'You want mē to go out on my own, find a mad walking dead bloke, go to your repossessed and probably locked house, break in, find the padded cell and lock him up?'

'Yes. If you wouldn't mind. And he's not mad; he's unnerved. Scared. Confused. But if you could just be there for him, until I'm well again. You can dress him in those clothes you bought. That'll be nice, won't it?'

'He's not a doll,' I said. 'He's a human being now. A living, breathing man. He could be capable of anything.'

'With a brain like his I imagine he would be. You're good at looking after people, Camille. This is where you really could shine for this experiment!'

My mouth wouldn't close. 'But I don't even know where he is.'

'My guess is he's gone down to the beach. Or the woods. Somewhere he once knew very well. He won't have gone far. Take Louis with you if you're concerned. He will help you, won't he?'

'What, help me find my naked would-be boyfriend, capture him and lock him in a padded room? Yeah, I should think so,' I said, not knowing what else to say.

'I wouldn't tell him that my father's brain is alive though, not just yet. I'm not sure he'd quite understand.'

'No, okay,' I nodded, as the thought of Herbert West drifted back into my mind. And not just the thought that I didn't have to write that English essay any more, now that college had burned down.

One thing had uttered a nerve-shattering scream; another had risen violently, beaten us both to unconsciousness and run amuck . . .

He was out there, Sexy Dead Boy. He was out there somewhere in the town. Doing goodness knows what. Maybe whooping in a treetop. Maybe strangling pensioners. And starkers too. How on earth was I meant to catch him? Pin him down? Drag him all the way up the steep streets of Clairmont Hill and up the gravel drive into Zoe's house? Up the stairs? Into the padded room? I couldn't even coax my Jack Russell puppy down from a tree.

'I'll try my best,' I said and turned to leave.

'Camille,' said Zoe.

I turned back to look at her. 'Yeah?'

'Thank you.'

'Lutwyche's BRAIN? You gave the thing Lutwyche's brain?'

So I told Louis when we were in the hospital car park waiting with Damian while he finished his cigarette. I didn't mean to. I just thought he ought to know. So he'd know what to expect.

'Oh my god. There's a madman on the loose. He's

gonna be a madman, just like Loopy Lutwyche! You should have told us this, Camille. This changes everything.'

'What do you mean, changes everything? It doesn't change *any*thing. I always knew that I would need to look after him once he came to life.'

I looked around the car park. Nothing but cars and wheelie bins and a strong midday sun beating down onto the concrete. Pee Wee was sniffing inside a chip box. But beyond that was the hills. And the woods. And somewhere, the human formerly known as Sexy Dead Boy. Now, I guessed, his name was Thomas, like Zoe's dad.

Louis walked up to me and held my wrists. 'He's going to be off his head. Maybe dangerous. We really don't know what we're dealing with now.'

'He won't be mad,' I said. 'He might be scared though. We've got to go and find him and look after him.'

'Camille, you should have said something . . .' He looked across at Damian. I looked at Damian too. 'What do you think?'

Damian took one long drag on his cigarette and blew smoke out slowly through his nostrils like a dragon. 'As I see it there's only one thing we can do.'

'What?' said Louis.

'What?' said I.

'Kill it,' said Damian.

'What?'

'WHAT?'

'Well, no one knows he exists except us four,' he explained. 'Princess, you said the quack had no idea there was someone else in the gym, right?'

'No, she didn't know anything about . . . '

'Right, so the cops don't know about him. And Zoe's in no fit state to know what's good for her so I suggest we leave her out of it for now. And we go and find him. And we end it.'

'Kill him?' said Louis. Pee Wee scurried over to him and hopped up and down by his boots to be picked up. 'You can't just kill another human being, Dame.'

'Oh look, we can all get happy-clappy and Friends-of-the-Earth about it later if you want but the fact remains that there is a dangerous dude on the loose and that is our fault. We're all to blame for whatever he does. And the right thing to do now is locate the target and frag it. End of.'

'He's not a target, he's a real live boy and he's called Thomas!' I shrieked. 'We've just spent the last I-don't-know-how-long putting him together. There's no way I can kill him. There's no way I can kill anything! And there's no WAY I'm going to stand by and let you kill him either. No wayski.'

'We ain't got a choice, darlin',' said Damian, flicking his cigarette into a wheelie bin and lighting up another. 'We don't know what Oliver Twisted's capable of, do we? He could be out there right now, tearing people limb from limb. Kids. Old dears. You really want that on your conscience?'

'. . . or he could be crying somewhere or shivering underneath a bush or something,' I argued.

Damian shook his head as he took another long drag. 'I say we finish the maniac before he gets started.'

'No, I want to help him,' I said.

'And how do you plan on doing that, princess? Reanimated psychos don't tend to go in for all that soul-searching rehab cobblers you've got in mind. The only language they understand is a shovel to the face. That's my kind of therapy.'

Louis laughed and then he stopped laughing when he saw my face.

'Come on,' said Damian, looking straight at me. 'You've read the books. And you've seen the movies.' He looked at Louis. 'You know how this ends.'

'Aren't you in enough trouble?' said Louis, as Pee Wee licked his chin. 'You're already odds on for a criminal record and a few months' community service. You really want to add murder to your charge sheet?'

'It won't *be* murder, will it?' said Damian. 'How can you murder someone who's already dead? Everything he's made of is dead. He's a dead head, a dead body, dead hands . . . no one knows he exists except us.'

'And those cops. They know,' said Louis.

'They know nothing,' said Damian, folding his arms. 'We can get away with that if we just stick to our story and say Zoe was the only one in the gym. Right? So who's with me? Who's gonna help me kill a killer before he kills?'

I took a deep breath. 'I've promised Zoe I'll look after him and take him back to the house. I can't go back on a promise.' Louis was looking at me like he wanted to tell me how big my arse looked without hurting my feelings. Damian was looking at me like he couldn't wait to tell me how big my arse looked. 'You're just afraid of him because he's fitter than you are,' I snipped, folding my arms.

'Do you really think I'm that shallow?' said Damian, his face darkening.

'No,' I said.

'Is he?'

I shrugged. 'You've seen him. He's pretty cute.'

'Look, we just need to find him for now, before the police get to him and before they start asking awkward questions,' said Louis, putting Pee Wee on the ground and reaching for my hand.

'Awkward questions like what?' I said.

'Awkward questions like why he's naked or why his hands are falling off.' said Damian.

'They won't fall off,' I said. 'Zoe is a brilliant surgeon. She doesn't make mistakes like that.'

Damian pouted and looked at Louis. 'Lou?'

'What?' Louis frowned.

'Kill or cuddle? What's it to be?'

Louis looked at me and took ages to answer. 'Maybe Dame's right. If he's off his head, we need to stop him. We can't explain this away to the police. They'll want to know who he is and . . . '

'Please, Louis,' I said.

'I'm going home to tool up,' Damian announced, folding his arms. 'You two can sit here having a coffee morning about it if you want. I'm going.'

'Tool up with what?' I called after him.

He swaggered back to us. 'Weapons, of course. We got ourselves a real live dead guy to bag and tag. Now, for the last time, who's with me?'

This wasn't right. This wasn't what Zoe wanted. This wasn't even what I wanted, not after all our hard work. I hadn't even seen Thomas properly yet. I felt sure if I could catch him and get him into Zoe's house, into that padded room, we could train him to be something good, something human. Like I'd trained Pee Wee to bring back balls and eat doggy treats and Pot Noodles, *not* poodles.

I felt my spine straighten. I felt myself grow an inch taller. I felt my heart pound stronger than ever, like a big brass band marching down the street, knowing exactly where it was going, exactly what tune it was playing. I knew what I had to do now.

'I said, who's with me?' Damian repeated, putting his hand out in front of him.

Louis put his hand on top. 'I'm in,' he said with a deep sigh. I could tell that killing things was not in his nature at all. Dead things he could deal with, but he wasn't the sort of boy who was used to making things get dead.

'Camille?'

'Yes,' I said. 'I'm in.' And I put my hand on top of theirs even though I didn't mean it at all, not one little bit. I threw Louis a look as I rubbed his hand in the hand pile, then took mine out of it. I would make my excuses and as soon as the boys were out of the way, I was going to go straight to the woods and find Thomas, on my own if I had to, and lead him to safety. I'd never been more sure of anything ever ever. Maybe I'd be good at it too, working with the recently undead. Zoe had said I was good at caring. Maybe that was my vocation.

'Right,' said Damian, rubbing his hands together. 'We'll

go to my house, get on the hard stuff for a bit of Dutch courage, grab anything metal with a point on it and track this psycho down . . .'

'Dame . . .' Louis began.

'No, I don't wanna hear anymore, Lou. The time to hesitate is through. We've got a town to save. Come on, let's fucking DO THIS, people!'

Acknowledgments

To Barry Cunningham for shocking this book back to life many times.

Imogen Cooper, Rachel Hickman, Rachel Leyshon, Esther Waller, Elinor Bagenal, Tina Waller and all at Chicken House. Miranda Baker, for her totes excellent editorial support. And my friend Laura Myers, for your endless enthusiasm for Louis.

My sister Penny Skuse, for always reading and always laughing, even when you're not supposed to.

The Snead Crew – Maggie, Roy, Emily and Matthew who always reads it early and always enthuses, even when it's crap.

The Skuse Posse – Jamie, Angie, Alex and Josie Skuse who helped me to work out how heavy a corpse was. And to Joshua Skuse, because you ask with every book when you're going to be in it. So the Three Joshes are in this one, just for you.

To book bloggers the world over who have reviewed my books and helped to spread the word, particularly Laura Heath at Sister Spooky Book Fangirl. Consider yourself totes awesies.

My internal soundtrack masters, who this time round were AC/DC, Avril Lavigne, Boyce Avenue, The Chemical Brothers, The Cure, Dizzee Rascal, Dresden Dolls, Ed Sheeran, Embrace, Evanescence, Ke$ha, Lissie, MGMT, My Chemical Romance, The Naked and Famous, Nero,

Nicki Minaj, Oingo Boingo, Owl City, Paramore, Pendulum, Pink, The Prodigy, RHCP, Rihanna, Sleigh Bells, Zero 7.

Robert Louis Stevenson, H.P. Lovecraft, Mary Shelley, Stuart Gordon, Peggy Webling and John Hughes, because they all got there first and did it mucho, mucho better.

Frances Bean Cobain, Lisa Blackwell, Jack O'Connell, Josh Hutcherson and Gerard Way. Although you didn't know it, your body parts gave life to Zoe, Camille, Damian, Louis and Professor Lutwyche. So cheers for that.

Praise for ROCKOHOLIC

*... intensely funny ... Laugh-aloud slapstick with a
dash of romance. It's terrific.*
BOOKSELLER

*Pure brilliance! I loved this one ... If you want to read a
British book this year make it this one.*
BOOK MOGUL blog

*... funny, and accurate about the way teens
think and speak.*
THE TIMES

*... I absolutely loved it ... I truly recommend the novel.
Be prepared: you will want to listen to a lot of rock music
while reading this novel ...*
THE BOOKETTE blog

Oh Man – I loved this book! ... Superb!
I WANT TO READ THAT blog

*I am in love with this book. It makes me smile ... the last
line is absolute perfection! And it made me cry.*
WRITING FROM THE TUB blog

*... seriously? A teenager who KIDNAPS HER
FAVOURITE ROCKSTAR? ... dude, who *wouldn't*
want to kidnap their favourite rock star?! ...
YOU HAVE TO READ THIS.*
LOVEREADINGX blog

… a heart-warming tale of what it's like to love something so much it hurts, the reality of coming face to face with what you love and realising that sometimes you have to stop having a dream and start living the dream …
SISTER SPOOKY BOOK FANGIRL blog

… Rockoholic is a really fresh YA novel that will have you absolutely gripped … If you've ever been crazy about a celebrity or you simply love to read YA, you must get a copy.
MOSTLY READING YA blog

… a whole lot of fun. Jaw-droppingly off the wall in places, I lost count of the times I laughed out loud while reading it …
I WAS A TEENAGE BOOK GEEK blog

… very excellent … I am a big fan of Ms. Skuse, who also wrote the superb Pretty Bad Things. *Give* Rockoholic *a whirl – it is incredibly funny.*
MY FAVOURITE BOOKS blog

… pretty darned awesome …
CICELY LOVES BOOKS blog

… Rockoholic *is one of the funniest, most entertaining and highly original books I've read in a long time …*
I can't recommend Rockoholic *highly enough …*
NARRATIVELY SPEAKING blog

This is one of those books that made me laugh and cry ...
The relationship between Mac and Jody is just gorgeous ...
I really did love this book ...
SERENDIPITY TEACHER blog

A rip roaring story about the perils of fame and the
reality of all that glamour.
JULIA ECCLESHARE, LOVEREADING

... humorous and touching, shocking and reassuring,
this story is a joy to read.
BOOKTRUST

Praise for PRETTY BAD THINGS

… Skuse's fast-paced, edgy debut … conveys the twins' powerful connection through their affecting dialogue and recollections of childhood. Readers should be fully invested in their whirlwind tour of the Vegas strip, right up to the unexpected ending.
PUBLISHER'S WEEKLY

… a cultural pick 'n' mix of influences spanning the decades … There is an impressive filmic quality to the novel – you can literally see it rolling out before you as you read … altogether a pretty damn good read.
TELEGRAPH

… skilfully drawn teenagers, street smart but vulnerable. Their complimentary but strikingly different voices, coupled with exuberant dialogue and a fast-moving plot kept this reader enthralled … An impressive debut.
GLASGOW HERALD

… the best YA thing I've read in ages … Fantastic story, wonderful writing, and the characters are just SO good … It's so good, I'd even recommend it to people I don't like.
KEVIN BROOKS

… vastly enjoyable debut … does a great job of establishing voice – laconic, teenage, contemporary – and attitude – disrespectful, impatient, funny …
KEREN DAVID

… almost bursting with its own driving energy … excellent … its pace and ambition … carry it triumphantly through. The author is clearly someone to watch.
NICK TUCKER, CAROUSEL MAGAZINE

… a fast-moving and exciting novel … sassy, clever, pacy … sings off the page…
ADELE GERAS, CRIME CENTRAL blog

This breathtaking, rollercoaster book flings the reader head first into the action from the opening page and doesn't let up until the closing paragraphs. This is teenage rebellion and recklessness in its rawest form…
INIS, IRELAND

Pretty Bad Things *is one of the most important YA debuts of 2010. It was refreshingly funky, pacy and rude. I loved it!*
JOHN MCLAY, BATH KIDS LIT FEST

… slick, hip and anarchic … this is fresh and effortlessly readable.
BOOKSELLER

Dynamic characters, wisecrack jokes and exhilarating read, Pretty Bad Things *is a brilliant novel ... and I would recommend it to anyone who enjoys Young Adult fiction with a twist.*
CHICKLISH

... this book could do what Catcher in the Rye *has done for more than a generation of readers but unlike J.D. Salinger, let's hope the author continues to deliver a knock-out punch with each new book that's published ...*
LOVEREADING.CO.UK

... C.J. Skuse's writing is among the best I've read in the past few years, and her words are brimming with snark, wit and humour ... cool, edgy and daring ...
WONDROUS READS BLOG

... a fabulous debut ... Skuse, female, writes with a lot of balls ... she has arrived on the scene with a voice that I for one will be longing to hook up with again.
ACHUKA

... bat shit crazy awesome ... Full of sass and sweet-toothed criminality ...
IN THE LIBRARY OF LADY VIOLET blog